The Heart to Love

A Novel

Shauna Jamieson Carty

Island Novel

Divine Word Communications, LLC, *Roselle, New Jersey*

The Heart to Love
A Novel

This novel was first published in 2010 under the title
About Wendy, by Jamieson Carty

Island Novel Publishing is a division of Divine Word Communications, LLC, a publisher and promoter of Christian literature. Our products can be purchased in bulk at a discounted price. Please contact us for details at prayerpartnersnovels@gmail.com.

This book is a work of fiction. All of the characters, names, incidents, organizations and dialogues in this novel are either the products of the author's imagination or are used in a fictitious manner.

Scriptures are taken from the New King James Version of the Bible. Copyright © 1982 by Thomas Nelson, Inc. Used by permission. All rights reserved. Old English verses are taken from the King James Version.

Printed in the United States of America

ISBN-10: 0991643399
ISBN-13: 9780991643394

DEDICATION

I dedicate this book to God who is love (1 John 4:8), to the love of my life Ricky who God blessed me to love and marry, to our five children who God is blessing us to nurture and love, and to my mother who has always inspired me with her love.

BOOKS IN THE
PRAYER PARTNERS SERIES

The Heart to Love
By Shauna Jamieson Carty

When a teenage boy says he has the heart to love a girl for the rest of their lives, can she believe him? Wendy's mother believed Wendy's father and ended up pregnant and alone. Now Wendy is 17 years old and saving herself for her high school sweetheart Paul. Paul promises to marry her after graduation and enter a covenant of everlasting love. Wendy's mother withholds her blessings and cautions them to wait. Now Wendy is about to find out where her father stands: beside her as she walks down the aisle or by her mother.

The Heart to Live
By Shauna Jamieson Carty

College life isn't the "happily ever after" that Wendy and Paul dreamed of when they were in high school. They attend the same university, but nothing seems to be going according to their plans. "Remember to pray for me," Paul tells Wendy. Wendy covers Paul with her prayers, but their security is shattered and depression sets in because of a tragic shooting on their college campus. Will sharing their faith help to restore the peace and give them and their peers the heart to live joyfully again?

The Heart to Forgive
By Shauna Jamieson Carty

Love is everlasting, except of course when our loved ones hurt our feelings and it's just too hard to forgive. At the center of Paul and Wendy's faith is the belief that they can pray to God and ask for forgiveness for the things they have done wrong. God will forgive them and they must forgive others. They and their friends Constance and Sergio pursue different paths after college, but they share a common loss and continue to get together for a memorial benefit concert once a year. Can they get past the pain of hurtful relationships? Will they have the heart to forgive themselves and each other and embrace God's unfailing love?

Dear Readers:

Thank you for spending time with us. I pray that your faith in God will be built up as you read the Prayer Partners Series of novels.

The Lord gave me the vision for the three novels in this series many years ago, and it took many years and many stages to manifest. This novel was first published under the title, About Wendy, by Jamieson Carty. This is the same story, except for a new beginning and subtle changes. I've given it the new title The Heart to Love in order to make the series more unified. To God be the glory! Praise the Lord! Alleluia! Thank you, JESUS!

Submit your relationships to God, seek His forgiveness, and trust Him to reconcile broken hearts.

"Now all things are of God, who has reconciled us to Himself through Jesus Christ, and has given us the ministry of reconciliation, that is, that God was in Christ reconciling the world to Himself, not imputing their trespasses to them, and has committed to us the word of reconciliation."
(2 Corinthians 5:18-19 NKJV)

Please write to us at prayerpartnersnovels@gmail.com; we'd love to hear from you.

Peace, love, and God bless,

Shauna

ACKNOWLEDGMENTS

Praise the Lord! Alleluia! Thank you, JESUS!

Thank you to my mommy who set an unforgettable example for me as a writer when she typed her first 500-page manuscript on a typewriter on the back verandah of our home on the island of Jamaica. *Centre of the Labyrinth*, by Rosetta J. Jamieson, is still my favorite novel.

Thanks to my husband Ricky for believing that I should use this gift of writing that the Lord has placed in me and for supporting me in doing so every step of the way.

Thanks to our children for cheering me on, for reading my work, and for the many writing projects of their own that I love to read.

Thank God for my church family at Second Baptist Church in Roselle, New Jersey, and for all the people who remember me and my family in their prayers. "...The effectual, fervent prayer of a righteous man availeth much." (James 5:16)

Thanks to my cover models who inspired me and became wind beneath my wings as we worked on this project. The books are fiction and do not reflect our experiences, but like the characters, we know the power of God to mend broken hearts.

Special thanks to my sister in Christ, Pauline Finley, for expecting nothing less than three novels in this series.

Thanks to biblegateway.com and all the other Bible references on the Internet that make it easy to find a scripture for every moment of our lives.

CHAPTER ONE

A hummingbird fluttered its wings and pressed down its long beak to sip nectar from the center of a hibiscus flower. The plant swayed gently rustled by a light breeze as sunlight beamed down from the clear blue sky casting a shadow of the bird's long twin tail. The scene could be frozen in a picture frame and used to lure tourists from the chilly spring season in New York to the warm, tropical weather on the island of Jamaica.

That scene outdoors was an unhurried, natural part of God's creation. Inside, two teenagers were in a rush. They were getting too close, too soon, too fast—undaunted by the knowledge that their actions would permanently change their lives.

Devon Douglas switched off the television and turned to face the girl seated on the sofa beside him. The movie they had been watching ended in typical fashion for a Hollywood romance, stirring a longing in them for a deep passionate kiss. Marcia Tapper gazed back at him, wide-eyed and trusting, her lips parted, expectant. He kissed her, his intensity matching the characters they'd watched on television.

Marcia sighed. She had never been kissed like this, but she had known that when the time was right, Devon was the only guy she would allow to get this close. At seventeen, he was the sole object of her fantasies, the prince in the fairytale she conjured up in her head.

His taut muscles flexed as his fingers caressed her cheek, traveled along her bare neck to skin just below her shoulder, where the neckline of her blouse plunged. She should stop him now, but she thought she deserved this. She desired to be the girl he was holding, the one with whom he shared his deepest secrets, his most intimate thoughts.

"Marcia," he whispered her name.

Her eyes flickered open to meet his. This wasn't a fantasy. His touch was real. Her body tingled with an unfamiliar sensation that caused her to

1

lean toward him. "Stop," her mind screamed remembering that she had been taught that intimacy outside of marriage was wrong. She wouldn't stop yet, not until he told her how much he loved her.

Devon kissed her again, leaning her ever so gently back on the couch. His eyes focused on her chest as he unbuttoned her blouse.

"Devon." Her voice was soft, as she said his name.

"Yes, babe," he replied, forcing himself to focus on her eyes. Concern registered on his face. He felt that at almost seventeen, she was ready, like a juicy mango waiting to be picked from the tree and savored until the owner licked the last drop of its succulent juice from his lips. Was she going to forbid him to taste her fruit?

"You'll stop when I tell you to stop, right?" she asked shyly.

He nodded and kissed her gently. "Honey, if you tell me to stop, I'll stop. I'll never force to do anything you don't want to do."

She exhaled slowly, relieved, but as his hands roamed along the curves of her body, she inhaled short, quick breaths.

"Marcia, I miss you so much when we're away at school."

"You do?" She watched as he pulled the cotton t-shirt he was wearing over his head. She had seen his bare chest so many times before when they went swimming, but this moment was different. She sat up, letting her own shirt fall away from her body.

"You're the only person I'm able to talk to without you judging me," he replied, holding her close. "Everyone else has these expectations of how I should behave, what my goals should be, what I should do with my life. After all, I am Donovan Douglas' son," he concluded, deepening his voice.

She smiled at him and ran the tips of her fingers across his brows. Impulsively, she quickly and firmly kissed his bare shoulder.

"That's what I love about you. You make me feel like I can just be me. All the other girls I've dated care about is how much property my parents own, what kind of car I drive, and how it would feel to be the First Lady of my parents' hotel."

"Are you seeing anybody now, Devon?"

"What do you mean?"

"Do you have a girlfriend?"

"No, I don't." Their eyes met and for a moment they gazed at each other conveying an unspoken bond of trust. "No, Marcia, I don't have a girlfriend. Would you be my girlfriend?"

"Why?"

Devon wasn't surprised by Marcia's question. They had grown up together like brother and sister, and he knew she wouldn't take his proposition lightly. He wouldn't deceive her either; he had always been her protector. "I want you to be my girlfriend because I love you, Marcia. And I love you because you care who I am, not what my parents' money can buy. I love you. I love you. I love you," he declared, punctuating each statement with a kiss.

"I love you too," she exhaled her response. She had waited all her life for this moment. She wanted him to kiss her deeply, passionately. He did. She wanted him to touch her again. He did.

Devon Douglas loved her, and just as they had been together since childhood, she knew they would always be together. Sure, they would both go away to college just like they did for high school, but wherever she went she would carry his love with her. She was sure he would do the same.

After college, they would get married. Perhaps, they would return to live in the house in Jamaica where they had grown up. Maybe, they would settle in New York. All that mattered was that they would be together, and she knew they would because Devon loved her.

She gasped as he touched her intimately. They should stop now, she knew, but she was reluctant to ruin the moment.

Devon kissed her again. He expected her to tell him to stop, and he paused to read her expression as he touched her. The passion he saw burning in her eyes caused him to charge ahead, forgetting that she would stop him, forgetting that he should stop them.

He'd had other opportunities, but he never let himself get this close to the girls he dated. He was always afraid that they would use this to trap him; that they would aim to get pregnant for him, just so they could own him. Marcia was different, and that's why he loved her.

He sighed, or was that her? It seemed they were both now breathing as one. Ever so slowly and gently, their bodies met and they became one. He looked at her and saw the tears seeping from the corners of her eyes. His instantly filled with tears too.

"I love you, Marcia Angelique Tapper. Don't forget that. Okay? I love you."

She sniffled. "I love you too."

So this was it: the intimate experience that their parents and their church had taught them was wrong unless they were married. Any pain Marcia felt had been soothed by the love she saw in Devon's eyes.

Afterward, as they showered together in Devon's private bathroom, he was concerned that he might have hurt her. Did she regret what they had done? He wanted to know.

In that moment, she didn't. Euphoria. That's what she felt. Removed from the reality of life around them, as though—like the characters in the movie they had watched—she felt she was guaranteed a happy ending.

Devon held her a lot. His fleeting touch or gentle caress made her feel secure. When their eyes met and held, she felt like they were unveiling their souls. They hid nothing from each other in that moment. Never had they been so close. He placed his palm against her lower back as he escorted her downstairs to the room she shared with her mother when she was home from school. They were conscious that his parents would soon return from the romantic date they had gone on in celebration of his father's birthday. And as he kissed her, she felt grown up, content, and in love.

Her mother's return served as a sharp reminder that she was still a child who shared a bed with her mother in her mother's employer's house. Ruth Tapper entered the room humming softly the tune from a hymn she sang at church.

"Marcia. Wake up, girl. Strange. Gone to bed so early on a Saturday night."

Marcia heard her mother come in, but hoped that she would let her sleep. She felt uncomfortable facing her mother so soon after what she and Devon had done.

"Mm," she mumbled, turning away, snuggling into the pillow.

"Wake up, child. Everybody at church asked for you this evening. Pastor and his wife said to tell you hello."

Marcia sat up in the bed and placed the pillow in her lap. She watched her mother remove her church dress and put on a floral, cotton housecoat with snaps down the front. Ruth folded the bright orange polyester dress she had taken off and placed it on a shelf under her cream-colored broad brimmed hat. During the week, she would hand wash the dress, along with the laundry she manually scrubbed for the Douglas family.

"I'll see them tomorrow," Marcia replied.

"Good. I'm glad that you still plan to come with me in the morning."

"Of course, Mommy. I said I would."

"Yes, but this would not be the first time you change your mind and go off with Mrs. Douglas and her family." Ruth plopped down on the bed beside her daughter. She had gained a lot of weight in the years since she had dropped out of school and given birth to Marcia. Hard work had roughened her hands, but her face was round and soft, and her broad smile dimpled her cheeks hinting that she had once been an attractive woman.

Ruth was still beautiful now, but Marcia's constant embarrassment at having a mother who labored as a maid prevented her from noticing. It annoyed Marcia when people suggested that she looked like her mother. She didn't see the resemblance. She prided herself on being slender and moving with the gracefulness of a dancer. She described her mother as being plump and would view her disdainfully as she trudged into a room like a market woman accustomed to carrying a heavy load. Marcia's skin tone faded into the weak hues of a pink sunset while her mother's possessed the potency of midnight. Yet there was no denying that Marcia's eyes replicated her mother's, dark and mysterious, revealing an indelible likeness between them.

She hadn't wanted to attend church with her mother on Easter Sunday. Earlier that day, as she and Devon had shopped and spent time together, she had been planning to tell her mother she would attend church with Devon and his family instead. But now she felt obligated by guilt. She had done something that her mother would never approve of, and this was her way of redeeming herself.

On Easter Sunday morning they awoke to the sound of a rooster crowing outdoors. Wearing the dress that Devon bought her the day before, Marcia boarded a bus with her mother and arrived at church before the start of Sunday school. Devon and his family rose hours later and enjoyed a leisurely breakfast before leaving home. Their chauffer drove them to church in his father's Mercedes Benz. As soon as the service ended, Devon's family returned to the house while Marcia had to coax her mother to leave an after-church social by telling her she needed the extra time to finish packing before she returned to school.

When they finally got back to the house, she only had an hour before she and Devon had to leave.

"How was church?" Devon asked, smiling at her, feeling pleased that she was wearing the dress he had selected. He thought that the color caused her tanned complexion to glow.

Ruth responded before Marcia could. "The preacher had a word of caution for you young people today," she said, as she cleared the table after having served her daughter and the Douglas family an early dinner. "You should hear the sermon and take heed to what the Lord says in Romans, chapter..."

"Ruth, we don't have time for any sermon right now," Mrs. Douglas interrupted her. "We all already went to church today. You know that the drivers are waiting. Marcia and Devon, get your bags. It's time to go. Darling, did you already give them some pocket money?" she asked her husband.

"Yes, dear," Mr. Douglas responded, slipping an arm around his wife's waist. "I took care of everything."

"Of course, you did," she said giving him a quick kiss on the lips.

They treated Marcia like their own daughter, paying for her education and activities in the same manner that they did for their son. They even paid separate drivers to transport Marcia and Devon to their boarding schools, even though the schools weren't far apart. Although tradition dictated that school children in Jamaica were on holiday during the week after Easter, both Marcia and Devon were returning to school so they could participate in the swimming championship. The chauffer who transported each of them also carried other students from their swim team.

"See you soon," Devon said, sharing a brotherly hug with Marcia as he usually did in front of their parents. "Good luck with the swim meet."

"You too," she replied. "When is the next time you're coming home?" she asked, feeling a little worried that their separation would threaten the love they had declared for each other a day earlier.

Devon shrugged, reaching for his bags.

"Come on, children. Let's go," Mrs. Douglas urged them.

Ruth wiped her hands on her apron before pulling her daughter into a tight embrace. "May the Lord bless you and keep you safe from all hurt, harm, and danger, seen and unseen, my child," Ruth prayed. "Remember, Jesus loves you and so do I."

Marcia hugged her back before pulling away. "I love you too, Mommy."

"Be a good girl now, you hear," Ruth instructed her.

"Yes, Mommy," Marcia replied with her back to her mother as she followed Devon outside.

After the competition, Marcia resumed her regular routine of attending classes, participating in sports, dance, and music lessons, and acting in the drama club. And as usual, Devon didn't call. Leading separate lives while they were away at school was the norm.

Three weeks later, Marcia threw up at breakfast. She rinsed her mouth out with Listerine and hurried off to class. Perhaps, she ought to take her mother's advice and drink something warm in the morning, she thought. Her mother had taught her that the warm liquid would get the gas off her chest and make room for her to retain her first meal, but a quick bowl of cold cereal in the morning always seemed more convenient.

The next morning, she drank a mug of sweet, hot, mint tea. It helped, and she decided to make the warm drink a daily habit. She vomited a few more times, but it was sporadic and it wasn't always after breakfast. She told her roommates she had picked up a stomach virus. But something else was different. Only she could feel the tingling and notice her tender, swollen breasts.

That was the first sign of pregnancy she noticed, as she busied herself with preparing for graduation. Growing up with Devon's mother, she had learned a lot about pregnancy. First, she knew that not every pregnancy resulted in childbirth. Devon's mother had miscarried many times during the years Marcia lived in their home. She had even given birth to a baby girl who lived for only a few hours. Those experiences taught Marcia that the fact that she was pregnant now didn't necessarily mean that she was going to be a mother, so she tried not to worry.

Graduation day arrived and she was relieved that the figure forming dress she had picked out months before still fit comfortably. It clung to her waist, accentuated her flat stomach, and flared at her broad hips. Her back up plan, if her stomach bulged by then was to keep on her cap and gown after the ceremony, in spite of the heat of the day. If anyone enquired, she would have attributed it to her sense of pride at having graduated from a prestigious high school.

Marcia had only two guests at her graduation ceremony: her mother and Mrs. Douglas. Her mother wore one of her church dresses, with her broad brimmed hat and soft rounded black shoes. Mrs. Douglas wore a linen pants suit with a silk shirt and a pair of high heels. Mr. Douglas was too busy working at their hotel and would only take time off for his son's commencement exercises. And Devon's social calendar kept him busy at school.

The Catholic sisters who ran Marcia's girls high school left students boarding there with little opportunity for a social life. The uniform they wore—all white to the underwear—was a symbol of the life of chastity and purity the *nuns* expected the girls to lead. In actuality, the girls behaved in a manner that was far from that ideal, but on their own time. Under the *nuns'* watch, they appeared to abide by the rules.

Devon's school, in spite of its reputation for academic excellence was also known as a party school for upperclassmen. Senior year there involved many outings and intermingling between male and female students in a manner that was forbidden at Marcia's school. Marcia had not expected that Devon would be able to get away from his campus for her graduation considering that his was the next day, but she had hoped he would.

At the end of the ceremony, the graduates dispersed, and Marcia sashayed toward the two women.

Her mother smothered her in a tight embrace.

"Hallelujah! Thank you, Jesus! We are proud of you girl." Ruth could not contain her excitement. Her skin jiggled as she did a little jig.

Marcia smiled, but stood erect clasping her hands before her, her head angled slightly upward, her chin jutted out. She turned to Mrs. Douglas, embarrassed by her mother's exuberance.

Mrs. Douglas extended her right hand to shake Marcia's. They leaned toward each other to share a kiss on the cheek, but their faces didn't touch.

"Congratulations, Marcia. We are proud of you. Well done." She handed her a bouquet of flowers.

"Thank you. I wouldn't be here without the support of you and your family. Mommy and I can never thank you enough."

"Witnessing you graduate at the top of your class is thanks enough," Mrs. Douglas replied, smiling.

"Thank you, Jesus! Hallelujah!" Ruth did a little dance around them.

Marcia glanced uncomfortably around her to see if any of her classmates were watching. The chairs the graduates had been seated on were empty now. Marcia's classmates focused their attention on their own families. Still, Marcia felt self-conscious. And as she had for many years in the presence of Devon and his wealthy peers, she found herself wishing that Mrs. Douglas had been her mother instead of the undignified woman prancing before them.

"Okay, Ruth. Get a hold of yourself," Mrs. Douglas recommended.

"You have to excuse me, Missis. I can't explain how I feel. Me glad bag bust," she explained, lapsing into the broken English dialect that she was most comfortable speaking. "Only by God's grace this day has come. You wouldn't understand how I feel, but I have to praise the Lord." She waved her open right hand in the air. "Hallelujah! Thank you, Jesus!"

Both Marcia and Mrs. Douglas felt an urgent desire to leave before Ruth completely lost control like she was feeling the Holy Spirit at a church revival. There were teachers and administrators Marcia should have introduced her mother to, people her mother would have been grateful to meet. Instead, she and Mrs. Douglas exchanged a look that conveyed that they were in agreement.

"The driver is waiting," Mrs. Douglas said coolly. "We should go."

With that they escorted Ruth away from the crowd, down the walkway toward the street where the cars were parked.

The chauffer dropped off Devon's mother at a hotel near Devon's school where she planned to meet her husband. Then, he drove Marcia and her mother back to the Douglas family's house. The next day, after Devon's graduation, he and his parent left on a night flight to London. Marcia learned about the trip from her mother. Devon hadn't told her he was going. They had not spoken to each other since Easter.

She was three months pregnant, and she felt alone, afraid, and insecure.

CHAPTER TWO

Marcia was just too tired. That was the first sign of pregnancy Ruth detected in her daughter. She had slept all the way on the drive back to the house after her graduation ceremony. Ruth had expected her to be too excited to sleep. They unpacked, showered, and turned in for the night. Marcia slept all night, but the next day her mother noticed her sitting up straight at the kitchen table fast asleep.

Ruth peered at her daughter's body in the tank top she was wearing. She didn't look like she had gained weight, but her breasts were fuller than they had ever been. As though Marcia sensed she was being watched, her eyes flickered open.

"Mommy?" Marcia sat up straighter and as she met her mother's gaze, she became alert. "It's so hot. I can't believe I fell asleep and I'm supposed to be doing my chores." She stood up and attempted to busy herself as her mother grabbed her by the wrist.

"Marcia Angelique Tapper. You are pregnant." It was more of a statement than a question. "Lord, have mercy on us." Ruth collapsed into a chair. She clasped her hands together and placed them on top of her head. In that one revelation, her dreams for a more prosperous future for herself and her daughter were shattered. She had endured a life of servitude since she had become pregnant with Marcia at age sixteen. She had not expected this from her daughter who was on a different path. Marcia had graduated from high school without getting pregnant, or so Ruth thought, until now. She had a full scholarship to attend university. She would establish herself in her career before she married and had children. Wasn't that what they

9

had always discussed?

Ruth envisioned herself serving as a nanny to Marcia's children one day, so her daughter would not be tied down at home and could excel at her career. That's what Marcia had always said she wanted. Until now. "Lord Jesus, but you see my dying trial."

Tears flooded Marcia's eyes. She didn't deny the truth.

"How, Lord? How? When? What a crosses on us now, Lord!" Ruth didn't look at Marcia or direct her questions to her. She stared off into space, a look of deep sorrow in her eyes. Her shoulders slumped, her stomach contracted as though she had received a physical blow. She could only see the black future that had faced her at age sixteen. Marcia was only a year older than she had been when she became a mother. "Not again. Lord Jesus." She shook her head. "Heaven help us."

Marcia fell on her knees before her, tears streaming down her face. "I'm sorry, Mommy." She sobbed. "I'm sorry."

Ruth rested her head on the palm of one hand, and with the other, she gently stroked Marcia's hair. One thing was certain. She would not abandon her daughter the way her parents had abandoned her. Of course, Marcia could no longer stay at the Douglas' house. But Ruth prayed that one day, after the baby was born, Marcia would get her life back on track and fulfill her goals and dreams.

There was only one person Ruth could call for help. Her sister, Pat Harrison, lived with her husband and daughter in New York, but they owned a house in Kingston, which they rented out to tenants. They kept a section of the house for personal use. Ruth asked Pat if Marcia could stay there and Pat agreed.

"What is wrong with these young girls?" Pat asked when Ruth broke the news to her over the phone. "Why can't they keep their legs closed? Don't they realize that teenage pregnancy is too high a price to pay? And where is the boy who got Marcia pregnant?"

Ruth was silent. She didn't want to tell her sister that history was repeating itself in more ways than one. Marcia and her mother were alike in that neither of them revealed the identity of the father of their child. Ruth had her suspicion, but she hadn't confronted Marcia with it. There was nothing to gain. She needed her job working with the Douglas family. She couldn't make demands of them. If anything, she owed them for all they had done for her daughter.

"Mm mm mm," Pat continued. "Somebody set a curse on you all. What would possess Marcia to go lie down with a man when she knows her mother does not even have a bed to call her own?"

Ruth listened with tears running down her cheeks, but said nothing.

"I'm sorry this happened, but I will help out in any way I can. We women always pay the higher price. How many months did you say she is?

Almost four. Well, her body is about to go through some changes. That alone should help her realize that it was not worth the sacrifice to rush into lovemaking. She never listened all those time you told her that love never make to run away. Why don't these young girls wait until they are emotionally, physically, and financially ready to handle the consequences? I hope my daughter is listening to this conversation and will take heed, so she does not find herself in the same predicament."

"How is Blossom?" Ruth asked, hoping to shift the focus of the conversation from her daughter to Pat's. She needed her older sister's help, but she felt like Pat was giving her a verbal beating. After all, she had tried her best to ensure that her daughter didn't repeat her mistake.

"Blossom is fine, praise God. I had hoped that she and Marcia would be together this summer in New York. The application I filed for you and Marcia to migrate to the United States should have been approved by now. You will get through soon though."

"Good. I will continue to pray."

Neither one mentioned what impact Marcia's pregnancy would have on any plans for migration.

"Anyway, I will ask the caretaker for the property to bring you the key. Marcia will have a bedroom and bathroom to herself, but there is no telephone service in there."

"That's okay. I'm just grateful that she will have somewhere safe to go. That's more than I had after..." Ruth sobbed as memories of her own painful experience came rushing back.

"I know. We'll get through this by the grace of God." Pat knew her sister was hurting. She more than anyone else knew how much sacrifice Ruth had made for her daughter. Some women sat around waiting for Prince Charming to rescue them, but not Ruth. Ruth had worked hard and tried to mold her daughter so that Marcia's generation would be better off than she was. Ruth owned nothing but her clothes and the privileges that came with being employed by people as kind as the Douglas family. The little money she earned could only rent her a room in a tenement yard. Marcia was on the verge of elevating both herself and her mother socially and economically. Until now... "We'll talk soon. Let me know when you get the key and move Marcia into the place."

"I will"

"And, Sis..."

"Yes."

"Have faith in God."

Marcia spent the summer alone, locked away in her aunt's house. A year earlier she had pictured herself vacationing in New York during the summer. She had imagined that Devon would have been in the city too and could have given her a tour of the university he would be attending. Otherwise, she could have been socializing with her former classmates at graduation parties and basking in the sun with them on the beach. There had even been talk of Mr. Douglas giving her a job at his hotel, so she could earn some money before starting her college education. She had visualized herself working there alongside Devon.

Instead, she had no idea where Devon was, or what he was doing. He should have been back from London by now, but she didn't dare ask her mother for him. She passed the time re-reading her textbooks and trying to figure out what was happening to her body.

By August, she could feel the baby moving, or at least that's what she thought she was feeling. At first, it felt like the flutter of butterfly wings along her lower abdomen. As the weeks progressed, the movements became more forceful, like an occasional thump or jerk. Her stomach was protruding now, her skin itched, and there were changes in her complexion. Most of the time, she felt scared, daunted by the realization that there was another human being growing inside her.

Devon came to see her in the middle of the month after asking her mother where she was and obtaining the address. Ruth told Marcia he was coming, and Marcia dressed in her best summer dress that she could still fit in and sandals as she waited eagerly to see him. The tenants who shared the house escorted Devon to the side door and Marcia let him in.

"Finally," she said, greeting him with a smile. "I was wondering if you would ever come to see me."

Devon scrutinized her from head to toe, his eyes resting for a long time on her bulging belly.

She had hoped that he would hug her and spend time just holding her in his arms, apologizing for not finding her sooner, and reassuring her that he would always be there for her.

Instead, he stood before her like a model of casual wealth in his designer jeans, boat shoes, and polo shirt.

"Say something," she appealed softly, unable to bare the coldness of his silent stare.

"What do you want me to say? I can't believe you did this to me. To us," he declared.

"What did I do to you?" she shrieked, caught off guard by his response. "I'm the one who is having a baby!"

"You turned out to be worse than all the other girls. I knew the other girls wanted to have a baby for me, so that I would be forced to commit to them, but not you. I did not expect this from you," he said in disgust. He had been shocked and hurt when he first heard the rumor that Marcia had disappeared from the social scene because she was pregnant.

Marcia knitted her brows, her eyes filling with tears. She couldn't believe that Devon was reacting this way and wanted to cover her ears. She had expected his support, not accusations.

"Why didn't you tell me the moment you found out you were pregnant?" he asked.

"I didn't know where you were," she replied. "You left the island without even telling me your family was going to England."

"You should have told me the moment you knew," he demanded. "We had other options. No one needed to know but us. We could have gone on with our lives the way we always planned."

Marcia shook her head, tears streaming down her face.

Devon brushed his hand over his hair. "I'm leaving for college in New York in a couple days, so don't think your having my baby is going to change that."

"Who said I'm having your baby?" Marcia retorted, feeling like someone else had asked the question and not her. She heard her own voice and felt her lips move, but she no longer felt like herself and Devon was not acting like the guy she loved. She wouldn't wait for him to reject her. Her only defense was to reject him first. She inhaled deeply and asked in a stronger voice, "I am having a baby, but who said it's yours?"

Devon knitted his brows and stared at her in disbelief as a wave of emotions washed over him. He hadn't doubted it was his baby when he heard the rumor. As far as he knew Marcia hadn't been intimately involved with anyone else. Yet, she had kept her pregnancy from him. Could her reason for doing so be that she was carrying someone else child? As the hurt of her betrayal pierced his heart, he also saw a way out.

His voice was soft and hoarse as he spoke. "You're right. You didn't do anything to me. You did it to yourself. Good luck." He turned away from her, yanked open the door, and slammed it shut behind him as he left.

Devon returned to his parents' house feeling relieved. Now that he knew he was not going to be a father, he could start his life in New York with no concern that had shirked his responsibilities back home. If Marcia wanted to throw away her life like that, that was her problem. They were such close friends that he had thought they were made for each other. Now that she had betrayed him, he made up his mind not to give her a second thought.

CHAPTER THREE

Ruth was waiting anxiously for Devon to return from his visit with her daughter. Would he admit to his parents that the child Marcia was carrying was his? Or would he confide in her and provide financial support while keeping the truth a secret from his parents?

Instead, Devon said nothing to anyone about Marcia upon his return.

As Ruth pondered his silence, she reached the same conclusion. He had to be the father. Marcia wouldn't let any other male get close to her. It was true that Ruth had been wrong to think that Marcia would wait until she was a college graduate and married before getting pregnant. The entire situation revealed that there was a lot that Ruth didn't know about her daughter. Yet, she felt convinced that Devon had been her daughter's only lover.

As she watched him packing to leave for college, fury and frustration built up inside her. Her daughter too should have been getting ready to leave for college, not waiting to have a baby that she could not financially support. It had taken two people to make that baby. It wasn't fair that Marcia had lost her college scholarship, while Devon faced no consequences for his actions. She felt certain that he was involved.

On the day before Devon left for New York, his mother asked Ruth to prepare a special dinner for him. Escovitch fish and bammy was Devon and Marcia's favorite dish. Ruth fried the fish and soaked it with vinegar and sautéed onions and green pepper. She set it on plates alongside the bammy, flat bread made from cassava. Ruth had served this meal to them often at the end of each summer before they left for boarding school.

14

Marcia's absence from this farewell dinner left a tremendous ache in Ruth's heart.

Ruth served the Douglas family with a smile plastered across her lips, but emotional turmoil raged within her. She was mad at Devon, but she had known him since he was an infant and thought it unlikely that he had forced himself on her daughter. Any intimacy between them would have taken place because Marcia consented. That thought left Ruth feeling angry with Marcia. Marcia knew better. Forget the fact that she had been taught that it was better to wait. Didn't she want a better life for herself? Was the opportunity to lie down with Devon so tempting that she couldn't control herself? Yes, unless Marcia's lover had acted against her wishes, Marcia was ultimately to be blamed. But it still took two to make a baby and it wasn't fair that Marcia alone had to live with the consequences.

What were his parents thinking? Ruth wondered if they didn't suspect that their son and Marcia had been lovers. Probably not. He was their one and only: the prince in their private kingdom, the heir to the Douglas throne. They were so proud of him that they would probably condemn anyone who said or did anything to sully his image.

Ruth tried not to focus on them. They were her employers and she needed her job. The fact that she could not discuss the situation with them as an equal only added to her frustration.

Sometimes, she found herself asking how God could let this happen —in spite of all her prayers. The same answer kept coming back to her: God gives people a choice, to serve Him or not; to do things His way, or not. Ruth had read again and again all that the Bible said about intimacy between a man and woman. Two becoming one was a special gift that God reserved for those who entered the covenant of marriage. Outside of that sacred covenant, uniting as one flesh was common, but the Bible said it was wrong. Neither she nor her daughter had resisted this temptation. Now Ruth could only pray that God would be even more merciful to Marcia than He had been to her.

Still, the fury and frustration she felt mounted within her, in spite of her prayers. It was like a pressure building inside her and she had no outlet for releasing it. Like a cartoon character who could blow his top, Ruth felt like her head would explode.

Marcia entered the final phase of her pregnancy in relatively good health, even though she had not seen a doctor and she was extremely depressed. She counted the months since she and Devon had been together that Easter weekend and determined that the baby would be due sometime in December. The skin of her stomach itched, she assumed, because it was stretching. She massaged it with Vaseline daily, using her mother's cure-all for every skin ailment. After Devon's visit, she had even more difficulty sleeping because she would lie awake crying and worrying. Eventually, she couldn't lay comfortably in bed because her stomach got in the way.

She felt like she was cut off from the world. The tenants next door had children, and she often heard them playing, but kept to herself. She spent most of her time indoors. When she did go out, she wore a straw hat and sunglasses. Looking young worked to her disadvantage, she thought. She was certain that if strangers saw her face they would know that she was going to be a teenage mother and she felt ashamed.

Often, she cried because she never heard from Devon again. All through September, October, and into November, she wondered what he and her peers were doing. What was college life really like? She was certain they were all excelling and she was being left behind.

Occasionally, one of the tenants would knock at her door to tell her there was a phone call from her mother or her aunt. They were the only people who knew how to contact her. They asked how she was feeling and urged her to call on her neighbors if she felt any pain. Marcia promised them that she would.

Her mother came to visit her in November. During the visit, Ruth laid her hands on Marcia's belly and prayed. Tears streamed down her face as she asked God to protect her daughter and grant that the baby be fearfully and wonderfully made and not die but live and declare the works of the Lord. She believed that there was power in praying the scriptures, and she based her prayer on the Psalms.

"Have you been reading your Bible?" she asked.

Marcia replied honestly, "No."

"Read it," Ruth commanded, placing her palm against her daughter's cheek. "I can't take away the sadness you're feeling now, or the pain you're going to feel during childbirth, but I promise you this. When everything else fails, call on Jesus. He will see you through."

Marcia nodded.

"I'm sure you don't fully understand now. But I was once in your shoes, alone and afraid. I didn't know I would live to see this day when my daughter was all grown up and graduated from high school. In spite of all the struggle, God has been good to me."

Again Marcia nodded.

"You'll probably be here alone when you go into labor. Use the money in this envelope to pay someone to take you to the hospital. Maybe one of the neighbors will take you. If not, call a taxi. We've already told the neighbors that you may wake them in the middle of the night to use their phone. They also have the phone numbers to call me and Aunt Pat to tell us you're on your way to the hospital. I wish you didn't have to be alone, but I can't take time off from work yet. Mrs. Douglas promised to give me a week off when you have the baby, but only God knows exactly when the baby will come."

"I know, Mommy." A sob escaped her lips.

"Pray, Marcia. The more scared you feel, the more you should pray and ask God to help you."

Ruth held her daughter. It wasn't just a hug. She held her gently like she was her baby girl again. There was so much more she wanted to say to her, but she didn't want to make her feel any more nervous than she was already feeling about delivering the baby.

Ruth worried that it was a matter of life and death. Both the mother and baby were at risk. But in the best situation, both pulled through in good health. Ruth prayed for the best.

After she left, Marcia cried hysterically. She hoped that sleep would come to interrupt the thoughts that caused her so much pain. When it didn't she got on her knees with the Bible open to the page her mother had been reading.

Underlined in pencil were these words: Be anxious for nothing, but for everything by prayer and supplication with thanksgiving let your request be made known to God and the peace of God which surpasses all understanding will guard your heart and mind through Christ Jesus.

She closed her eyes and silently let the tears flow. Gradually, a sense of calm came over her and she climbed into bed releasing her fears in sleep.

Marcia went into labor one December morning. It was not that her water broke in the dramatic fashion that she had seen so often in the movies. Instead, she felt intense pain. One contraction after another, the pain became excruciating. When she knocked at her neighbor's door, no one was home who had a car, so they called a taxi for her. As Marcia was leaving, she reminded her neighbor to call her mother.

For the next eleven hours, Marcia longed for someone to hold her hand, to whisper words of comfort and support. Once, when she felt she could not tolerate the pain, she screamed, "Devon!"

A nurse with sympathetic eyes touched her shoulder and said softly, "He is not here yet, Miss."

When the baby was born, the same nurse held her for Marcia to see before she placed her gently in her arms. Tears streamed down Marcia's face as she stared at her little girl in awe. That this person had come from inside her was truly a miracle. Marcia praised God. She was hurting physically still, but there was another pain—a deep dull ache in her heart as she longed for someone she loved to share this moment with her.

No one came to the hospital. When she and the baby were released, they took a taxi back to the house. Her neighbors fussed over her, and she let the Grandma of that family hold her baby while she borrowed their phone.

She called her mother, but it was Mrs. Douglas who answered the phone. It was their first contact with each other since Marcia's graduation, and Marcia marveled at how much her life had changed. She had many regrets, but as she looked at the tiny baby before her, she decided that little Wendy was not one of them.

"Hello, Mrs. Douglas. This is Marcia. How are you?"

"Marcia. Dear child. I'm so glad you finally called. We didn't know how to reach you. The only number we could find in your mother's room was your aunt's. Have you spoken to her?"

"Who?"

"Pat Harrison. Your aunt in New York."

"No. I was calling to speak to Mommy. Is she there?"

"No. Ah. Call your aunt. She will tell you everything."

"Is everything okay, Mrs. Douglas? Where is Mommy? Is she okay?"

"Please, Marcia. Call your aunt. Once you've spoken to her, if you want to call me back, I'll be here."

Marcia called her aunt but didn't get her immediately. She hadn't expected to because it was the middle of a workday. Later that day, Marcia found out that as she lay panting in labor in the hospital, her mother breathed her final breath. Her aunt had called her on that day but didn't leave a message because she didn't want Marcia to hear of her mother's death from someone she hardly knew.

Why hadn't her mother ever told her that she suffered from high blood pressure? Why hadn't she ever noticed her complaining about headaches? Why had she suffered a massive brain hemorrhage on the day of her granddaughter's birth? There had been no hospitalization, no chance for recovery. She had been hanging clothes outside behind the Douglas family's house when she collapsed.

Marcia reached for her baby. "Wendy," she said softly. She snuggled her close, trying to suppress the anguish she felt inside. "Wendy," she repeated as the baby gazed back at her and smiled. "My daughter Wendy. You're all I have now, my baby. Wendy."

CHAPTER FOUR

SEVENTEEN YEARS LATER

Wendy reached for her thick, heavy, hardcover Economics book and slammed her locker shut. As the second bell rang signaling the start of class, she hurried down the hallway, trying to make up for the time she'd lost when she stopped by the gym to see her boyfriend. Her classroom was on other end of the high school.

Senior year seemed to be going too fast, and Wendy had a major problem to solve before graduation. She needed to find her father. Growing up in New York with a single mother never bothered Wendy until last summer when she and her boyfriend Paul Chambers began to talk about getting married once they finished high school. Wendy had no doubt that it was in God's plan for her to marry Paul and eventually move to Africa with him to work as a missionary. They not only daydreamed about this. They prayed and read the Bible together, and agreed that this was where God was guiding them.

She and Paul knew each other from church, where their mothers had attended since they were babies, but their mothers didn't agree that they should be in such a rush to get married. The more Marcia resisted the idea of her teenage daughter getting married, the more Wendy longed for her father to be present in her life, to witness her graduation, and to give her away at her wedding.

Up until recently, Wendy had been satisfied with the love she received from her family. She had grown up in the Bronx, north of Manhattan with its skyscraper buildings and south of Westchester County with its suburban homes. Wendy's family lived in the northern-most part of the Bronx which was urban in its access to public transportation, yet suburban-like with green grass and trees and mostly multi-family homes.

The red brick building where Wendy's family lived had three floors, each with its own apartment and was adjoined to others like it that lined an entire block. Wendy and Marcia shared a one bedroom apartment on the ground floor. Above them lived Marcia's cousin Blossom and her husband. Aunt Pat and her husband Trevor watched over them from the top floor and played the role of grandparents in Wendy's life. Yet, they always told her stories of her Grandma Ruth, Marcia's mother, who had passed away around the time of Wendy's birth.

Every Father's Day, Wendy made cards for the two father figures in her life: Uncle Trevor and Uncle Steve. She had grown up hearing the same short story about her own father. Her mother told her that her father's family own a hotel on the island of Jamaica, and her mother and Grandma Ruth used to live with them until shortly before Wendy was born. With that information, Wendy was launching her own search for her father.

The door to the classroom door squeaked open and Wendy said a sheepish, "Sorry, I'm late," to the gentleman standing by the chalkboard. Her regular teacher was out on maternity leave, and like her classmates, she didn't pay too much attention to the substitute teacher. She noticed that her regular seat was taken and looked around the room for an empty seat. Her classmates never followed the seating plan when they had a substitute teacher. They paired up or formed groups, ready for a chat session.

"Turn to page 265 in your textbook," the substitute teacher said.

"Can I go to my locker?" a student called out.

"Me too," said another.

"I got to go to the bathroom," another student announced. "Hey, Teach, can I get the hall pass?"

"Everybody sit down," the teacher demanded. He was accustomed to disorderly conduct from the students when he met a class for the first time, but it didn't take them long to realize that he would take no nonsense.

"I need the hall pass." The boy standing by his desk was persistent.

Wendy watched as the teacher shook his head. She pulled out her notebook ready to tune out her peers and the teacher while she worked on the letter she was writing to her father. Her mother had finally told her the name of the hotel that her father's family owned in Jamaica. She prayed that God would make a way for her father to receive the letter when she mailed it there.

"Sit down," the teacher said in a deep, stern voice. "You'll get the hall pass when your classmate gets back."

The boy rolled his eyes and sluggishly returned to his seat.

"The topic in this chapter of your textbook is entrepreneurship. I'll be teaching and testing during this period. We will discuss the principle, you will provide me with some examples to indicate that you understand the topic, and then I will give you a quiz. Your average from these quizzes will count as twenty percent of your final grade."

The class let out a collective groan.

"You can't do that. You're just a substitute," one student shouted.

"Mrs. Mason never gave us a pop quiz," complained a girl in the front row.

"Mrs. Mason is on maternity leave," the substitute teacher reminded them.

"Are you going to fill in for her all the time?" asked the boy who was waiting to go to the bathroom.

"We'll see," the teacher replied, as the missing student returned with the hallway pass.

"I hope not," the boy mumbled, as he snatched the hall pass from his classmate and headed for the door.

"What did you say, young man?" the teacher demanded.

"I said, I'll be right back," the boy replied.

His classmates snickered.

The period progressed exactly as the teacher described, and the students quieted down and paid attention. This was an advanced placement class where the students were concerned about test scores and the caliber of college they would get into. When the bell rang, they handed in the quiz and rushed from the room.

The teacher stopped Wendy as she was passing by his desk. He took her quiz from her and said her name.

"Wendy Tapper, right?"

She nodded.

Seeing the puzzled look on her face, he quickly got to the point.

"Are you Marcia Tapper's daughter?" he asked.

"Yes. Do you know her?" Wendy responded, surprised.

"I used to, quite well. We grew up in the same place." He paused, uncertain that he should proceed. This was too much of a coincidence. Would months of searching be brought to an abrupt ending with a chance meeting of his daughter in a high school classroom?

If Wendy had been a younger child, he would have waited to talk to her mother first. Yet, he had already missed seventeen years of her life, and she was almost an adult. He resolved that he had waited long enough.

"What's your father's name, Wendy?" he asked, feeling a lump rising in his throat.

"Devon Douglas. Do you know him too?" Wendy asked, staring at her substitute teacher.

"I am Devon Douglas."

Wendy opened her mouth to speak, but couldn't. She looked up at the man standing in front of her. The girls who had been seated near her had called him a cutie, and she agreed. He stood over six feet tall, with low cut hair and a lightly bearded face. Now, she studied that face. There was something familiar about those thick eyebrows and hazel eyes. Suddenly, she tossed her backpack on the desk between them and searched frantically for her wallet. In it, she had a picture of her parents as teenagers that she rarely looked at, but felt secure knowing it was there. She gazed at the picture, then at the man standing in front of her. The beard was different, but all of the other features were the same. Noting the resemblance, she gasped and slapped her right hand over her mouth.

"Oh my goodness. It is you!" she exclaimed. She stood on the opposite side of the desk and just stared. "Thank you, God," she whispered. God had heard and answered her prayers in a miraculous fashion. He had brought her father to her, even before she mailed her letter to Jamaica in the hope of finding him. Here was her father in the flesh, standing in front of her in her high school classroom in New York. "Praise the Lord!"

Devon smiled in wonder and awe, as he gazed at his own offspring standing in front of him. As he dwelled on her features, he noticed both his traits and her mother's. He wasn't a religious man, but as he heard his daughter's words, he said, "Yes! Thank God." This was the type of miracle only God could orchestrate.

His daughter knew who he was and even carried a picture of him around in her wallet. Perhaps, getting to know her would not be as difficult as he had anticipated. Perhaps, if her mother had told her about him, she would not be averse to their meeting.

After they had stared at each other for a moment, he said, "Your mother. I'm going to need to talk to her."

"Yes, yes. Of course," Wendy grinned at him, believing yet not believing her father was really there. She couldn't wait to tell Paul.

She gave her father the phone number and best time to call her mother. In exchange, she accepted his business card.

The bell rang again. Another set of students entered the class.

"We'll talk later. I promise," he reassured her.

She nodded as she left the classroom and rushed down the hallway to find Paul.

Paul reacted with suspicion to the news that Wendy found her father, so Wendy decided to wait until she got home to call her mother. Her mother worked as a Home Health Aide and was in the middle of helping her patient get dressed when her cell phone rang.

"It's Wendy," Marcia informed her patient, before answering her phone. Her patient knew that Marcia always kept her phone on to be accessible to her teenage daughter. Marcia frequently bragged about her daughter to Mrs. Briggs.

"Mommy. Mommy, guess what?" Wendy shouted breathlessly into the phone.

"What, Wendy? Are you okay?" Marcia asked.

"Yes, I'm fine. I just can't believe it. You'll never believe me when I tell you who I saw today." Wendy chatted quickly. "Oh my goodness. I can't get over this."

Marcia giggled. Her daughter spotted a celebrity today, she thought. While she wanted to play along, she had to hastily wrap up the conversation, so as not to keep Mrs. Briggs waiting too long.

"Okay, honey. I want to hear every detail, but later. I'm helping Mrs. Briggs."

"Mommy, this can't wait. I saw Daddy today."

Shocked into silence, Marcia almost dropped the phone. "What did you say?"

"I saw Daddy today. At school. He was the substitute teacher in one of my classes. Praise God, Mommy! Can you believe it? He recognized my name, but he waited until after class to tell me. I can't believe it. Can you believe it? Daddy, mommy! Of all the unlikely coincidences. This is a gift straight from God." The words raced from Wendy's mouth and she would have rambled on if Marcia hadn't stopped her.

"Wendy?"

"Mommy, Daddy is not in Jamaica. He is here in the United States, right here in New York. He is so handsome. I think I have the most handsome father in the world. And he wants to get to know me."

"Wendy. Stop. Look, Sweetie, I'm busy now. I'll call you back. Better yet, we'll discuss this when I get home."

"Okay, Mommy, but hurry home."

"I'll do my best. Don't let anyone into the apartment. No one. Go upstairs to Aunt Pat and Uncle Trevor, or to Blossom's apartment, if you need anything. Okay?"

"Yes, Mommy. I love you. Hurry home so that we can talk about this."

"I love you too."

Marcia resumed the task of dressing Mrs. Briggs. Her patient lived alone and had lost the use of most of her limbs. Physically, Mrs. Briggs was weak, but her mind was sharp and she retained details, like the name and age of Marcia's daughter.

"Did something happen to Wendy?" she asked.

"No, Mrs. Briggs," Marcia replied, appreciating her concern, but hoping her patient wouldn't pose any questions she couldn't answer. "She's fine."

"But you are not. Your facial expression changed so severely just now. Certainly, something terrible must have happened to cause you to look so worried."

Marcia smiled, but she was sorry that her face was so expressive. "Nothing has happened, Mrs. Briggs. Wendy ran into someone today. Someone who... Someone I..." She sighed. "I... I'm just surprised. That's all."

"Shocked is more like it," muttered Mrs. Briggs, but she didn't probe any further.

Wendy hung up the phone and turned up the music on her CD player until it vibrated the walls of the tiny apartment. So far, her mother and her boyfriend, the two people closest to her, didn't seem to understand why finding her father was such a great cause for celebration. Yet, their reaction did little to dampen her mood.

She bellowed out the words of the song that was playing and danced around the living room. "Somebody told me that we overcome by our testimony." She started to call Paul back to thank him for the CD that he'd made for her with some of the latest gospel hits, but hung up. This song, "Love Him Like I Do," by Deitrick, Mary Mary, and Ruben Studdard was one of her favorites.

The phone rang and Wendy sensed that it was Paul. There was such a close connection between them that she felt he must have been longing to talk to her at the same moment that she was thinking about calling him.

She picked up the receiver and kept on singing the song that was expressing her love for the Lord.

"Girl, you better sing," Paul said, and started singing along with her.

Wendy smiled as she pictured him dancing around his apartment. She stood in place as she belted out a part by female gospel artists Mary Mary, "God, He led me through a test, and he brought out the very best of me, and now I'll never forget to tell the world what You mean to me..."

Paul picked up back on the male vocals. As the song came to an end, Paul said, "Instant replay. Rewind and come again."

Wendy laughed, but she pressed replay and turned the music down. "So, are we going to do this song in the talent show this year?" she asked.

"Yeah! It would be good if we could get some of the guys from the youth group at church to join us."

"We could try, but you know they're living that double life. They love the Lord inside the church, but outside the church, they don't want anybody to know it."

"That's a shame."

"It is," Wendy agreed. "And you know, Jesus said, if we're ashamed of him, he's going to be ashamed of us."

"Preach, Sister Wendy. Preach," Paul said jokingly.

"I wasn't trying to. I'm just saying, though, you know all the kids we go to church with never want to take a stand when we see them around the high school."

"True, but we've been praying about that for years now, so maybe this year will be different. God knows we're graduating. Maybe he'll surprise us with support from our peers. After all, look what he did for you today."

"Yeah, can you believe it? Paul, I met my daddy today."

"I know. He sort of looks like you too."

"Did you see him?" she asked excitedly.

"Yeah. I went by the class and peeked through the glass at the door. He looked like he could very well be your father."

"That's because he is my father. Didn't he look like the picture I showed you?"

"He did."

"Well then?"

"All right. No doubt. You found your pops."

"He found me. Praise the Lord! Hallelujah! Thank you, Jesus!"

"Yes, praise God. But you should try to play it cool until you see what he's about."

"What do you mean?"

"Well. You don't know anything about him. Where has he been all your life? Why did he suddenly appear now?"

"I told you I've been praying. You've heard me asking God. This is nothing but a gift."

"Okay, but be careful. Guard your heart."

"Whatever."

"What?"

"Can't you just be happy for me?"

"I am."

"You're not acting like it."

"You're right. Turn up the music. Let me get in on your praise party. As a matter of fact..." He located his copy of the same CD, put on the music and blasted it.

Later that night, Marcia reflected on her conversation with Wendy as she waited for the New York City subway. An icy wind gust whipped across the outdoor platform, down the stairwell, and into the enclosed level of the subway station where she huddled waiting to catch the train.

As the train screeched to a halt overhead, Marcia bounded up the stairs and boarded the front car. She felt safer there with the engineer, less likely to become a victim of crime. Crime on the subway at night wasn't common, but it happened, and Marcia's habit of walking fast and riding near a uniformed worker helped to reduce her risk of being targeted. But on this night, it was Wendy's revelation that threatened Marcia's sense of security.

Marcia kept hearing Wendy's voice as she said, "I saw Daddy today."

Wendy's statement resounded in Marcia's mind as she exited the number five subway-train, descended the stairs and almost ran the distance between the train station and her apartment. She tugged at her wool scarf to cover her nose and mouth as an icy breeze fanned her face. It was almost midnight when she unlocked the door to her apartment, but she knew Wendy would be waiting up for her.

"Hey, Mommy." Wendy seemed to leap from the sofa-bed in the living room to the front door in one long stride.

"Hi, honey," Marcia replied, removing her outerwear. She hugged her daughter, then sat on the floor and pulled off her boots. Marcia's cheeks, nose, and ears were tinged red from the cold.

"I made you some hot chocolate," Wendy said, moving into the kitchen while her mother went to the bathroom to wash her hands.

The apartment was compact, so neither one had to raise her voice to talk to the other. The front door opened into a dining area that could only fit a circular table for four. Behind it was the bathroom, and next to that a slim corridor formed the kitchen. A tiny living room and equally small bedroom completed the unit.

"Thanks for the hot chocolate," Marcia said, taking a sip. She placed the mug on the dining table and sat down. "Now, what did you have for dinner?"

"Uncle Trevor made stew peas and rice. Aunt Pat sent a plate down for you, if you're hungry."

"Thanks. Did you eat? I know you were probably too excited."

Wendy nodded and sat in a chair next to her. She had been restless all evening as she waited for her mother to get home.

"Mommy, you have to see him. You know the picture you gave me of daddy that was taken when you guys were teenagers?"

Marcia nodded.

"Well, he looks just like that, but older and more muscular."

Marcia smiled, happy for her daughter, but she felt confounded by what the day's events might mean for her. She sighed and ran a hand through her hair. "Tell me everything that happened," she said.

Wendy breathlessly relayed the details of the meeting with her father. "We didn't have much time to talk," she concluded. "It was my last period, but he had to teach another class. We exchanged phone numbers. He wants to talk to you. I still can't believe this. I feel like I'm dreaming."

"Me too," Marcia replied, placing one hand over her daughter's. "Now, take a deep breath and try to relax." She silently prayed for the right words to say.

"I can't relax, Mommy. I didn't tell you this before because I didn't want you to feel bad, but the closer I was getting to graduation day, the more unhappy I felt that my father would not be there. I had started writing him a letter that I was going to mail to the hotel in Jamaica that you told me his family owns."

"God answered your prayers by bringing him to you instead." Marcia spoke, thankful for the calmness in her voice. She remembered how she had lied to Devon when they were teenagers. While she was pregnant with Wendy, she'd told him that the baby she was carrying wasn't his. She had not seen nor spoken to him since.

"Mommy, you're crying," Wendy said, interrupting her thoughts.

"I'm sorry." Tears filled Marcia's eyes as she tried to sort out her feelings. "It's been a long day and I'm exhausted."

"Are you crying because of Daddy?" Wendy asked. "I want to get to know him, but he'll never replace you. You know that right?"

Marcia nodded and held on tightly to her daughter. Devon's emergence would change a lot between them, but it would never hinder their love. "You have a right to know your father and his family, Wendy. I've taught you that you should allow yourself to become the woman God calls you to be, but part of that comes from knowing your background."

"So you will talk to Daddy then."

"Yes." Marcia nodded and stood up as she spoke. "Let me take a shower, and we both need to get some sleep."

"Daddy said you could call him at any time."

"I'll call him in the morning."

"Thank you, Mommy. I love you." Wendy hugged her again, and again they held on tightly to each other.

"Now get some sleep, or you'll be falling asleep in your classes tomorrow."

"I don't think I can sleep."

"Try," Marcia said, steering her daughter toward the bedroom. "I'll take the sofa-bed tonight."

By the time she got out of the shower, Wendy was sound asleep.

CHAPTER FIVE

Devon drummed his fingers against the table as he waited. He and Marcia had talked briefly that morning and decided to meet at one of the many Jamaican restaurants in her neighborhood. This one was located in a strip mall. The dining area was immaculate, the tables decorated with frilly white tablecloths, and a vase with a single carnation sat on each one. Customers formed a line at the cash register ordering takeout, but few bothered to sit down. Devon felt his stomach rumble as he inhaled the scent of curry, but it was the woman he was meeting and not the food that was on his mind. He had selected a table close to the window, surrounded by empty tables nearby. This setting offered him and Marcia the comfort of meeting in a neutral place without sacrificing the privacy they needed to talk.

Marcia entered the restaurant and paused just inside the doorway to remove her hat. There was no greeter or hostess, so she approached the seating area scanning the faces of the people sitting at the tables.

Devon recognized her immediately, as he saw her face. Her face looked the same as the pretty teenage girl he once new. He rose from his seat just as she looked in his direction. Their eyes met and he waved. She smiled, and as she walked toward him, he felt his heart begin to race.

Approaching him on shaky legs, Marcia resolved to appear unaffected by this man. He was Wendy's father—nothing more. When they were teenagers, an intense look from him would make her blush. His voice would send waves of warmth up and down her spine. His touch would make her quiver. But this man had also caused her great pain.

"Devon Douglas. Long time no see." Her heart lurched, but she smiled coolly and reached out to shake his hand.

"Hello, Marcia. I'm glad you came." He shook her hand, but also leaned forward to kiss her cheek. A wave of memories washed over him and he felt the urge to pull her into his arms, but instead, he pulled back. Their eyes locked and held.

As he helped her remove her jacket, his eyes roamed slowly along her body, delighting in its form beneath her black turtleneck sweater, jeans, and matching boots. Her lips parted in a smile that still made him feel like she smiled just for him.

She felt her confidence wavering and sat down.

"You should have told me the truth," he blurted out as he sat down.

"You should have known," she retorted, glaring at him. "What kind of girl did you think I was? No matter what others thought of me, I thought you would have known better. We were friends for so many years." Her eyes were sad, exposing her emotions far more than she had planned. She looked at the menu in front of her.

"You're right. I'm sorry. I was so preoccupied with leaving for college when I heard you were pregnant, I didn't think twice about it once you said the child wasn't mine."

She never stopped thinking about him, and here he was confessing that he had not spared her a second thought. She felt so angry, she could have drenched him with the glass of water that sat on the table in front of her. "You're telling me that you didn't know I was a virgin on the day you slept with me. And you really thought that in a matter of weeks I would have moved on to someone else. You knew me better than that," she whispered.

"I wasn't thinking," he replied, realizing now how uncharacteristic of her that would have been. Had he been more concerned about her, and not just himself, he might have realized that back then. He felt like a jerk. During the past six months, he had done nothing but think about her. Yet, he couldn't explain that seventeen years ago, he hadn't really cared, and still expect her to grant him access to their daughter. "I was getting ready for college," he continued, as though that was a good excuse.

"So was I," she retorted.

"I know. I'm sorry. I just remember being so excited and apprehensive about moving to New York, but I still took time to check with you," he hesitated, "to find out if you were carrying my child."

"What would you have done if you had known from the beginning?" Her eyes held his challenging him.

He looked down.

"You would have insisted that I have an abortion."

"I'm glad you didn't." His eyes met hers once again. "Wendy is such a beautiful girl, I mean young lady. I'm sure she owes it all to her mother."

Marcia blushed, but was infuriated by the fact that Devon could win her over so easily with the slightest compliment. Sparks were still flying between them, but she had already played with fire and gotten burned. She sipped water from her glass, determined to cool down.

He exhaled deeply and leaned back.

They both needed a breather. Neither had intended to plunge into conversation about the most intimate part of their lives. The waiter came over, took their order, and left with the menus.

"Wendy is a beautiful girl. She looks a lot like you."

"No, she doesn't." Marcia refused to let another compliment chip away at her guard, especially one that didn't ring true. To her, Wendy looked like Devon. Wendy had inherited her father's height, dark brown complexion, and dark hair. Like his, her nose was straight and prominent above full lips. "Wendy looks like you, and from what I remember, she has a lot of your personality."

"But she has your eyes, Marcia. Intense. Dark and mysterious. I feel like I could lose myself when I look into your eyes."

Marcia cleared her throat and took another sip of water. Either the heat was turned up too high in the restaurant, or his closeness was making her warm. In spite of all the pain his abandonment had caused her, she wanted him to kiss her while she ran her fingertips along the muscles that rippled beneath the slacks and button-down shirt he wore. Her feelings didn't make sense. She felt like sixteen again, and he was the guy she had always had a crush on.

"You haven't changed much, have you, Devon Douglas?"

"I have."

"Why are you here?" she asked, looking directly into his eyes and displaying confidence she did not feel.

Devon knitted his brows, but his eyes held hers as he declared, "I owe you."

Marcia shook her head. "You owe me nothing."

Devon tried to choose his words more carefully this time. "I want to get to know our daughter."

"Fair enough, but why now?"

The waiter returned, placing two orders of jerked chicken, coleslaw, and slices of hard dough bread in front of them, giving Devon time to think before he answered. When he finally spoke, he made reference to the last time they saw each other.

"Do you remember that my family went to England right after graduation?"

"Yes, I was terrified about being pregnant and it broke my heart when I found out that you had left the island and hadn't even bothered to tell me."

Devon's eyes searched hers and he knew an apology was inadequate but he said the words anyway. "I'm sorry." After a brief pause, he continued, "Do you remember my grandfather who was living in England."

She nodded. "Of course. I used to love when he came home on holiday and took us to country to his farm."

"I liked that too," Devon agreed, feeling close to her as he remembered and regretting even more that they hadn't remained close. "Well, he retired the year we finished high school, so my parents and I went to help him settle his affairs abroad and prepare to move back to Jamaica. I wish he was still there, so he could see you again and meet Wendy."

"He passed away?" Marcia asked softly.

Devon nodded.

"I'm so sorry," Marcia said sincerely.

"Thanks. He was ninety-nine, so... Anyway, before he died, he told me that it's about time I took responsibility for my child. He said he had fathered many children in his lifetime, with different women of course, and was proud that he had financially supported every one of them. He remembered all their birthdays and kept in touch with them and their mothers. Through that network of people, he learned what happened to you and your mother because my parents and I had only told him that your mother died suddenly and you had left. It wasn't until last year that he finally found out that you had gotten pregnant right before you left, and no one could convince him that the baby's father was anyone but me."

"He sounds like a wise man," Marcia said, smiling.

"Marcia, the funny thing is, I hadn't thought about you in recent years, but the moment he mentioned my child, I knew. I guess subconsciously I always knew. Can you ever forgive me?"

Without hesitation, Marcia replied, "I already have, considering I'm not exactly an innocent party here. Besides, Wendy needs you."

"She does?" The thought that his daughter needed him resonated with Devon on many levels. He felt guilty because he should have been there all along. Yet, he felt grateful that Marcia openly acknowledged that need and that he was there now to fulfill it. He also felt anxious to catch up on lost years and to compensate for his absence by giving wholeheartedly of himself now. His feelings overwhelmed him and he focused on the food as he tried to regain control. He cut off a piece of the spicy chicken and ate it with a bite of bread. Was it Marcia's presence, or their conversation, that was emotionally breaking him?

"I sincerely mean that you've done a great job without me," he added looking up and making eye contact with her to convey his sincerity.

"By the grace of God. Only, by the grace of God."

They both ate a few mouthfuls, giving themselves time.

Devon noted how Marcia wore her hair differently now. As a teenager, she had always kept it straight, with bangs that fell across her forehead. He like this look, with her hair braided and pulled back, away from her face. He longed for the closeness they used to share and imagined himself soothing the dark lines of her brows as he stared into her eyes.

Marcia blushed under his scrutiny. Devon's look had always been intense, but there was a time when she knew what he was thinking. She wondered where his thoughts focused now. Again, she quelled her insecurity and tried to remain in control of their conversation.

"I'm trying to break the cycle," Marcia finally said.

"What cycle?" Devon asked.

"Teenage pregnancy. My mother had me at sixteen, and I was sixteen when you and I... Let's just say, I barely turned seventeen before Wendy was born. Now she is seventeen and poised to go off to college as I was when..."

"Surely, Wendy is too levelheaded to do anything foolish," he interjected.

"I would like to think so, but I can only think of myself at her age. I was a brilliant student at the best girls' high school in Jamaica. I had a full scholarship to attend the University of the West Indies. My mother never thought I would be foolish enough to ruin everything by getting pregnant."

"You weren't foolish."

"Oh, but I was. I made the biggest mistake in my life when I let you get too close to me, but I don't regret having Wendy. She has been the center of my world ever since."

Her comments bruised his ego, but he understood that she was being honest. He knew she was right, but it hurt to admit that the intimacy they shared, which he once thought of as a conquest, had been a mistake. He regretted now that so many years had gone by without him being a part of their lives.

"Does Wendy have a boyfriend?" he asked.

"Yes. She is developing a serious relationship with a guy she has been friends with since childhood. She says they are not lovers and I believe her. Wendy is a born again Christian. When she was seven years old, she committed her life to the Lord, and she has been living to please Him ever since."

"Really!"

"Really. It's certainly made parenting a lot easier for me. She hasn't pushed the boundaries the way many teenagers do because she fears God. She prays about her decisions, reads her Bible daily, and tries to live in a way that pleases God."

"Wow! The attractive, energetic teenager I met yesterday?"

Marcia nodded.

"So, why are you worried? She doesn't sound like someone who would rush into lovemaking without a commitment like marriage."

Marcia cleared her throat. "First of all, I was a churchgoer myself when I got pregnant. In the eyes of both our mothers, I was an angel. That's why they were both so disappointed in me when they found out."

Her voice shook when she spoke about herself, but steadied as she continued to talk about Wendy. "Wendy says she is saving herself for marriage. The problem is that she and Paul are thinking of getting married after high school. They have applied to the same colleges and are planning to live together, once they get married of course."

Devon almost choked on his food. "Over my dead body. No one is ready for marriage at their age."

"If you take that approach with Wendy, you will alienate her. You need to get to know her before you begin to make judgments about what she should do with her life."

"Are you saying that you approve of this impending marriage? When I think of myself at her age, there was no way I was ready for marriage. In fact, my fiancé of three years recently left me because at thirty-five, I'm still not ready to get married, at least not to her. I can't stand by and let my daughter make the mistake of marrying so young."

So he was engaged, but he hadn't been married. The facts registered on Marcia's brain for a split second before she retorted, "Your daughter? Funny. It's been almost two decades and I don't remember you sharing any of the responsibility of raising her."

Her comments silenced him. He wanted to say that was not his fault, but in a way it was. It was absurd of him to step in and expect to play the role of a protective father who had been there all of Wendy's life. But it was just as ridiculous of Marcia to think she could dictate what role he would play now that he was there.

"I don't understand you," he said. "You said you wanted my help to prevent Wendy from making the same mistake you did. Yet, when I agree with you, you get defensive. Look, I know life must have been difficult for you as a teenage mother, but do you think it's easy for me to meet my daughter for the first time when she is almost an adult? Can you imagine what it was like to find out about her last year and not have a clue whether or not I would ever find her? I didn't sleep last night because I was afraid to wake up and find that meeting her was a dream."

Marcia pushed her plate away, completely losing interest in her food. She wondered if he really expected her to feel sorry for him, after all that she had been through. The nerve of him to speculate about how hard life must have been for her as a teenage mother. He couldn't even begin to imagine… Her voice was soft when she spoke. "Fine, Devon. If you care so much about Wendy, you need to remember first and foremost that she is our child, not yours. I've been mother and father to her all her life, and she is all that I have. I believe that God has brought you into our lives in answer to our prayers, so I don't expect that you're here to hurt her."

"I would never do anything to hurt either one of you."

"Right," Marcia replied, her tone tinged with sarcasm. She looked at her watch. "I have to be at work in Manhattan at three o'clock, and I need to give myself at least an hour to get there. So, that only gives us another fifteen minutes."

"I could drive you to work."

His offer changed the tone of their conversation and made him seem like her friend again.

"No thanks. It would probably take longer in traffic than it does by train."

"Fair enough." He smiled at her, thinking he wanted them to be friends. "Where do we go from here?"

She sighed. "As I said before, I'm glad you're here. Take time to get to know Wendy. She already loves you just because you're her father. I read somewhere that when a girl is close to her father, she is more likely to wait instead of rushing to be intimate with a boy."

"You didn't know your father, did you?"

"No." She placed a few dollars on the table and stood up.

He pushed them toward her and said, "Please don't insult me. Lunch is on me."

"No thanks," she replied squaring her shoulders. "I pay my own way. I stopped being a Douglas family charity case a long time ago."

"This has nothing to do with charity, Marcia. I invited you to lunch."

Marcia hesitated for a moment, and then walked away, leaving her money on the table.

He took care of the bill and met her at the door.

"It's freezing out there," he said as he zipped up his jacket. "Let me drive you to the train station."

"Thanks, but no. I need this walk to clear my head."

He reached for her hand and took a step closer to her, so that their bodies were almost touching. "We used to be friends."

She gazed up at him. "Friends are equals. I was always your domestic helper's daughter."

He thought it would be better to apologize than to argue with her. "I'm sorry." He paused. "For everything."

She nodded and pulled her hand from his grasp. Holding the door open behind her, she stepped outside. Turning to see that he had followed her, she said, "This is not about me. It's about Wendy." She cleared her throat. "Our daughter," she said, emphasizing the first word. "Call her later. She works part-time after school, but she should be home by eight-thirty. I won't try to control your relationship with her. She plans to be living in another state by the end of the summer anyway, and there will be little I can do to influence her at that point. I can only trust that God will guide her."

"May I call you in the morning to let you know how things are going?

I might need your advice."

She looked back at him, and lingered for a moment longing for a time so long ago when they were close friends who relied on each other for advice. "Sure," she replied. "I have to go."

He watched her stride across the parking lot, cross the street at the traffic light, and disappear around the corner before he returned to his car.

CHAPTER SIX

The matriarch of Marcia and Wendy's family was Aunt Pat, and she was known to assess a problem and mow down any obstacles in her way with the destructive force of a hurricane. Marcia expected that her aunt would view the resurgence of Wendy's father as just that, a problem to be eliminated. So when she heard her aunt return home on Saturday evening, she braced herself for a confrontation.

"Marcia. Marcia Angelique Tapper." Pat Harrison trod heavily down the stairs, through the foyer and to the door of Marcia's apartment. A full-figured woman, she weighed in heavily in stature and in matters affecting her family. Traditional and Christian in her values, she let her husband lead, but her influence swayed most decisions.

"Come in, Aunt Pat. I was expecting to hear from you the moment you got home." Marcia embraced the older woman who hastily pushed her away.

"Have you taken leave of your senses? How do you mean to have Wendy out with that strange man this time of the night?"

Marcia smiled at her aunt who had been more than a mother to her and sat next to her at the dining table. "That strange man is Wendy's father, Aunt Pat."

"Father? Father? It takes more than a one-night stand to earn that title. The Douglas family has been nothing but trouble to you, and here you've gone and invited trouble back into your life."

As far as Aunt Pat knew, Devon had caused nothing but trouble in Marcia's life. She knew little of the friendship they had shared and of the days when Devon had protected Marcia like a big brother should. Yet, even if Aunt Pat had known Devon in those days, any favorable image of him would have still been tarnished from the day she found Marcia locked away in a filthy bedroom with her baby.

Aunt Pat remembered clearly how she and her daughter Blossom had flown to Jamaica from their home in New York. They arrived on the island and took a taxi to their house in Kingston. They let themselves in through the front gate and waved to an elderly couple sitting on the front porch. Aunt Pat had spoken to them the night before, so they were expecting her. She and her daughter walked around to the side of the house and unlocked the door to the bedroom where Marcia had been staying with Wendy.

As she opened the door, the stench of feces hit her.

"Yuck," her daughter declared scornfully and held her nose. She took two steps backward and waited in the yard.

Aunt Pat stepped inside the bedroom. "Lord, have mercy," she appealed softly, as she caught sight of Marcia sitting on the floor, her back upright against the bed.

Marcia's hair was matted together and sticking up. Her red eyeballs enclosed in puffy eyelids surveyed Aunt Pat as though she were in a daze. A spaghetti strap of the loose, discolored dress she was wearing hung off one shoulder. She reached out to pick up a dirty diaper. There were many strewn all over the floor. Marcia got on her hands and knees and reached for the others, as though she felt a sudden, urgent desire to clean up.

Aunt Pat dropped her bags and started walking toward her niece when she was distracted by the gurgling sound of the baby. She turned instead toward a white, frilly basinet at the foot of the bed. In it, the baby lay on her back, dressed in a light cotton blouse accentuated with embroidery, gently moving her legs and arms. She smiled, as Aunt Pat bent forward to get a closer look.

"Little Wendy." Aunt Pat reached out and picked her up. The diaper the baby wore looked full but held no foul odor. In fact, the baby smelled like fresh powder. Aunt Pat held her close and turned to face Marcia, puzzled by the contrast. At first glance, Marcia looked like a mad woman, yet, her baby showed no signs of neglect. One thing was certain; Marcia needed help.

"Blossom," Aunt Pat called out to her own daughter.

"Yes, Mommy." The seventeen year-old peeped inside for the first time since she had arrived with her mother. "Oh, my goodness!" she gasped as she scanned the bedroom, quickly holding her nose again.

"Help your cousin into the bathroom. She needs to take a bath, wash her hair, and put on some clean clothes."

Blossom hesitated, pointing to Marcia with manicured fingers. She was impeccably dressed in a brand new summer dress and chunky heels. With each turn of her head, her hair bounced.

"Yes. Help her. She is your cousin," Aunt Pat replied. "You and her are the same age and look at the difference between you. You see what happens when you young girls make a boy turn you into a fool." Aunt Pat's words were harsh, but her eyes welled up with tears. Still holding the baby close, she shook her head and sniffled. "God blessed you and your mother with such good brains," she said to Marcia. "First, my sister made young boy mash up her future, and now you." Aunt Pat continued to shake her head, as she instructed her daughter. "Come, Blossom. Help her now."

Blossom reached out her hand to Marcia. "Hi," she said, and knelt beside her on the floor. She displayed a genuine friendliness that she had not felt at first. "So, after all these years of talking on the phone we finally get to meet." She put an arm around Marcia's shoulder. "Marcia, come. I need to freshen up, too. And I'm dying to see what you really look like. I know my pretty cousin that I've seen in pictures all these years is somewhere under this mess."

Blossom smiled, and Marcia smiled back. She still had a dazed look in her eyes, but she trusted these women.

"Thank you, Jesus," Aunt Pat said, as Marcia accompanied Blossom into the bathroom. As they closed the door behind them, Aunt Pat continued to plan and to pray.

Their family had suffered too many losses, Aunt Pat thought, taking count. First, Marcia had graduated from high school, but lost her college scholarship because of her pregnancy. Then, Marcia's mother had died suddenly on the day that Marcia gave birth to Wendy. Now, feeling responsible for her mother's death, Marcia had sunk deeper and deeper into a state of depression.

Aunt Pat preferred to count her blessings, and resolved to not wait around for her family to take another loss. She planned to act quickly to rescue Marcia and Wendy before another tragedy occurred. She and Blossom would take them to live with their family in New York, before Marcia did something desperate. Marcia's words on the phone had prompted Aunt Pat to come immediately. Marcia had said she deserved to die like her mother had. She said she blamed herself for her mother's death because she had caused her mother so much stress which probably led to the brain hemorrhage that the autopsy revealed had claimed her mother's life. Aunt Pat hadn't taken Marcia's words lightly, and now that she saw the condition Marcia was living in, she knew she needed to act fast.

The immigration papers she had filed years before to petition for Marcia and her mother to live in the United States had been approved just in time. When Aunt Pat first told Marcia the news on the phone, Marcia replied that she did not deserve the opportunity that her mother had not lived to grasp.

Aunt Pat spent a week in Jamaica. She and Blossom cleaned up, packed up, and straightened up Marcia's affairs before escorting her and Wendy back to their home in New York where they lived today.

"It's hard to explain what's happening, Aunt Pat, but it has to be

God's will. The way Devon found Wendy at this point in her life..."

Aunt Pat knitted her brows as she gazed at her niece with concern registered all over her face.

"If it makes you feel any better, Aunty, Paul is with them. He and Wendy had their usual date tonight. All they did was ask Devon to join them. They went bowling."

Aunt Pat grunted and shook her head. "You're asking for trouble, if you ask me. After all the pain and suffering you went through while Devon went off to college living like a prince on his parents' money. Do you think he even thought twice about you? Do you think he ever shed a tear over you and the baby he helped to create? And after you did a fine job of raising her on your own, you're going to let him waltz into her life and parade himself off as her father."

Marcia sighed. "Wendy wants to know her father, Aunty, and I have no right to stop her. She is almost an adult and she plans to marry Paul and move away in a few months, anyway. Maybe as a team, Devon and I can get her to reconsider."

"The whole thing just does not make any sense to me. God blessed you and Wendy with such good brains. First, you were a straight "A" student until you let Devon ruin your shot at a college education. Now, history is repeating itself with your only child."

"Aunty, Wendy's situation is different. You can't compare her falling in love and getting married to what happened to me. Paul is a responsible young man who loves Wendy very much. I just wish they would wait and get married after college."

Both women sat, silent for a moment. Aunt Pat shook her head as Marcia toyed with the plastic rose that stood in a slim vase on the dining table.

"Maybe Devon can make a difference, Aunty. I never had the influence of a father in my life. Maybe it's not too late for Wendy's father to be a positive influence in hers."

Her aunt grunted. "Let's hope."

"I've been praying about this for a long time, Aunty."

"And you believe God has sent the man who broke your heart and never looked back, until now, in answer to your prayers." Aunt Pat shook her head again.

Marcia felt doubtful as she spoke to her aunt, but inside, she still felt convinced. "We've invited Devon to church with us tomorrow, and to family dinner. Promise me you'll give him a chance."

Again Pat grunted.

"Aunty?"

"All right. All right. People can change, but as they say, 'Once bitten, twice shy.' You ought to bear that in mind before you find yourself falling for him again."

Marcia tried to dismiss her aunt's parting words, as she got dressed for church the next morning. After all, the renewed relationship with Devon was not about her; it was about Wendy. Wendy needed her father. It was that simple. And in self-defense against future heartbreak, Marcia had long devoted her life to raising her daughter and serving the Lord. Not even propositions from men inside the church had caused her to waver. Yet, as the doorbell rang, she felt her heartbeat quicken. She reached for her coat, deciding it was the winter clothes and not thoughts of Devon that was making her warm.

A blast of cold air whizzed past her as she opened the front door.

"Good morning." Devon greeted her with a smile and a single yellow rose.

She squinted at him as he handed it to her.

"I just wanted to say thanks for sharing Wendy with me and for letting me into your life."

Marcia smiled back, flushed. She tried not to think of the rose as a personal gesture from Devon to her, but as a token for their daughter. "Thank you, but this is really not necessary. You are Wendy's father, and to say that meeting you has made her happy is an understatement."

Their eyes locked and held for a moment. "Wait here while I place this in some water inside." Marcia left Devon standing in the foyer. Inside her apartment, she tossed the plastic rose aside, filled the vase with water, and placed the rose Devon had given her inside it before leaving it on the dining table.

"Let's go," she said as she passed Devon without looking at him and led the way outdoors. Brilliant sunshine brightened the morning but failed to warm the frigid air. Marcia waved a gloved hand at a neighbor who was also leaving for church.

When they were seated inside Devon's car, she gave directions to the church. Devon blew on his hands in an attempt to warm them.

"Cold?" Marcia asked.

"Freezing. I forgot my gloves. No matter how long I live here, it seems that I can't accept the fact that a sunny day can be this cold."

Marcia laughed. "It took me a long time to learn that too. I still remember the first time I got caught unprepared. It was shortly after I left Jamaica and came to New York for the first time. I had taken the bus to meet Aunt Pat at her job one day and got off at the wrong stop. At first, I thought I was in the right place, so I started walking down the street through the slush. Icy water soaked through my boots and socks, and my toes started freezing. I had never been so cold in my life. Then, the breeze started blowing and I didn't have a scarf on, so it felt like the wind was blowing right through my chest and penetrating my bones. I thought I was going to freeze to death. I started crying and that only made matters worse. It seemed like icicles were forming on my cheeks and my nose. Anyway, to make a long story short, I called Uncle Trevor from a pay phone and by the time he picked me up, my whole body was freezing and my fingertips were turning blue. I thought I was going to die." She shuddered. "I still can't stand the cold."

Devon chuckled, surprised and pleased that she felt comfortable enough with him to reminisce. He remembered that side of her: talkative and animated, punctuating her sentences by waving her hands. The moment endeared her to him. He wanted to park the car and give her his complete attention. As he steered, he glanced in her direction.

"So, that's why you're always so bundled up," he said.

"Always," she replied, tugging at her scarf for emphasis. "So, tell me, how did everything go last night?"

"Well. Thank God. We laughed a lot, bowled a few strikes. Laughed some more. Our daughter is a regular comedian, and so is Paul. I like him. He really seems to be a nice guy. They seem to be well suited for each other."

Marcia sighed, causing Devon to glance at her, momentarily directing his attention away from the roadway.

"What?" he asked, wondering if something he said upset her.

Marcia shrugged. "Turn here," she said. "It's the big white church on the left, a couple blocks down."

"Got that. Now, will you tell me why you sighed?"

Marcia observed his profile. His complexion was smooth like milk chocolate. When he looked at her, she saw compassion in his eyes. All her resistance vanished, as she stared at his handsome face, admitting to herself that he still affected her just as he had when they were teenagers. She was determined to never let him know that. This relationship was solely about Wendy, and she spoke with that in mind.

"Wendy and Paul. They are well suited for each other, and sometimes I believe her. When I spend time with them, I almost find myself accepting what she defines as God's plan for their lives. Yet, the practical side of me says they are too young. Too inexperienced. Naïve. Even people in church get divorced. No one has everlasting love, and Wendy is setting herself up for heartbreak. Do you understand?"

Devon steered the car into a parking spot, switched off the ignition and turned to face her. He had launched his search for Marcia last year because he wanted to meet his daughter, but the more time he spent with Marcia, the more he found himself wanting to be there for her. She was beautiful, and he could see why he had been attracted to her as a teenager. He was even more drawn to her right now. Her eyes looked a bit tired, and she knitted her brows as she spoke. He reached out, but stopped himself before he stroked her forehead to soothe away the lines.

"Let's go inside," she said, reaching for the door. She felt relieved as she climbed out of the car. Sitting that close to Devon and staring into his eyes caused her to feel like she was being pulled back in time to the days when she was a teenager and a life with Devon meant more to her than anything else. "We don't want to be late."

The parking lot was almost full, and Marcia waved and greeted other churchgoers as she and Devon walked side by side to the door. She didn't hold his hand but glanced at him and smiled. He smiled back and seemed comfortable. Confident. Perhaps, he even looked a little arrogant as he held the door open for her and two other ladies who followed. She watched as their eyes lingered on him, clearly savoring the view.

As they entered the well-lit sanctuary, Marcia nudged him and pointed toward the choir stand. Wendy, dressed in a burgundy and white robe, waved vigorously at them, a broad grin on her face. They waved back and filed into a row near the front. Marcia kissed Aunt Pat, who was already seated there, and blew a kiss to her cousin Blossom who was seated nearby. She whispered an introduction to Devon who nodded his head in their direction and waved slightly. Their attention was drawn to the speaker standing in the front below the pulpit, but not before Marcia noticed Blossom giving her a thumbs up. She rolled her eyes in return and focused on the speaker.

"Does anyone else have a testimony this morning? We all have a story to share about what God has done for us? He woke us up this morning. He gave us health and strength to be here when so many others are lying in a hospital bed. The least we could do is praise him."

"Brother Bruce." A feminine voice came from behind him.

"Yes, Sister Wendy." Brother Bruce approached her and handed her the microphone.

"Praise the Lord, church," Wendy said enthusiastically. "Hallelujah! Thank you, Jesus. I'd like to tell you what God did for me this week." She held the microphone in her right hand and raised her left hand as she spoke. "My father, my heavenly father brought my earthly father into my life for the first time." She placed her left hand on her chest. "You see, all my life, my mom has been the only mother and father I've known. And although she, my aunts and uncles filled my life with love, I was never lonely, but I was curious. I was praying that somehow God would make a way for me to meet my dad, and He has."

A voice in the congregation shouted, "Hallelujah!" and others followed.

"Praise the Lord, Sister Wendy," Brother Bruce said and reached for the microphone.

"One more thing," Wendy said, beaming, and looking directly at Devon. "Daddy, I just want to let you know I'm happy that you're here." She closed her eyes. "Hallelujah. Thank you, Jesus!" With that, she handed over the microphone and returned to her seat.

Wendy's words shook Devon at the core of his being. This was the pinnacle of an emotional week that had reordered his priorities and caused him to question his sense of self. Days ago, he had known he was a father and was determined to shoulder financial responsibility for a mistake he hadn't even realized he had made. Now, pleasing his daughter and her mother had become so important to him that they felt like his reason for being.

He cleared his throat and swallowed hard. A hand covered his, and he looked at its owner who was smiling at him. His heart raced as he searched her eyes. Marcia nodded and looked toward Wendy, squeezed his hand and drew hers away as the service began. She was lost in her own thoughts. Wendy's exuberance in praising the Lord was familiar. It reminded Marcia of someone she had been ashamed of; Wendy was a living reminder of Marcia's mom.

Devon listened to the words, as the choir belted out songs ranging from traditional to contemporary.

"Amazing grace, how sweet the sound, that saved a wretch like me," they sang.

Devon usually dismissed the lyrics of this legendary hymn as being suitable for someone who lacked self-esteem. But on this Sunday morning, he found himself thinking of the wretch he had been. He had been intimate with Marcia as a teenager and had not cherished the occasion. He hadn't thought of her all these years as he went through his promiscuous twenties and finally settled into a long-term engagement with his college sweetheart as he entered another decade of his life.

He realized now that while he was playing and partying, Marcia had been raising a child. His child. She must be an excellent mother, he concluded, as he looked with pride at the beautiful young lady singing in the choir. Wendy had some of his features, but she was her mother's child and owed him nothing for the woman she had become.

The next song brought Marcia to her feet, arms outstretched heavenward. He listened to the lyrics. "Your grace and mercy brought me through; I'm living this moment because of You. I want to thank You, and praise You too." She sang along with the choir, "Your grace and your mercy brought me through." Marcia was one of a few well-dressed, otherwise dignified, church ladies on their feet shouting, "Hallelujah!" by the time the choir finished singing.

"We never try to quench the Holy Spirit," Reverend Walker said as he approached the pulpit. He paused and closed his eyes, and gradually, the women quieted down. Reverend Walker directed the congregation to turn in their Bibles to Revelation, chapter twelve, the eleventh verse, which he read. "And they overcame him by the blood of the Lamb and the word of their testimony, and they did not love their lives to the death."

During the sermon, the preacher explained the importance of testifying. "Your story could save someone's life," he said. "Someone could be sitting in this congregation this morning who is going through hell in their marriage, hell on their job, because of their health, or because of a loved one. You strengthen their faith when you tell them your story. When you stand up and say that you've been there, but God brought you through, you give them hope that they can hold on. Don't be ashamed to tell them that God brought your marriage back from the brink of divorce. Our Lord is a God of reconciliation. Don't be ashamed to tell them He supplies all your financial needs. Our Lord is a provider. Don't be ashamed to tell them He healed the sick and saved your loved ones from a fate worse than death. Our Lord is a Healer and He will deliver the righteous from every affliction."

Wendy listened to the preacher and was happy to have her convictions confirmed. She looked over at Paul who was seated at the keyboard and he nodded. Then, she focused on her parents noting that they too seemed to be listening attentively.

Devon thought about Wendy as he listened to the preacher. He had expected her to resent him for being an absentee dad. He had braced himself to have to break down walls of resistance to get to know her. Instead, she openly praised God for him. That humbled him. He glanced at Marcia, wondering what she thought about him, and whether she would ever allow him to get close to her again.

CHAPTER SEVEN

After church, the family fell into their weekly routine. Wendy had tossed a salad and made fruit punch the night before. Marcia had cooked brown stew chicken. Aunt Pat had risen early Sunday morning to boil rice and peas and her daughter Blossom roasted a slab of beef. The traditional Jamaican cuisine was served up in minutes, hot and fresh, shortly after they got home from church. As they gathered around Aunt Pat's dining table, she asked Devon to say grace.

Beneath his dark complexion, he blushed a deep red. He felt Wendy grasp his hand from her seat next to him. His eyes found Marcia sitting across from him and she smiled. They closed their eyes. "Dear Lord, thank you for this meal and those who prepared it. We pray your blessing upon us, in Jesus' name," he said softly.

"Amen," everyone chorused.

Aunt Pat grunted.

The clanging of utensils ushered in the first bit of conversation.

"Pass the rice, please."

"Roast beef?"

"Chicken thanks."

"Mm, good."

"Is who cook this? Marcia? Your hands turn sweeter every week. Who tell you say you can't cook?" The comment was a running joke between Marcia and her Uncle Trevor. When Marcia joined their family, Uncle Trevor had been the only person with enough nerve to tell Marcia that her food lacked flavor. Aunt Pat guarded her niece's self esteem too carefully to say anything. With his trademark humor, Uncle Trevor made Marcia laugh at her mistakes while the retired chef taught her himself. The cooking lessons congealed the father-daughter bond they shared.

"Thanks, Uncle. Your tips are still paying off."

Uncle Trevor took Sundays off, but he cooked most of the meals during the week.

"Hey, Uncle Trev. Dad loves to cook too. Dad, Uncle Trev used to be a chef." Wendy chatted, quickly turning her head from one man to the other. "Uncle Trev, Dad's family owns a hotel in Jamaica, and even as a child, he had to work different jobs. He worked as a cook, did housekeeping, handled reservations, the works."

"Really? Is that fact or fable? I never expected that your father was ever required to work in his life." Aunt Pat made the statements under her breath, then jabbed the roast beef with her fork and lifted a chunk to her lips. Uncle Trevor heard from the other end of the table and cast his wife a disapproving glance. Marcia shook her head, but Wendy kept on chatting cheerfully as though she had not heard Aunt Pat's response.

"So what caused you to make the transition from your hotel to teaching?" asked Blossoms' husband.

"Uncle Steve is the principal at PS 42," Wendy interjected.

"I performed community service once working with a group of youths who didn't even know how to write their names," Devon replied. "I decided that I wanted to make a difference, to do something more meaningful with my life."

"So you abandoned your family's business in spite of the fact that it bought you an Ivy League education and all the creature comfort money can buy. Your parents must be proud," Aunt Pat retorted, her voice rich with sarcasm.

"Mom!" Blossom nudged her, urging her to quiet.

Aunt Pat met her husband's disapproving look head on.

Steve shook his head, and Marcia's glance darted from Devon to Wendy to assess their response.

Wendy's cell phone rang before anyone else spoke. "Sorry. Excuse me," she said and got up from the table to answer it. "Hey Paul. What's up?"

"We're ready. Are you still coming?" Paul asked.

"I want to. Let me find out." Wendy put Paul on hold and returned to the table. "Mom. Dad. It's Paul. This is the weekend we usually take his mother to the nursing home to see her sister. May I go with them, please?"

"And this is your first dinner with your father, ever. Don't you think you need to stay here?" her mother replied.

"It's okay, Marcia. Let her go," Devon suggested.

Aunt Pat grunted loudly.

"Thanks, Dad." Wendy replied cheerfully kissing him on his cheek. "Meet you out front in five minutes, Paul," she spoke into the phone. She grabbed her plate, kissed her mother and father and blew kisses to everyone else. "Love you, guys," she shouted as she hurried down the stairs to get her coat.

Aunt Pat shook her head. "Mm, mm, mm. Seventeen years." She looked down at her plate in an attempt to suppress an outburst.

"I hadn't expected her to even want to go today," Marcia said, looking apologetically at Devon.

"Really, I don't mind. She and Paul told me the other night that they have been doing this for years. His aunt looks forward to their visits, so I didn't think it was best to stop her from going."

"You didn't think it was best," Aunt Pat fumed. "Apparently, you didn't think about her at all for the past seventeen years, and now you waltz in here and start talking about what's best for her. Marcia might be impressed by your sweet talking, good looking façade that has her head spinning like she isn't a day over seventeen herself, but you don't fool me, young man. I don't know what you're up to, but I don't like it. If Marcia had a father, he would have fired his shotgun by now and sent you running, after the way you broke his daughter's heart. I may not be her father, but I'm not about to sit idly by and watch you hurt her and Wendy."

Blossom folded her arms.

By now all but Steve had stopped eating. He gulped mouthfuls as he watched the exchange.

Uncle Trevor placed a protective hand over Marcia's and nodded in agreement with his wife.

"I have no intention of hurting either one of them, Mrs. Harrison." Devon's voice was husky as he spoke, first making eye contact with the older lady, then meeting Marcia's steady gaze. "I... I am sorry, sorry about the past. I can't deny that I've been foolish, selfish, and immature, but I wouldn't be sitting here if I didn't want to change." He paused. "Wendy is giving me a chance, and I'm asking that you do the same."

Aunt Pat grunted and Blossom placed a hand over hers. This time Aunt Pat said nothing.

Marcia lowered her gaze to focus on her plate.

Uncle Trevor finally broke the silence. "I made some bread pudding for the occasion," he said. "What do you say we clear the table and move on to dessert?"

Wendy longed to talk about her father as she sat in the back seat of the car traveling to the nursing home with Paul and his mother, so she was glad when Paul's mother raised the subject.

"Your father seems like quite a gentleman, Wendy. I didn't get a chance to talk to him, but I was observing him at church this morning," said Madge Chambers.

"He's really nice, Mrs. Chambers. I still can't believe he's here. Like, my father is at my house right now. After all these years. God is so good!"

"I'm surprised you were able to get away," Paul interjected.

"I know. He's really cool. Mommy didn't want me to go because she thought it was rude of me to leave, this being the first time I ever had dinner with my father and everything, but Dad said yes. Cool, huh?"

Paul's eyes met hers in the rearview mirror. He nodded. He prayed that Wendy's father planned to stick around and wouldn't drop in and out of her life and break her heart.

"Where does he live, Wendy?" Paul's mother asked.

"In Mount Vernon. Close to the Bronx border. It's incredible to think he was living so close by and I didn't know he was here. I thought he was living in Jamaica."

Wendy's voice, the look in her eyes, her body language, everything about her radiated how happy she felt about meeting her father. When she spoke again, Paul knew it must have taken great effort for her to change the subject.

"Mrs. Chambers, did you finish the quilted blanket you were making for your sister?"

"Yes, I did. It's in that box on the seat beside you."

"She's going to love it," Wendy suggested.

"I think so. Let's just pray that it will bring back some of the memories she's forgotten."

They were lost in their own thoughts, as they remained quiet for the rest of the drive.

Later that evening, Marcia walked Devon to the front door. She bit her lips as they stood face to face in the foyer.

"Thanks for everything," he said. "I really enjoyed the day."

"Yeah right," she said, smiling. "Would that include the threats and the interrogation?"

"Your aunt loves you. She made that clear. A tongue lashing is the least I deserve for abandoning you like I did when we were teenagers." He reached for her hands and stepped closer to her. "I really am sorry, Marcia. Even if I thought your baby wasn't mine, I should have been there for you as a friend. I don't doubt that you would have stood by me if it had been the other way around and I needed a friend."

Marcia nodded and looked away, focusing instead, on the top button of his coat. The back of her eyes burned and she fought back tears. Her aunt was right. One look and she wanted to fall into his embrace. "Our relationship is about Wendy," she declared.

Devon reached out and gently lifted her chin, so that she would look up at him. "True, but you have feelings too. What kind of man does not respect the mother of his child, especially when she has made so many sacrifices in raising her?" He paused as their eyes locked and held. "Thank you. And thanks for letting me in."

Marcia nodded and stepped back, trying to shake off any feeling of intimacy between them. She opened the door. "I'd put a hat on if I were you. It's mighty cold out there."

He covered his head. "Good night, Marcia."

She extended her hand for a handshake. "Good night, Devon. Get home safely," and with that she closed the door.

Devon walked slowly back to his car. He didn't bother to cover his neck with the scarf that was draped across his shoulders. The temperature had plummeted thirty degrees since the afternoon high when they left the church, and it was now well below freezing. The frigid air functioned like a cold shower cooling the sensual awareness that tingled throughout his body. Had Marcia been a prospective lover, someone he had met and dated while he was in his twenties, he would send her flowers daily with a joke written on the card to make her smile. He would dine with her at Manhattan's finest restaurants and together they would watch a Broadway play. If she really played hard to get, he would fly her to Jamaica for a weekend. And then, he would have her until she no longer distracted him with intense desire.

But romancing Marcia was not an option. Spending time with her and Wendy was creating a new consciousness of God's grace in his life. As he drove home, he thought of how much they had given him in the last week that he had not earned. They embraced him with their ready acceptance and their warmth. From their first meeting, they had replaced his former fiancé, best friend, and parents as the central figures in his life. Right now, he didn't know how he would bridge the two worlds and he didn't care. Yet, he needed to talk to someone, someone he could trust.

He entered the two-family house that he purchased years before as investment property, but later moved into one of the apartments when he accepted a teaching contract in New York. He had learned the value of real estate from his parents, who owned and rented out similar property throughout the state. As he climbed the stairs to the second floor, he decided whom to call.

He couldn't call Tricia. During the three years of their engagement, he and Tricia would talk for hours, often because they disagreed with each other on important issues like where they should live, where he should work, and what he should do with his life. She had loved him enough to give up an apartment on the Upper East Side of Manhattan to live with him in Mount Vernon, which was to her a major social fall that she planned to endure only until they got married. She had loved him enough to tolerate his decision to teach, a poor man's profession in her book, but she tried her best to convince him that joining his father in the hotel industry would put him in a better position to provide for his family. Last summer, he returned from Jamaica with the news his grandfather had shared with him before he died. The news about Wendy and Marcia upset Tricia immensely, but it was Devon's determination to find them that finally sent Tricia packing. No he couldn't call Tricia.

He considered his best friend Troy with whom he discussed everything since the day they met at a Country Club in Kingston while growing up in Jamaica. Their parents had sent them there for tennis lessons. They were both bright, good-looking sons of elite Jamaican families. They attended the same boarding school and were inseparable until the year they went off to college. Troy stayed in the Caribbean and studied law at the University of the West Indies before joining his father's firm. Through Troy, Devon constantly had glimpses of the pampered lifestyle he could have if he acquiesced to his parents' wishes and moved back to Jamaica. Troy could not understand some of the decisions Devon made and told him so. But they were still friends and partied together often each summer while Devon spent time in Jamaica.

Devon picked up the phone and dialed his friend's number.

"Hello. Good night," Troy answered.

"Wha'appen, man?" Devon used a familiar Jamaican greeting.

"Dev. Funny you should call. We were just talking about you."

Devon could hear movement and a woman's voice in the background. "Good things, I hope."

"Depends on whom you ask. You know who is here? Tricia."

"Really? I didn't realize she was in Jamaica. Was that her voice I heard in the background when you answered the phone?"

"No, man. That was probably the cleaning staff. Trish went back outside. Mom had a garden party this evening. Fodder for the lifestyles section of the Gleaner. Trish was here with her schmoozing the press. You know your girl loves that stuff."

"She is no longer my girl, Troy, and you know it."

"Just checking."

"Did she bring a date?"

Troy chuckled. "I thought you didn't care."

"I'm just curious."

"Yeah right." His voice conveyed both humor and sarcasm. "No, she didn't bring a date. She came solo, looking as stunning as ever. To tell you the truth, she was my date for the evening, and she made me enjoy what would have otherwise been a dull event. She is quite a gem."

"She is. I'm glad you've remained friends. It makes sense considering how much time Tricia and I spend with you and your ever-changing dates. And, actually, Tricia is better off without me."

"I'd agree with you on that. At least until you come to your senses."

A pause and then, "Women like Trish don't remain single for long, Dev."

"I know. I'm sure Tricia won't have any trouble finding a man who can make her happy, something I was failing at."

"You were doing okay until you became obsessed with finding your baby-mama." Troy's tone was condescending.

"I found her." Devon's interpolation went unheard.

Troy spoke without pausing. "As if you're the first man to ever break a woman's heart and father an illegitimate child."

"You didn't hear me. I said I found them."

"What? When?" Troy asked in surprise.

"I'll tell you the details, but first you have to promise me not to share this with Tricia, my parents or anyone else. I'll tell them when I'm good and ready. All right?"

"Sure. Fine. Tell me what happened."

"Well, I just spent the evening having dinner with my daughter and her family. My daughter. It's funny to hear myself say that. The whole experience has been surreal. I don't know where to begin."

"At the beginning. You found Wendy, the girl your grandfather told you about. And you're convinced that she is your daughter?"

"No doubt about it. She looks just like me."

"Really? Hmm. And her mother?"

"Beautiful. A real babe. Has me thinking all kinds of thoughts I shouldn't be thinking."

"Really? Careful now. You've been down that road before, and she didn't have the morals to turn you down then. And I'm sure, one way or the other, it's going to cost you."

"What do you mean?"

"You've escaped child support for the past seventeen years, but certainly, if your," Troy cleared his throat, "daughter is college bound they'll try to get you to pay for her education."

"She is going to be her high school valedictorian, and she has a full scholarship to a local state college and a partial scholarship to my alma mater if she wants it."

"Wow! Impressive."

"Yes. And she has the sweetest disposition. I expected her to hate me."

"Maybe not hate, but resent you at the very least."

"Believe it or not, she has been so loving. So warm. Respectful. She has embraced me completely as a part of her life."

"How does her mother feel about that? If anyone should hate you, she should."

"If she does, she's doing a good job of hiding it. I like her. A lot."

"Devon," Troy warned, "Careful, now. Wendy's mother has every reason to play games with you until she gets what she wants. Once she realizes how much you're worth, she'll want something. At least you have two factors in your favor. Wendy is almost an adult and most of your assets are here. We could shelter them easily. In the meantime, if all the love and forgiveness they've shown you seems too good to be true, it probably is."

"They're Christians."

"And? So are we. That never stopped you and me from fornicating and breaking a whole host of commandments."

Devon chuckled, not because he was amused, but because he figured Troy wouldn't understand. Their way of thinking about religion was very different from the attitude he observed in Marcia and Wendy. As he thought about how to respond, he heard Troy speaking to someone else.

"Look, man. I have to go," Troy said, redirecting his attention back to Devon. "But as your lawyer and friend, I am urging you to be careful."

"As my lawyer and friend, I'm reminding you to respect my confidentiality."

"Haven't I been keeping your secrets for the past twenty years?"

"Yes."

"Later, then."

"Later."

CHAPTER EIGHT

The more Devon observed Wendy and her boyfriend as they spent time together, the more their relationship reminded him of himself and Marcia when they were teenagers. Wendy and Paul openly encouraged each other and enjoyed each other's company, but, unlike Marcia and Devon, they displayed no evidence of their physical attraction. They genuinely just seemed like good friends. When they were driving home after a movie one night, Devon asked them about their chaste behavior.

"Dad!" Wendy exclaimed.

"You guys are seventeen, not seven," Devon replied. "I need to know. Is this innocent act just for me?"

"No, Mr. Douglas," Paul replied. "It isn't an act. Many of our peers are making love with their boyfriend or girlfriend or even people they hardly know." He laughed nervously, uncomfortable with discussing this topic with Wendy's father. "Can I say that?"

Devon nodded. "Yes, I want you to be direct with me."

"Okay," Paul replied, more confidently now. "Some of our friends have been sleeping around for years already, but Wendy and I have promised each other that our... that our... You sure you want me to say this, Sir? I am talking about your daughter."

"Certainly."

"Okay. We promised each other that we would wait until after we get married. Our virginity is a special gift we want to give each other."

Devon stifled a laugh as he pulled over the car, switched on the ceiling light, and turned to face Paul who was sitting in the back seat.

"Oh, boy," Wendy said softly. "Dad, you're intimidating him."

"Am I?" Devon asked, flexing his muscles. "Paul." He slapped the teenager on his shoulder. "I understand when you say my daughter is a virgin. Some women like to wait, and I am glad my daughter is one of

53

them, but are you telling me that you, good fellow, have never made love to anyone?"

"No, Sir. I have not."

"You've got to be kidding me. Aren't you tempted to do otherwise?" Devon asked finding it hard to believe that Paul was as innocent as he seemed.

"I'm sorry, Paul," Wendy mouthed to her boyfriend. "Dad!"

"Hush, Wendy," Devon said, but kept his eyes locked with Paul's. "A father needs to know that his future son-in-law is honest about these things. I'm not expecting Paul to be a saint. I just want him to be a man of integrity."

"He is," Wendy insisted.

"I am, Sir. Wendy and I like to do things God's way. I love Wendy and I love God, who Himself is love, so how can I do otherwise?"

"And God says, 'No lovemaking before you're seventeen,'" Devon jabbed.

"No, Sir. He says, 'No fornicators will be welcome in His kingdom.'"

"And you believe that?"

"With all my heart," Paul and Wendy answered in unison, then, they smiled at each other.

"Dad. This is why I love Paul so much," Wendy said, reaching for Paul's hand. "He is for real. What you see is what you get. He loves the Lord with all his heart like I do, and that's why I love him."

Devon exhaled audibly. "Okay. I wouldn't want to argue with that."

"You know what, Dad? On Valentine's Day, the year we turned fourteen, our church had a ceremony celebrating God's unfailing love and a group of us committed to waiting until after we get married to make love exclusively to our spouse. Then, a year ago, Paul and I made a promise to each other. We want our first night together to be our wedding gift to each other, and we want to share something intimate that we haven't shared with anyone else."

Devon glanced at Wendy as she spoke, but most of the time, he kept his eyes focused on Paul. "And you're not tempted to do otherwise?"

"Of course we are," Wendy answered, but Paul placed a hand over hers and she stopped talking.

"This isn't just about pleasing each other, Mr. Douglas. I love your daughter, dearly. I've known her all my life and I don't want to live without her on this side of eternity or the next."

"What?" Devon asked as he looked from one teenager to the next. Never had he ever met anyone like them. He suspected that this wasn't just talk; they actually believed what they were saying. How different they were than he and Marcia had been at their age. And his life experience hadn't brought his viewpoint any closer to Paul's. He had approached the conversation as a father who had words of wisdom to offer a child, but as he listened, and so much of what they said was new to him, he realized that they could teach him something new.

"We're both trying to get into heaven," Paul replied.

"Yeah, Dad. And we would like to see you and Mom there too."

"Okay. All right." Devon appeared cool, but he was shaken by their conversation. "I got what I was asking for. I must say, I'm proud of you. Wendy, no father would want it any other way. And Paul, I wish I could say that I was half the man that you are when I was your age."

Devon dropped off Wendy and Paul and went home feeling pleased that as a father, he had been able to have that kind of discussion with his daughter and her boyfriend. In his teenage years, all his peers had displayed a casual attitude toward lovemaking. Perhaps they exaggerated or made up stories about their experiences, but no one he knew would advocate abstinence and quote scripture to back up their beliefs. Wendy and Paul's attitude toward lovemaking was rare, and while Devon believed they were sincere, he looked forward to discussing what he had learned with Marcia.

Every spare moment Devon had evolved around Marcia and Wendy. When he wasn't with them, he was thinking about them. He had known them for over a month now, but spent most of that time with Wendy and her boyfriend, not with Marcia. He chatted with Wendy after school each day as he drove her to her part time job. He attended her extra-curricular activities at school and at the church. And he accompanied Marcia and Wendy to church on weekends.

Devon was pleased that he'd bonded easily with Wendy, but her mother was harder to reach. He wondered if Marcia intentionally kept her distance. He hoped that time would once again mold a relationship between them that was as close as the one they shared during childhood.

The conversation with her father left Wendy feeling frustrated and embarrassed. It was bad enough that she and Paul faced ongoing ridicule at school from their peers because of their holier-than-thou attitude toward intimacy.

"Church girl."

"Holy Roller."

"Virgin Mary."

Mentally, she could hear the voices of other students calling her names each time she spoke up against their purported promiscuity. She didn't think it was wise for her peers to have already been intimate with multiple partners by the age of seventeen, and she said so. Girls cheated themselves when they let a boy get that close when they were alone, only to have him act like he didn't even know her once they were back in school. School was stressful enough without a girl having to worry that she might be pregnant each time her period was late. As far as she was concerned, being intimate with anyone at this point in her life would interfere with her studies, distract her from her goals and dreams, and make her life more complicated. She was glad Paul felt the same way.

"You're brave," Jasmine, a girl she knew from both church and school, had told her recently. "I agree with you, but I'm not going to let anyone at school know it, so they can make fun of me."

Wendy had never been popular with her peers, but she was well known. Everyone at school knew her as the brainy church-girl who could sing. She and Paul made their mark on Washington High School during their freshman year, when they entered the annual talent show and won, singing their rendition of an old classic Bebe and CeCe Winans' song "Addictive Love." Since then, she and Paul sang at many school events. Their songs were always Christian, and Paul would back them up by playing the piano, guitar, or saxophone. Even those who disliked them for Bible-toting and Scripture-quoting perspective respected them for their music.

Yes, she and Paul validated each other, and were comfortable with the way they were, so the last person she expected to come along and criticize them was her father.

As her mother arrived home from work that night, Wendy met her at the front door to complain.

"Mom. You should have seen the way Daddy interrogated Paul today. I was mortified!"

"Mortified! That sounds like an SAT word." Marcia chuckled, not realizing immediately how upset her daughter was. "I'm sure it wasn't that bad. It's only natural for a father to question his daughter's boyfriend. That's what fathers do, honey. That's why girls who have their father around usually get more respect from the boys they date."

"Paul has always respected me, Mom, even when I was being raised by a single mother."

"I know. That's why I love him. Paul is a good guy, Wendy. I'm certain he'll make a good husband for you one day. I've never argued with that. I just want you two to complete your education before you get married."

"What's wrong with getting married and then completing our education?" Wendy asked throwing her hands up.

"We've gone over this before. Once you get married, you'll be sleeping together. Once you're doing that, you might get pregnant. If you have a baby sooner rather than later, you might end up like me: age thirty-something, working full-time in a minimum wage job, and just now trying to get a college education." Marcia sighed.

Wendy sighed longer and louder. She thought she understood her mother's fears, but how could she make her mother understand that the relationship she and Paul shared was different from the one her parents had. She didn't doubt that her parents had loved each other as teenagers. For her and Paul, there was more than love. She and Paul were called to do God's work together, as husband and wife. She felt as sure of that as she was that she was female. But she didn't argue. "I'm going to bed now."

Marcia reached for Wendy's hand as she walked by her. "Are you okay, honey?"

Wendy nodded, but there were tears in her eyes.

"You're not okay."

"Mom, I'll be fine."

Marcia kissed her on the cheek. "I love you."

"I love you too."

The next day, Marcia's cell phone rang just as she got off the subway train and started walking toward the building where she worked.

"Hello."

"Marcia."

"Hey, Devon. I was expecting to hear from you."

"Yes. I wanted to call you last night, but I figured that it was too late and you wouldn't have any privacy to talk."

Marcia grinned as she glanced at the traffic that lined the Manhattan streets and skirted her way through the throng of pedestrians walking along the concrete sidewalk. "Yes. This setting is a lot more private. I'm just an anonymous face in the crowd."

"You're in the city."

"Yes. I'm almost at work, but I can talk for a few minutes."

"Good. I asked Wendy and Paul some probing questions about their relationship, last night."

"I heard."

"Do you think I was wrong to pry? A father wants to know, and given what you and I have been talking about, I just thought I would ask. What's your impression? I mean, Wendy is so in love with this guy that she is determined to marry him in a few months, yet I've never seen them kiss or express any form of physical attraction."

"Their love is not based on that, but that doesn't mean they are not attracted to each other."

"Yeah, but any normal, hot blooded seventeen-year-old guy who spends so much time with a beautiful girl is at least going to be tempted. We were."

"You're right, but let me give you the background on Wendy and Paul. Years ago, we started a program at our church aimed at encouraging our youngsters to wait. We've educated them about the risks and responsibilities associated with lovemaking. We start teaching them early because we live in a community where we have seen mothers as young as twelve years old. What does a twelve-year-old know about puberty, much less motherhood? It's tragic, really. Anyway, the program is primarily spiritual with prayer, Bible reading, and discussion, helping these youngsters to realize that it is a blessing to wait—to present their bodies a living sacrifice, holy and acceptable to God. We've had a positive impact on these youngsters. We encourage them not to go off and spend time alone as couples, not to set themselves up for temptation that they cannot resist."

"And it's working."

"As far as we can see, yes. Plus, the high school seniors have added another dimension to the program, led by Paul and Wendy. They have raised awareness about the times during their senior year when girls are most likely to get pregnant, like on prom night, or on the senior trip, and they are encouraging abstinence and prevention."

"Impressive, on the one hand, but at the same time, it sounds a bit extreme. Some amount of intimacy is normal. We made love at their age and it didn't destroy our lives."

"Speak for yourself, Devon Douglas. Had it not been for that one time, I might have been president of my own advertising agency by now? At the very least, I would have taken advantage of a free ride through college, instead of struggling now to pay for a few credits at a time toward my degree. Come to think of it, my mother might have been alive and well, enjoying the rewards of my success. So, don't minimize the impact of our lovemaking and teenage pregnancy."

"I wasn't. I didn't mean that…"

"Whatever you meant, we're talking about unfulfilled dreams. And you, you were supposed to be running a chain of hotels in the Caribbean by now. What happened to that dream?"

"We weren't talking about me or you. We were talking about Paul and Wendy," Devon said, frustrated by the turn the conversation had taken.

"Yes. We're talking about how they can learn from our mistakes."

"Okay. Okay. I'm the newcomer here, and there is a lot I have to learn. I know so little about what happened to you after the one time we made love, so I shouldn't make light of it."

"No, you shouldn't."

"I'm sorry."

"It's all right. I have to go."

"Because you're mad at me."

"No. It's time for me to work. We'll talk again some other time."

"I could pick you up after work," Devon offered.

"No thanks."

"It's better to have conversations like this one in person," he insisted.

"Some other time. Okay? Bye now."

Devon hung up the phone feeling insecure about his role as a father, and even more so about his relationship with Marcia. Marcia looked like the girl he once knew, but she had changed. Clearly she had been shaped by experiences she'd had since the last time he saw her. Experiences he knew nothing about. She looked good and seemed to be well cared for by her family who loved and protected her. However, he suspected that her life had not always been this way. Had he not once been like family to her, yet, when she needed him most, he had walked away?

CHAPTER NINE

Valentine's Day for Wendy and Paul was usually a time spent talking about their plans for the future. When they were selecting the colleges to apply to, they checked to see which ones provided housing for married couples. If the college didn't, they checked online to see how much it would cost to rent an apartment nearby. For the first time ever, when the day arrived, Wendy was preoccupied with a big date she had with someone else.

As Devon arrived to pick up Wendy for his friend's wedding on Valentine's Day, he followed the sound of music through the foyer toward the back of the building to the front door of the apartment Marcia and Wendy shared. The door was open, but he paused to knock before entering just as Marcia spun around to face him from the bathroom doorway.

"Honey, is that you?" she asked, her head bent forward as she wrapped her wet hair in a towel. The thigh-length robe she wore hung open revealing silky lingerie.

Devon cleared his throat just as Marcia looked up, saw him and squealed.

"You're here! How did you get in?"

"Steve was on his way out and let me in. Sorry I startled you."

He didn't look sorry. He looked downright pleased with himself, standing at her doorway grinning from ear to ear. Marcia pulled her robe together and secured it with the belt. "Wendy must still be upstairs. Blossom was helping her with her hair and makeup." She turned away from him and removed a tray of cookies from the oven.

Devon was conscious that he had invaded her privacy and felt even more intrusive as he scanned the entire apartment in one quick glance. The aroma of pastry brought his attention back to Marcia and the tray she had removed from the oven.

"Valentine chocolate chip cookies!" Devon exclaimed. "Your mother used to make these. I haven't seen these in years. May I?" He entered the apartment and stood behind Marcia as she was placing the cookies on the table.

She glanced over her shoulder at him. "Try the ones in the basket. They're cooler. Sit. Make yourself comfortable. I'll let Wendy know you're here."

Their bodies were close and as she tried to squeeze pass him, he held on to her hand.

"Wait. Remember how we used to eat these? Have one with me, please."

She wanted to decline, but lingered.

He sat at the table and reached for a cookie with one hand while the other pulled her to his side. He held the cookie out toward her, and she broke the heart shape in half, keeping her eyes focused on the cookie.

"We were friends then, right?" he asked, softly, remembering how she had denied their friendship when they met for the first time in the restaurant.

"What?" She looked at him with knitted brows that begged for him to soothe them.

He released her hand and ran his fingers lightly across her forehead. "Way back when we were kids. We used to eat these together all the time." His eyes met and held hers. "I'd give you my heart, or you'd give me yours, and we would share our cookies just like this." He took a bite. "Mm." And another. "This is really good. Just like your mother's with the miniature chocolate Kisses on the inside. You're bringing back a whole lot of memories." He glanced at her and saw her looking at the basket of cookies with tears in her eyes. Grasping her hand again, he pulled her to sit on his lap, and wrapped both of his arms around her. From their first meeting, he had wanted to take her in his arms like this. He hooked a finger under her chin and brought her face closer to his. "What is it?"

She shook her head and brushed away a tear, annoyed that she was crying. She felt his fingertips stroking her cheek. Later, she would be disappointed that she hadn't had the will to resist as she felt his lips meet hers.

He was cautious at first, certain that she would push him away. Their relationship was about Wendy, she'd told him at least a dozen times. He was Wendy's father, nothing more. But he remembered when they had been friends. Like brother and sister playing together beneath their mothers' watchful eyes. And later as teenagers, sneaking that first kiss. He kissed her now and felt her lips part as his met hers. No, this wasn't what he had planned, and he hadn't expected her to accept him, but she felt good.

Marcia had grown up a lot in seventeen years, but her reaction to Devon Douglas had not changed one bit. As their kiss deepened, she realized that she still wanted to be his girl.

He removed the towel and toyed with her wet hair, inhaling its fresh scent.

She sighed and pulled away from him, shaking her head. She stood up, but still he held on to her hand, trying to read her expression.

"Did I cross the line?"

She nodded. "Let's not make the same foolish mistake."

"Is being attracted to each other a mistake?"

"For me, it has been a costly mistake. I can't afford to let that happen again."

He sighed. "I'm sorry. Sorry that at seventeen I was too blind to see how much you loved me."

"Loved you?" Her voice was soft, barely audible.

"Yes, loved me. Since I found you again, I've done nothing but think about us growing up together, realizing now that you gave so much of yourself to me. Memories. You were like the daughter my mother never had. She treated you like her own child, dragging us both along to all the places that she thought were good for us."

"I was the daughter of your domestic helper and your mother had a very kind heart," Marcia said, her voice shaking as she spoke.

"Your mother was like family to us."

"She was your maid." Tears streamed down her face.

"Technically, yes. But our mothers were also friends, and you were mine."

Marcia sobbed, and in a split second Devon stood up and pulled her into his arms. This time, she pulled away and ran into the bedroom, closing the door behind her.

Three strides brought him to the door and he knocked. "Marcia. Babe, let's talk."

She didn't answer. Instead he heard Wendy shouting as she descended the stairs. "Dad? You're here. I just looked out of the window from upstairs and saw your car. When did you get here?" Her voice was carefree as she sashayed into the room.

Wendy stood face to face with her father, almost his height in heels. Devon saw his features and complexion reflecting back at him, but as his eyes met hers, there was no mistaking the reminder of her mother. He gasped, taken aback by the realization that this elegant lady standing before him with the poise of a fashion model was his daughter. "Wendy! You're beautiful."

She smiled and hugged him. "Thanks. That's a great compliment coming from my dad. Where is Mommy?"

He pointed to the bedroom.

"Mom?" Wendy shouted.

"I'll be right there, honey," Marcia responded, with a tone that Devon recognized was forced cheerfulness.

Marcia opened the bedroom door. She had changed into a sweat suit and held a camera in front of her eyes. "Say cheese."

Wendy smiled and posed.

"You look so pretty," Marcia told her.

"Let me get a picture with Dad." She held his hand and dragged him into the living room where they positioned themselves beside a potted plant.

"You need to get going," Marcia said after she had taken a few shots.

"Let me take a picture of you and Wendy." Devon's hands touched Marcia's as he reached for the camera.

She drew back, but said cheerfully. "Not with me looking like this." She held her arms out to Wendy and hugged her. "Have a great time."

"I will. Mommy, are you going to be okay?"

"I'm fine. Will you two get out of here before it gets any later?"

Wendy's eyes darted from one of her parents to the other. "Mom, your eyes are red."

"Perhaps from the shampoo. Now go." She held up Wendy's coat and helped her into it.

Devon walked back to the table and retrieved his belongings. As they joined him near the front door, he said, "Marcia, these are for you. They are from Wendy and me. Happy Valentine's Day." He had meant to give her the yellow roses as one baby step in his long-term plan to regain her friendship. He wanted the platonic familiarity they had once shared, but finding her in her bathrobe making his favorite cookies had thrown him off guard. He kissed her on the cheek and stood back so Wendy could do the same.

Marcia blinked back tears as she reached for the dozen roses and tried to remain composed in front of Wendy. "Thanks."

"Love you, Mom."

"Love you too, honey."

As she locked the door behind them, she burst into tears.

She was interrupted almost immediately by a knock at the door.

"Who is it?" she asked, trying to sound normal.

"It's Blossom." Blossom took one look at her as she opened the door and added, "I thought you might need a friend."

Marcia sat heavily on the sofa and propped her chin up on her knees.

Blossom started to follow but stopped short. "Yummy. Valentine cookies. May I?" She helped herself. "One for me, and one for the baby," she said, patting her protruding stomach. Placing the cookies on a plate, she joined her cousin on the sofa. "Want to talk about it?"

Marcia shook her head.

"Well, I'll just sit here with you because my husband went out and it's lonely in my apartment." Blossom swallowed a mouthful of cookies and got up to fill a mug with milk. Returning to her seat, she ate quietly, watching Marcia, before adding, "I imagine that you're feeling lonely too."

Marcia looked at her with her face still wet, but said nothing.

"I'm not a mommy, yet, but I imagine that when this baby I'm carrying grows up to be a lady like little Miss Wendy, and finishes high school, I'll be crying too. Add to that, Wendy's announcement that she wants to marry Paul and move in with him, I'd be bawling hysterically. Then, throw in the fact that her daddy arrives out of nowhere and claims her affections. I'd be fit to be tied by now. Girl, I don't know how you're coping, but I just thought you might need a friend."

Marcia said nothing, but fresh tears streamed down her face.

Blossom gulped down some milk and took a bite of the second cookie. "These cookies are good. Did you let Devon try them? Any man who knows you can bake like this would marry you in a heartbeat."

Marcia laughed. "Very funny, Blossom. That's more reason why I shouldn't have given him any."

"Oh, so he likes your cookies."

"It's a long story."

"I have time."

"I don't know where to start."

"With the cookies."

Marcia sighed. If there was anyone she could confide in, it was Blossom. Although they had hardly known each other as children, Blossom stood by Marcia's side like a sister in the years since Wendy was born.

"He loved the cookies," Marcia said, finally. "Always has."

Blossom arched her eyebrows.

"Mommy used to make them for us this time of year when we were growing up. His mother would engage him and me in some kind of craft while my mother worked in the kitchen. We would all sit down for lunch though and talk over milk and cookies."

"When was that?"

"Oh, up until high school when we started boarding out. Devon and I used to play together a lot. His mother would read to us, and she would take us out often during the day, and sometimes in the evening with his father. I'm ashamed now to admit it, but God already knows that I used to wish she was my mother." Marcia cried openly now. "I mean, I loved my mother, but she was the housekeeper, the maid. Devon's mother was this sweet sophisticated lady who smothered me with attention, and I loved her for it. When there were visitors at the house, I always felt ashamed that it was the domestic helper and not the lady of the house that was my mother. Do you understand that?"

Blossom nodded.

"But I still loved my mother."

"Girl, you're not the first person to ever feel ashamed of your parents. Trust me on this one. We all have our moments. So, you're saying that you and Devon were like brother and sister."

"Yes, when we were small. As a teenager though, my feelings changed. I started to notice how cute he was, and to feel jealous when I heard about or saw the other girls who liked him. But I always had a conflict because I could dress like them, talk like them, and go to school with them, but I wasn't one of them, and they knew it."

"You mean because of Aunt Ruth?"

Marcia nodded. "Yes. When Devon had a birthday party at the house and all his friends came, I was included like all the other teenagers, but they knew my mother was working in the kitchen. At those parties, it was always some rich man's daughter that Devon would cut the cake with, even though I was supposed to be his closest friend. As I got older and wiser, I began to feel more like a charity case than a part of the Douglas family."

"So, if you and Devon grew apart, how did you end up getting together?" Blossom asked. "I mean you had to get really close in order to make Wendy."

"Ha, ha. We were home on Easter break. I still remember how good I felt about being alone with Devon that weekend. My feelings for him ranged from resenting him for letting our social class distinction come between us to fantasizing about marrying the guy one day. Yes. I was one messed up teenager. Academically brilliant, but socially, a major misfit."

"So, what happened that Easter weekend?" Blossom asked, raising and lowering her eyebrows playfully. She had always been curious, but when Marcia and her baby came to live with her and her parents, Marcia was in such a fragile state that she didn't dare ask. And as the years passed, it hadn't mattered, until now.

Marcia sighed again, but she felt less burdened. The only time she had ever talked this over was in her prayers to God. "We were both home, and he hadn't brought his best friend Troy home with him as he did on many visits, so we spent a lot of time talking and doing things together like we used to. We talked about the future, our plans for college, and we talked about the past, about how we both had changed since we were kids. We went shopping for stuff for school, his treat, and he bought me a really gorgeous dress. That Saturday afternoon when we returned to the house, everyone was out. It was an extremely hot day, and we decided to go swimming. We were lying by the pool talking when he asked me if I ever wondered about us. One thing led to another and soon we were kissing."

"How romantic! You made love by the pool."

"Nope. I see now that God gave me a whole lot of time to change my mind, but I didn't. I went back to his room with him to watch a movie after we'd showered and eaten dinner. And the rest is history."

"So, wait a minute. Are you saying that he took advantage of you and then pretended that nothing happened?"

"No. Devon was always very sweet, very attentive, immediately afterwards."

"If he was so sweet, why didn't he step forward like a man and take responsibility once you found out you were pregnant?"

"I told him the baby wasn't his."

"Girl! Why? What were you thinking?"

"That he wouldn't want it. That I had shamed mommy and disappointed Mrs. Douglas. That I was worthless and foolish to let this happen. That I wanted to die. You have to understand that I was my mother's only hope for a future in which she wouldn't have to work so hard. I was her one-way ticket out of poverty and I let her down. I broke her heart worse than Devon broke mine when he believed the rumors about me being promiscuous and not knowing who the baby's father was. And Mrs. Douglas, I don't know what she stood to gain, but she'd spent a whole lot of money on me. Ballet lessons, music lessons, tuition for boarding school. I couldn't even begin to repay her and her husband. I had disgraced them all. But I feared God more than I feared humiliation, so I knew an abortion wasn't the answer."

Blossom rubbed her hand over the mound of her bulging belly. "No, that wasn't the answer." She paused. "You're a survivor, girl."

"By the grace of God and the forgiveness of Jesus. Praise God for Aunt Pat, Uncle Trevor, and you."

Blossom placed a hand over hers. "And just look at little Miss Wendy today."

Marcia smiled. "She looked gorgeous. Thanks for styling her hair."

"No problem. Sit back and relax. I'll style yours too."

CHAPTER TEN

As Devon spent more time with Wendy, he would check with Marcia for permission before he made decisions that affected their daughter, but not necessarily before they shopped. Although Wendy still talked about marrying Paul that summer and traveling with him to Africa to work as a missionary, she was enjoying the extra money and gifts her father gave her. Devon bought her an expensive pearl necklace and matching earrings as a belated birthday present for all the years he'd missed. He opened up a credit card account for her, which she used to shop for clothes and accessories for the prom and the senior trip.

The apartment where Wendy lived with her mother had one small closet that they both shared, so Wendy took over one of the bedrooms at her father's house and stored her extra clothing and supplies there. She didn't sleepover, but it thrilled Devon to see his daughter's personality reflected in the posters on the walls, the pictures on the dresser, and the new bedding and curtains. Marcia never visited Devon's apartment and didn't interfere with the close bond they were forming.

Wendy called her at work one evening with an announcement that could not wait until she got home.

"Mommy, Daddy is going to buy me a car!"

"He is?" Marcia asked in surprise.

"Yes! He said he will take me after school one day when I don't have to work and we'll start looking."

"Wendy, you don't even have a driver's license."

"That's okay. Daddy will teach me how to drive. I just need to go get my permit first."

"You said you didn't have time for that. You know what, let's talk about it later. Okay?"

"Mom!"

"Let's talk later, Wendy. I'm at work. Remember? Okay, honey? I love you."

"I love you too, Mom," Wendy replied sullenly.

Marcia could hear the disappointment in her daughter's voice. She fumed. How dare Devon make Wendy such an offer without consulting her? She couldn't allow Wendy to accept a car from him. It was only natural that Wendy would be upset. Devon had set her up to be the unpopular parent. That night, when she was sure her patient was sleeping, she called him.

"Hello."

"Devon Douglas. Why did you make a decision like that without consulting me?"

"Marcia. Hi. I planned to call you tonight, but I thought you were still at work."

"I am."

"Oh. Wendy spoke to you about the car."

"Wendy called me this afternoon excited that you are planning to buy her a car. Now, I have the burden of telling her she can't get one."

"Why not? I'll pay for it."

Marcia sighed. It was just like Devon to throw his financial weight around, she thought. "It doesn't matter who is paying for it," she said, in the calmest voice she could muster. She had to work for another two hours before riding the train and taking a brisk walk home, so she needed to remain composed.

"So, what's the problem?" Devon asked, in a tone that matched hers.

You, Marcia thought, but didn't say so. "The problem is that Wendy doesn't need a car right now. A car was not even on our radar. Her senior year has been a busy one—like every other year, actually—and last summer, Wendy said she didn't have time to read the driver's manual in order to pass the written test and get her permit. Now, you've filled her head with this urgent desire to get a car."

"Excuse me. Have you ever considered that, just maybe, she wanted a car all along, but didn't pursue it because she knew you didn't have the money to buy her one?"

Marcia closed her eyes as the possible truth of Devon's words painfully hit home, causing her to wonder how well she knew her daughter. "Wendy doesn't need a car," she repeated, sorry that her voice trembled like she was going to cry. "And even if she did, Devon, I wouldn't just hand it to her. She would have to save her money and contribute to its cost. That is my way of teaching her to be responsible."

Devon thought for a moment before he responded. Marcia made a good point about teaching Wendy responsibility. Yet, he disagreed, "Wendy works hard and has shown that she is responsible. I think she deserves to be rewarded for that. I'd like to buy her a car, Marcia."

"You've bought her everything else. Must you throw your money around so? You don't need to buy her affections."

"I'll ignore that," Devon replied, hurt by Marcia's accusation that he would try to buy his daughter's affections. "If I buy Wendy a car, she won't need to rely on people to pick her up and drive her around. As you just acknowledged, she is busy. Between school, her extracurricular activities, her job, and her responsibilities at church, she has pulled Uncle Trevor out of retirement and into a job as her chauffer."

"Uncle Trevor has never complained."

"Lately, I've been driving her around, anyway, and we have talked extensively about this. Wendy wants a car."

Marcia breathed out a loud sigh of frustration. "Don't pick at my words, Devon. Wendy doesn't need a car. Please don't buy her one."

"Let me pick you up from work and we can talk about this face to face."

"No." She paused and tried not to let her tone convey the aggravation she felt. "No, thank you."

"Why not?"

"I prefer to get home on my own, and I have no intention of changing my mind about the car."

"Wendy has two parents now."

Marcia wanted to scream. How dare he? He had not been there all those times when she had wished that there were two. Like at the hospital when Wendy was born, and during the months of sleepless nights that followed. When Wendy sat up on her own for the first time and took her first steps, she had wished he was there. She had cried for weeks when Wendy started saying, "Dada," and he was nowhere around. She had longed for him to share her deepest feelings, as he had when they were younger. More than anyone else, she'd wanted him to be there to share her dreams, her joy, and the things that made her cry. Instead, she'd been left with a void when he became the cause of her pain.

She sniffled but insisted, "Don't buy her a car, Devon."

"Okay, Marcia," he replied softly. A pause and then, "I never intended to make you cry."

Marcia nodded, forgetting that he couldn't see her because they were talking on the phone.

"Let me pick you up tonight," he offered again.

"No."

He sighed. It wasn't easy fitting in, finding his place in their unofficial family of three. "Marcia, I know you think of me just as Wendy's father, but I also care about you."

Marcia closed her eyes again, this time, to hold back the tears and the emotions that Devon was stirring up. She could not, would not, allow him to get close to her again.

"I want to make you both happy," he said. "I don't want to hurt either one of you."

Marcia sobbed. "Devon. Please. Let's talk about this some more another time."

"Okay. Are you sure you don't need a ride home?"

"I'll be fine. Thanks."

They said goodnight.

Devon hung up the phone and ran his fingers over his hair. He wanted to take action, but wasn't sure what to do. As he looked around his room, his eyes rested on a baby picture of Wendy that she had framed and given to him. He reached for it and sat down in an armchair.

What had he been doing during the first year of Wendy's life? He pictured himself in college, excited about the opportunity to live in the United States. He remembered being puffed up with pride because he had been bright enough to get accepted into an Ivy League university when so many other applicants hadn't. He settled in on campus and studied hard, but by mid-semester, he had also developed an active social life. He went club hopping all over Manhattan on Friday nights and dated brilliant young women from around the world. Many were just friends he would hang out with, but others became lovers.

Until now, he had always reflected fondly on those college years, but tonight, he realized that a miracle had been taking place then without him. It hurt now to imagine that a part of him had joined with his first lover and become new life, and had been growing—would grow up—without knowing him. No matter how many stories he heard, or pictures he saw, he could never revisit those years. He would never hear the sound of a baby cry and thank God for his beautiful baby girl. Would she have held on to her daddy's little finger the way babies do, he wondered? Did she say "Dada" or "Mama" first? How old was she when she walked? What presents had she wanted each time she had a birthday? He could have given her so much more if he had been there.

On the following Sunday morning, Devon explained to Wendy in her mother's presence why he would put off buying her a car. She politely said she understood, but later, she exposed her deepest feelings to her closest friend.

"Daddy said he realized now that I had too much on my plate to find time to study for the permit and practice driving for the road test," she told Paul.

"True."

"But I don't think that's it. I think Mommy must be feeling threatened by all the money Daddy has been spending on me."

Paul faced her fully. They were sitting in his mother's car, parked outside of his house, but the engine was running. They always spent time alone there just talking before he took her home.

"That's possible. All your life it has been just the two of you. Life is tough for single mothers, especially when they don't make a lot of money like your mother and mine. When I was growing up my momma was so broke, she couldn't afford to pay attention."

Wendy smiled feebly at the over-run joke.

"Seriously though," Paul continued, "I know there were times when my mother cried because she wanted to buy me things that we could not afford. I don't mean extravagant items either. I'm talking about basics, like new clothes for school, and my first bicycle. If your mother had similar experiences, it's hard for her not to feel inadequate with your father spending so much money on you now." Paul didn't add an explanation that he too worried that she would learn to love being pampered and no longer be interested in the frugal lifestyle they would have to maintain as missionaries in Africa.

"I love my mother and she knows it. I haven't been asking Daddy for a lot of stuff. He just feels he has to provide for me. It's like he's trying to make up for all the spending he didn't do in the last seventeen years."

"Well, he can't. That time is lost forever. All you and your father can do is make the best of the time you have now."

"And it isn't much, is it? Pretty soon we'll be graduating and getting married and going away."

"If Pastor agrees to marry us," Paul reminded her.

"He said we could start pre-marital counseling soon."

"He also said he wouldn't marry us against our parents' wishes."

"And our parents don't wish for us to get married."

Paul reached forward and stroked her hair. "They don't understand our love."

"They don't. It's outrageous really. When they were our age, they were making love. If my parents hadn't, I wouldn't be here. Yet, here we are, waiting because God said we should, and they act like we're the ones doing something wrong."

"Maybe they're afraid that's the reason why we're in such a rush to get married. My mother asked me that just yesterday."

"Asked you what?"

"If I'm rushing to marry you just so we can make love."

Wendy giggled and blushed. "She did!" she exclaimed. "What did you tell her?"

"That I love you. That I have loved you since I was a little boy and you were running around the church in pigtails and glasses. I still remember the first time I heard you sing."

"I was so scared, but I remember that before the youth choir went into the sanctuary, we all joined hands and you volunteered to pray. That was the first time you prayed for me, Paul. We were little children and yet you helped me realize that this wasn't entertainment; we were praising God."

"You sang beautifully that day. Still do."

"Thanks. You inspire me so much, I always feel like I can soar."

"And you inspire me. As God would have it, we ended up in the same music class at school. You made me realize that I needed to use my gift for playing instruments to praise God in the church."

"How could you not, Paul Chambers?"

"I was a just a child. All the musicians were grown-ups."

"Until they recognized how well you could play every instrument in the church. You paved the way for other talented youth."

"Praise God, Wendy," he said, beaming at her. "Now, I need your help with the songs I'm writing for the Easter praise and worship celebration. The idea that you had of telling the story of Jesus' crucifixion and resurrection through the eyes of Mary is awesome. I wrote a song for Mary, the mother of Jesus, to sing as she helplessly watches her son dying on the cross. I also wrote one for Mary Magdalene to sing on Easter morning after she sees that Jesus is alive. I need you to tell me whether I've captured the intensity of their emotions."

"Knowing you, your songs will have the whole congregation in tears by the time they finish listening. Your songs are always so moving, Paul. How about we meet tomorrow, after school?"

He nodded, then suggested, "We'll read through the Bible stories first. I know you've been doing so on your own, but we should go over the scriptures together, so it will be fresh in our minds, and we'll ask God to help us stay true to His word."

"Cool."

Companionable silence, and then, "You know what, Paul?"

"What?"

"I imagine that the way I feel about you is how my mother must have felt about my father when they were young."

"Why do you say that?"

"Because they grew up together like we did. And as far as I know, she hasn't dated another man. Yet, she was so intimate with my father. Otherwise, I wouldn't be here. Right? So, she must have really loved him to go that far."

"Can you picture them back then?" Paul asked. "Pops would have been like, 'Yo, Baby. Come here.' No, no, no. Your father is way too proper. He would have said, 'Eh hem. Excuse me, Miss.'" Paul deepened his voice. "'I was observing you from across the room and I couldn't help but notice your radiant smile.'"

Wendy grinned at him and joined in the pretense. "Who me?" she responded, fanning her cheeks with her right hand.

"No one but you. Your eyes, I feel like I could lose myself in the warmth of your ebony eyes."

Wendy burst out laughing. "You sound just like him. Seriously though, whatever Dad said to Mom, his game must have been tight to win her heart, even for a moment."

"Well, if he had loved her like I love you, he would have stuck around to watch you grow instead of being missing in action all your life," Paul declared fiercely, bringing an abrupt ending to their playfulness.

Tears filled Wendy's eyes. "I know."

"Oh, baby. I'm sorry. It's clear that your father is trying to make up for not being there. There is no doubt that he loves you and regrets missing those years. He has told me so himself when we've talked. I look him in the eye when he's talking to me. No doubt, he's sincere."

"Do you think he loves Mommy?"

"I don't know. We don't know much about their relationship. Let's just continue to pray for them."

"Can we do that now?"

"Yes."

After they prayed together, Paul drove Wendy home.

CHAPTER ELEVEN

As Easter approached, Devon realized that being with Marcia and Wendy was the best way to show them how much he cared about them. This would be their first holiday together, his first holiday with his daughter ever. Yet, before meeting them, he had already made plans with his parents to travel home to Jamaica for his father's birthday which coincided with the Easter weekend that year.

Perhaps the memories Marcia had of her childhood affection for Devon's parents and her gratitude for all that they had done for her caused her to say yes. She would allow Wendy to travel with Devon to Jamaica to meet his parents and celebrate his father's birthday, but she wouldn't go herself.

They decided to break the news to Wendy together, over dinner, just the three of them at a Jamaican restaurant that was fancier than the one Marcia and Devon had lunch at on their first meeting. This one was designed to look and feel tropical. Potted palm trees swayed under the breeze of a concealed fan against one wall. Another wall displayed a ceiling-to-floor length painting of a sunset. Reggae and calypso rhythms played softly in the background.

Although it was dinnertime, Wendy ordered ackee and saltfish. It was customary to serve the Jamaican national dish for breakfast, but this restaurant made it available all day.

"Mm. This is so good," Wendy critiqued, as she lifted a forkful of the bright yellow fruit, bits of codfish, and a piece of boiled banana to her lips. "Mommy, why don't we make this at home?"

"It's hard to get ackee in the stores here sometimes," Marcia replied.

"We make it fairly often for breakfast back home," Devon commented, "especially on holidays and special occasions." Seeing that he had Wendy's full attention, Devon glanced at Marcia and noted that she nodded approval before he continued. "How would you like to have this for breakfast on Easter Sunday?"

"I would love it," Wendy replied, patting her lips with a napkin to conceal another mouthful. She was enjoying this meal with just her parents. It was a first. She had grown accustomed to having her father at their family dinners after church on Sundays, but there was something special about this moment with just the three of them that made her heart sing.

"Well, I could arrange that. How does breakfast with your grandparents on Easter Sunday sound?" Devon asked.

"Great! Are they coming to visit?" Wendy replied eagerly.

"No. I'm going to Jamaica for Easter and I'd like to take you with me."

Wendy squealed with excitement and threw her arms around her father's neck. "Awesome! Mom, we are going. Right?"

"Sure you can!" Marcia tried to sound upbeat in order to join in her daughter's excitement, but she felt a tinge of regret that she could not bring herself to travel with them. She was not ready and did not know if she could ever return to her birthplace that held so many unhappy memories for her.

Devon sensed her sadness, even though she wore a wide smile as his eyes met hers. "Wendy, honey. I'm going to take you to meet my parents," Devon cleared his throat, "Your grandparents, but since we're making the trip on such short notice, your mother won't be able to join us."

"Come on, Mom. Be spontaneous."

Marcia shook her head but kept her smile in place. "Maybe next time, honey. This time, you go. Enjoy, and take lots of pictures of the people and places so I can enjoy it with you that way."

"Yes! And video; I'll make sure Daddy records everything for you," Wendy added, ecstatic about their plans.

"Good. I like still pictures too though," Marcia reminded her.

Devon wasn't sure how to describe what he was feeling. Marcia and Wendy: they were his family. The three of them felt right to him in a way that none of his prior relationships ever had.

Both he and Marcia laughed heartily as Wendy started to dance a jig. "I'm going to Jamaica," she chanted. "I'm going to Jamaica."

Wendy had one hurdle to scale before she'd be free to enjoy her trip to Jamaica with her father. She and Paul had a tradition of playing a major role in the Easter presentation at their church. This year, they had convinced the adults to entrust them with the tasks of writing and directing the play for the first time. The closer they got to Easter Sunday, the more frequently Wendy, Paul and the other youth rehearsed.

Paul was also composing original music for the performance,

following up on Wendy's idea of telling the story from the viewpoint of two women named Mary. The first Mary was Jesus' mother and the other was a follower of Jesus who told others of Jesus' resurrection.

Paul was tinkering with the keys of his piano one evening when she arrived at his home. His mother let her in.

"Good evening, Mrs. Chambers," Wendy said, hugging her.

"Hello, Wendy. How are you?"

"I'm fine, thank you. And you?"

"Blessed and highly favored and thankful for another day. I'm just finishing up dinner in the kitchen and then I'll be ready to drive you and Paul over to the church."

"Okay. Thanks."

Mrs. Chambers returned to the kitchen while Wendy sat on the sofa in the living room facing Paul.

Paul turned his head to greet her and smiled. "Listen to this," he whispered, slowly stroking the keys of the piano. He played a sad melody.

"That sounds so depressing," Wendy said.

"Mm hmm," Paul nodded and kept on playing.

After a while, Wendy said, "If I listen to this much longer, I'm going to cry."

"Perfect. That's what I was aiming for," Paul said, grinning victoriously as he turned to face her. "How are you?" He joined her on the sofa and kissed her cheek.

"Fine. I see you've been working hard, as always."

"Yeah! You should hear the other pieces I've come up with. Remember how we were struggling because we didn't want to make up words for Mary to say that weren't in the Bible, but we wanted to focus on her long enough so that our audience will identify with her grief?"

"Yes."

"Well. This is it. We'll play this music softly in the background while she is standing near the cross weeping as Jesus is crucified." He retrieved a Bible from the side table and said, "Let's look at the scripture again. John, chapter nineteen, mentions Jesus' mother standing by the cross. See here in verses twenty-five to twenty-seven." Paul held Wendy's hand and they prayed for understanding and then read the scripture.

"Perhaps Mary wept hysterically as she watched her son's crucifixion. After all, he was bleeding to death right in front of her. What mother wouldn't grieve? Right, Mom?" Paul asked, as his mother walked through their living room at that moment on her way to her bedroom.

"Right, son," she replied.

"At the same time, though, we know when we read Luke, chapter one, that Mary believed Angel Gabriel when he told her that she would conceive Jesus Christ while she was still a virgin. She lived that experience, so she knew the power of God to make the impossible possible. So, perhaps, she felt the strength of God's peace that surpasses all understanding, even as she watched her son dying on the cross."

"Yes. She might have," Wendy agreed. "Perhaps the reason all four accounts of the crucifixion say so little about her is that she did not make a spectacle of herself because she knew this was God's plan. After all, as you said, she conceived Jesus while she was a virgin, so she had already experienced God's power working to bring about the impossible in her life. Imagine being pregnant and giving birth to a child while being a virgin. No one else ever experienced that."

"Right. So, let's not make her carry on hysterically, like we've been doing in rehearsal. Let's just make her weep quietly, and as the music plays, she can retell the story based on what we read in the Bible, without us using our imagination to enhance the story and risk distorting it."

"Good point," Wendy commended him.

"Praise the Lord."

"Yeah, praise God. So that's why you asked us to meet for rehearsal tonight."

Paul nodded. "Yes. We need to get it together for Pastor to approve."

"Right. We don't have much time." She paused and took a deep breath. "Paul, I have something to tell you before we go."

"What is it? Are you okay?" he asked, looking at her with concern.

"I hope you'll understand," she said softly.

"Tell me, Wendy."

"Daddy wants me to go to Jamaica with him for Easter weekend," Wendy blurted out. "He wants me to meet his parents and celebrate his father's birthday with them."

"What did you tell him?"

"You know I've never met my grandparents. And I haven't been to Jamaica since I left there as a newborn baby. There is a whole other side of my family that I didn't even know about until recently when I met Dad."

"You're going."

"I want to be with you for Easter as usual, especially with all we're doing this year, but there is so little that Daddy and I have shared, and so little time before I go off into the world with you as your wife." She sighed. "I'm going, Paul." She knew she was letting him down but hoped he would forgive her.

Paul nodded but said nothing. He felt hurt and disappointed. He wanted to feel happy for her, but she was so much a part of him and everything that he did that all he could think of was how much he would miss her. She played an integral part in everything he did, especially in this event that they had planned together. He couldn't imagine himself doing it without her. Sometimes he felt like her father was gradually pulling her away.

"It's only for a few days, and Desiree has been my understudy. She could easily fill in for me." Wendy tried to sound sympathetic, but she couldn't conceal her excitement about the trip.

"It won't be the same without you," Paul said softly.

"It will be just as good."

"I'll miss you."

"I'll miss you too. But I'll be back before you know it."

His mother emerged from her bedroom with her pocketbook in her hand.

"Ready, children?" she asked.

She dropped them off at the church where Desiree was excited to learn that she would be taking Wendy's place.

On a sunny but cool morning in April, Marcia drove Devon and Wendy to the airport. Paul came with them to see Wendy off and to keep Marcia's company for the return drive home. As they sat in Devon's car moving slowly in the traffic crossing over the East River on the Whitestone Bridge from Queens back into the Bronx, Paul broke the silence.

"This is Wendy's first trip without you, Ms. Tapper. You must be worried."

"Worried? No, Paul. I'm not." She told him about how she had grown up with Devon's family and trusted them fully with Wendy. After Devon had asked her for permission to take Wendy with him, she had prayed about it, and said yes, in spite of Aunt Pat's recommendation that they wait until summer to give everyone more time to adjust. "There is a bittersweet feeling in letting her go. I feel that this is God's plan for Wendy. And then, my family means so much to me that I couldn't dream of keeping Wendy from any part of hers. That doesn't mean that I won't be counting the days until she gets back, though."

"Me too," Paul agreed on a sigh.

Marcia giggled. "Lovesick already?"

"Truthfully? Yes. This is my first Easter without Wendy too."

Marcia hadn't given any thought to the fact that growing up together in the church, Wendy and Paul had spent every Easter and Christmas together. Her mind evoked a vivid image of herself and Paul's mother sitting near each other on Sundays, and later getting to know each other in the Mothers of Preschoolers group where their toddlers played together.

"Wendy was supposed to be my lead singer in the youth choir for the Easter praise and worship celebration and she had a major role in the play," said Paul. "The whole youth production was Wendy's idea and a special project we were working on together, and she just abandoned it without even asking me if I could manage without her."

"Oh, no. Sorry. I forgot about that. Did you have trouble finding someone to replace her?"

"No. We're blessed with so much talent that Desiree was glad for the chance to take Wendy's place. What bothers me is that Wendy just changed plans without even asking my opinion. Our work in the church means a lot to me, and I thought it meant a lot to her too."

"It does, honey. She's just so excited by this new relationship with her father that it's only natural for her to be distracted."

Paul had recently accepted the post of youth choir director, given to him by Reverend Walker. As the youngest person to ever serve as a choir director in the century-old church, Paul was confident and decisive, but humble enough to seek out the older and more experienced choir directors as mentors. Yet, what he valued most was the advice and loving encouragement that he received from Wendy.

Marcia glanced over at Paul noting the sadness that registered on his face. Come to think of it, Paul had been uncharacteristically quiet for most of the ride back. It worried Marcia to see Paul looking so dejected, knowing that somehow, she had willed the events that led to his sadness. She and Devon had no plans of permanently breaking up the happy young couple. They just wanted Paul and Wendy to come to their senses long enough to realize that they were both too young to get married.

"Hey, cheer up, guy," she said, nudging him. "They'll only be gone for a few days."

Paul nodded, but remained silent.

"And you'll talk to her often. She gave you the phone numbers, right?"

Again, Paul nodded.

They covered the rest of distance to Paul's house without further conversation. Marcia found herself wondering once again whether her daughter was right. Could an early marriage between Wendy and Paul be a part of God's plan? She prayed that God would give her and Devon wisdom to carry out, not interfere with, His plan.

The Easter praise and worship celebration took place in a high school auditorium, which seated over a thousand people and was filled to capacity. It was the largest audience Paul had ever played for and he missed Wendy. Desiree sang like an angel and her voice carried a note high enough to make the hairs stand up on the back of a listener's neck. The audience was deeply moved. Later, Paul's mother would tell him that there wasn't a dry eye in the place. God was glorified, Jesus was lifted up, and Paul felt grateful, but sad. He needed Wendy, and that morning when he had called the number in Jamaica to speak to her, she wasn't there.

He wasn't fond of the accolades that followed a production like this one, but they were customary. Reverend Walker took the microphone and commended everyone who played a part in the celebration. People were singled out and presented with bouquets of flowers and other tokens of appreciation. And Paul received a standing ovation as he was called up to the microphone.

"Praise God," he shouted, pointing upward. "Give God the praise. Hallelujah! Thank you, Jesus." When the crowd quieted down, he said, "The youth ministry would like to thank each and everyone for attending. We pray that you will never be the same, and that you have been moved by the word of God, and that you will go home and read the story of Jesus again and again for yourselves. Abide in God's word and He will give you the victory."

Applause.

"I just wanted to acknowledge that the idea for this production came from Wendy Tapper, as she would say, by inspiration of God. Wendy isn't here today," Paul swallowed hard, "but we could not have done this without her." He backed away and returned to his seat in front of the piano.

From her seat near the front of the auditorium, Marcia watched Paul. At a time like this, Paul should have been effused with so much joy that it would have brought uncontainable laughter to his and Wendy's lips. But as he had said, Wendy wasn't there, and Marcia could see that sadness weighed heavily on Paul even though he smiled and tried to appear upbeat. Once again, Marcia found herself wondering whether she and Devon had any right to interfere with the children's relationship. Yes, as parents, they liked to think that they knew what was best for their children, but at sixteen, hadn't she loved Devon enough to surrender everything to him?

On the following day, Marcia and Paul returned to the airport to pick up Devon and Wendy. Wendy glowed with a newly acquired suntan and chatted ceaselessly on the drive home. She loved her grandparents, and she'd enjoyed every moment she spent with them. Jamaica was beautiful, she said. She wanted to take Paul there. Perhaps, they could return in the summer. She was sure Paul would love it there too, and she told him so. She described how her grandparents reacted the first time they met her. Her grandmother cried while her grandfather boasted proudly about her to his employees. Paul just had to see their hotel on the beach and the house her grandparents lived in, Wendy told him. They even had a chauffeur who had driven her and her grandmother around while Devon and his father worked at the hotel.

Wendy's joy was contagious and Paul smiled sincerely as he listened to her. But the more he listened to her, the more insecure he felt. He felt concerned that the life he and Wendy had always discussed—living with material basics while working as missionaries—must seem less attractive to Wendy now, especially after indulging in such extravagance. He couldn't compete and that bothered him.

They dropped Paul off first, and then Devon drove the rest of the way home. He felt conscious of the fact that this would be Marcia's first visit to his house, and appreciated how much she had trusted him with Wendy. She had allowed Wendy to go home with him, first to his house in New York and then to Jamaica, when she hadn't checked out either place for herself.

Marcia's eyes recorded every detail as they entered the residential neighborhood where he lived. Neatly kept two-family houses lined the streets. Devon's house stood two stories high on a corner lot with an expansive driveway and lush green yard. Springtime showers had begun and dandelions sprouted their yellow flowers sporadically among the thick grass.

"Welcome," Devon said to Marcia, bowing playfully as he held open the door for her. Wendy bounded up the stairs ahead of them with a backpack on her shoulder and a small suitcase in her hand. Marcia smiled back at Devon and followed their daughter inside.

Devon's home was tidy and didn't show the signs of rushed packing that Marcia had expected to see. Marcia wondered if he hired a maid to clean up after him.

"Come see my bedroom, Mommy," Wendy beckoned her, leading the way down a small corridor.

Marcia dropped the bags as she stood in the doorway. She felt winded, not because of the luggage, but by the impact of seeing her daughter's bedroom. Wendy had everything that her mother had not been able to provide: a room of her own, spacious and furnished to her liking. As Wendy threw open her closet, Marcia approached slowly looking at all the new clothes Devon had bought her, then she paused at the dresser, her eyes drawn to Wendy's jewelry box.

"Mom, you have to see the necklace Grandma gave me," Wendy said undoing the top buttons of the blouse she wore. "The pendant has been in their family for generations."

A gold pendant in the shape of a hibiscus flower dangled from the chain. It was one Marcia remembered seeing Devon's mother wear when they were growing up. Marcia looked up at her daughter, hoping her eyes masked the insecurity she suddenly felt. She hadn't been able to give this to her daughter. From as early as Wendy's preteen years, Aunt Pat had offered them one of the bedrooms in her apartment for Wendy, but Wendy had said she preferred to stay downstairs with her mother. They were so close, sometimes living like sisters instead of mother and daughter. But as Marcia watched her daughter joyously indulging in all the comfort her father offered her, she wondered if Wendy had always longed for this but had concealed that longing to protect her feelings.

She was glad when a cell phone rang and Wendy answered it. Marcia needed to leave this room. She needed a moment to herself, and she needed to cry. She bumped into Devon coming out of his room as she entered the hallway. She tried unsuccessfully to blink back her tears.

Devon grasped her hand and led her toward the kitchen. "My mother sent you some escovitch fish, well seasoned and delicious. She made it herself, the way your mother taught her. Are you hungry?"

"No," Marcia replied in a hoarse whisper, thankful that Devon hadn't drawn attention to her tears. She tried to dry her face with her free hand as she followed him.

He guided her to the plush leather sectional in the living room where they sat side by side. "Mommy wants me to thank you for sending her granddaughter."

Marcia nodded, and although she tried to hold them back, fresh tears seeped out from the corners of her eyes.

"Both she and my father spoiled Wendy rotten for the time that she was there."

"I can imagine," Marcia said, sniffling.

Devon watched her carefully and kept talking, caressing her face tenderly with the look in his eyes. The trip to Jamaica with Wendy had brought back a lot of memories about their friendship, and he remembered now from their childhood that when Marcia cried like this as she confided in him, she wanted companionship, not pity.

"My parents were so impressed by how well you've raised Wendy. They see so much of you in her. Here you go." He handed her an envelope he had tucked under his arm. "Mommy wrote you a letter, so I'm sure she told you so herself. Do you want to read it now?"

"I can't." Marcia said on sob. She took a deep breath, and tried not to appear so upset.

Devon adjusted the section of the sofa that allowed him to lounge back and put his feet up. Then, he drew Marcia close to his side.

She rested her head on his shoulder.

"I don't know why they acted surprised. You were always so caring when we were growing up." He reached for a pillow, placed it in his lap and patted it for her to lie down.

She lay flat on her back and propped her feet up on the sofa.

He stroked her hair as she gazed up at him. Their position was familiar, drawn from their teenage years when they had long chats as they shared stories when they were home from boarding school.

A feeling Marcia had not experienced in a long time enveloped her. Contentment. She drew a deep breath and let it out slowly.

Devon made eye contact with her and held it. "You cared so much for me when we were younger," he said, stroking her face. "I am sorry I was not there for you when you needed me the most."

Fresh tears flowed from Marcia's eyes. She sniffled and found a tissue.

The tears were breaking him down, washing away any remains of the wall of resistance he had developed when he walked away from her as a teenager. He wanted to draw her close now, kiss her deeply, and declare his love, but he held back because he knew that she didn't yet trust him with her heart, and his actions would drive her away.

"Can you ever forgive me?" he asked softly, his head hung low, eyes meeting hers.

"I already have," she replied.

He smiled sheepishly. "I know. I just needed to hear you say it."

He leaned back and adjusted himself comfortably in the chair, all the while still stroking her hair. She turned on her side, with her head still rested against the pillow in his lap. They closed their eyes. Later on, as he drove her and Wendy home in the wee hours of the morning, they laughed about how all of them had fallen asleep.

CHAPTER TWELVE

Marcia had been saving money and making plans to celebrate hers and Wendy's birthdays long before their reunion with Devon. She would rent a car and take Wendy to Pennsylvania, where they would spend the night at a hotel, shop at the outlets on Saturday morning, and see a gospel play that evening. Wendy had been excited when they first made plans. She called it their grand finale because she planned to be away either at college or in Africa with Paul when they celebrated future birthdays.

When Marcia started planning their trip, she was offering Wendy a rare opportunity to splurge. Now, thanks to Devon, Wendy had grown accustomed to shopping sprees. He placed no limit on her spending and she hadn't had to look for bargains. Marcia knew Wendy was no longer eagerly anticipating their trip, but she had not expected her to completely cancel. Wendy announced her change of plans one Saturday evening when her father dropped her home after they'd bowled with Paul.

"Hey, Mom. Great news! Someone dropped out, so there will be room on the bus for me to go with the youth group to see the Mets and Yankees play baseball."

"Isn't that on the day we have our big birthday celebration planned?" Marcia asked, surprised that Wendy hadn't made the connection.

"Oh, I know, but Paul was so disappointed when I told him I couldn't go on the bus trip, and I felt badly after abandoning him at Easter time and all, so Daddy offered to take you out instead, so I could go on the trip with Paul. Isn't that great?" Wendy concluded, grinning from ear to ear, her eyes sparkling with joy.

Marcia wondered how Wendy could have forgotten the significance of the plans they'd made.

"Daddy is so cool. He fixes everything. And you won't even have to waste money renting a car, Mom. He'll drive you to Pennsylvania."

Disappointment gave way to anger, as Marcia turned away from her daughter and tried to remain calm. "How thoughtful," she quipped. She wanted to ask Wendy if she didn't realize how much the plans they'd made meant to her, but she knew she would end up in tears. Her conscience reminded her that it wasn't fair to lay a guilt trip on Wendy. When she was Wendy's age, Marcia had thought little of spending time with her own mother. Instead, she harnessed her anger for a confrontation with Devon.

She waited until she heard the water running confirming that Wendy was in the shower before she called him. "We need to talk," she said as soon as he answered the phone.

"Marcia? What's wrong?"

"I prefer to tell you in person. Are you home?"

"Yes. I just got here. Paul and I stopped to talk after we dropped Wendy off. Do you need me to come back there?"

"No. I'll come to you." With that, she hung up the phone and then called a cab. She knocked on the bathroom door and told Wendy where she was going.

"You're going to Dad's house?" Startled, Wendy turned off the shower and peered at her mother from behind the curtain. Marcia never went to Devon's house alone, but as Wendy read her mother's expression, she guessed why. "Mom, you're upset. I should have realized it wasn't a good idea to cancel our plans, but..."

"Don't worry about it. I'll see you later," Marcia said, closing the door behind her.

Wendy rushed to finish her shower. While she was getting dressed the phone rang.

"Dad, I'd forgotten how much the plans Mommy and I had made meant to her. This was supposed to be our special mother-daughter time together before I go away to college. She's really upset."

"Don't worry, honey. I'll smooth things over with your mother. Talk to you later."

Wendy hung up and called Paul to fill him in on what was happening.

"It sounds like we really hurt your mother's feelings. Sorry about that. Does that mean you're not going to go to the game?"

"I don't know. Daddy says he'll work it out with her. We'll see."

"Okay." He paused and then asked, "Are you alright?"

"Yeah. What are you doing?"

"Turning Chris Brown's 'Forever' into a gospel song."

"You are too funny. Did you finish all your school work?"

"Yeah, man. Listen." Paul sang as he danced to the upbeat rhythm of the music, but instead of the original lyrics, "Forever, on the dance floor," he sang, "Forever, I will praise You."

"That's pretty good," Wendy said after she'd listened to him for a moment.

"Now you drop some female vocals. Bring it," Paul requested.

"I'm so not in the mood."

"You're worried about your parents?"

"Not worried. Curious. Concerned."

"Okay, Ms. Vocabulary. Let's pray about it."

They prayed.

Wendy never found out exactly what happened when her mother went over to her father's apartment. Although her mother insisted that she and Paul should go to the baseball game, Wendy could tell that she wasn't happy about it. In order to try to make up for disappointing her, Wendy, Paul and Devon planned a surprise for that special day.

Wendy rushed out of the house early that morning after saying she had to cover for a friend who was going to be arriving late for work. She promised her mother that she would be back to spend time with her before leaving for the game.

Marcia went upstairs to chat with Aunt Pat, but the older woman shooed her, saying she had errands to run. So Marcia dropped in on Blossom and was helping her fold baby clothes when the doorbell rang.

"Will you get that for me? Steve left his keys." Blossom waved her hand toward the door.

"No problem," Marcia replied. She entered the stairwell and stopped abruptly, surprised by the sight below her in the foyer. Devon backed by Paul, Steve, and Uncle Trevor began a sweet serenade. They belted out a melodious rendition of "Happy Birthday," with pleasing harmony, and Paul threw in a comical rap that left Marcia and the women who were peeking out from the doorways behind her giggling. Marcia grew somber as Devon got down on one knee.

"Marcia Tapper. I'd be honored if you'd spend this day with me."

She looked away, searching the faces around her, and noticed Wendy standing with her hands clasped in a corner of the foyer behind them.

"Mommy, please," she mouthed inaudibly, but Marcia could read her lips.

"Miss T., we can't go to the game knowing that you're here alone instead of being out celebrating like you'd planned today," Paul said sincerely.

Marcia found herself wondering whether they had rehearsed this because their act was so well coordinated. "Remember, today is not actually my birthday nor Wendy's. It's just the day we had set aside to celebrate," she replied.

"I know, and I'm really sorry I messed up your plans," Devon apologized.

"Oh, just take her please," Aunt Pat muttered from behind her. "Get her out of the house. She has been getting under everybody's foot since morning."

"Aunty!"

"Girl, you better go. Steve and I would join you two if my feet weren't swollen and my belly didn't feel so heavy," Blossom added, with one hand on her pregnant tummy and the other giving Marcia a gentle shove.

Marcia shook her head, but she was smiling, amazed and amused that the people she loved most had teamed up against her so successfully. She took a deep breath. "Okay, okay," she said, throwing her hands up and they all cheered.

When they were seated in the car, she congratulated Devon on winning everyone over.

Everyone but you, he thought but didn't say so. His eyes met and held hers as he considered how beautiful she looked today. The melon colored shirt she wore made her complexion glow. "They love you," he finally said. "All they want is to see you happy."

"I know," she replied. "I'm blessed." As Devon drove off, Marcia looked out the window and waved goodbye to Wendy and Paul who were standing outside.

"Thanks for your help." Wendy smiled sweetly at Paul and hugged him.

"Any time." He held her for a moment, and then said, "We need to get going ourselves."

"Let me just grab my bag."

Paul started his mother's car, and as he waited, he selected Wendy's latest favorite music by the female trio, Trin-i-tee 5:7, for the short drive to the church.

"How come your mom let you have her car today?" Wendy asked when she was seated beside him.

"She went out with one of her girlfriends. She is going to pick up the car from the church parking lot when she gets back. So, by the time we return from the game, we're going to have to call her or your father for a ride."

"Cool. I don't expect my parents back anytime soon though."

"Alright."

"Paul, do you think they're in love." Wendy put great emphasis on her last word.

"I don't know. I love you," he said, also emphasizing the word 'love.' "You know, I feel that forever love for you."

"Right. Which is what I would want my dad to feel for my mom. Not in love today, out of love tomorrow. He already left her broken-hearted once when they were teenagers and she was pregnant with me. I don't think she can bear another heartbreak."

Paul listened carefully to what Wendy was saying. He too prayed that Wendy's father was sincere and would not leave either woman with a broken heart. He glanced over at Wendy. He knew she would be devastated if Devon were to walk away.

"You know," Wendy spoke, interrupting Paul's thoughts, "Mommy is always afraid that I'm going to repeat her mistake."

"Yeah."

"She obsesses about it sometimes. She doesn't want me to get pregnant like she and her mother did when they were teenagers. That's why she doesn't want us to get married this year."

"But we're not planning to have a baby."

"Yes, but it could happen."

"Once, we're married and making love," they both said at the same time.

"Right," Wendy continued. "And being broke, married and pregnant isn't much easier that being broke, single and pregnant."

"We're still broke," Paul agreed, chuckling.

"Right, and Mommy says we'd be making life very hard for ourselves."

"She's right."

"Yeah, but I just feel like if she and Daddy make up, and they get married and live happily ever after, it'll take the pressure off us."

"There is no happily ever after in the real world."

"You know what I mean. Daddy left her with a broken heart when she was my age. I've never seen her get involved with another man, so her only memory of romance is heartache. So that's what she expects to happen to you and me. But if Daddy can show her something else, I mean, if he stands by her now like he should have when they were teenagers, maybe it will help her believe that we'll be okay. That not all teenage love stories have an unhappy ending."

"I hear you."

By the time Wendy and Paul boarded the church bus with their peers, Devon was driving on the highway toward New Jersey. The New York roadway ran alongside the Hudson River, which on this day looked like a murky, cavernous, liquid valley dividing the two states. The George Washington Bridge loomed up ahead. Sunlight glistened off the water as they traveled the length of the viaduct to the other side.

Marcia felt free. The farther she got outside of the city of New York, the more she felt like a weight was being lifted off her shoulders. She tilted her head from side to side, removed a clip, and tousled her hair.

Devon kept his eyes on the road, willing himself not to be affected by her. Today, he aimed just to be her friend.

"Where are we going?" she asked.

"It's a surprise."

"Okay." She truly felt carefree as she adjusted the dial on the radio.

He chuckled. Seeing her happy made him feel good. Eventually, he steered the car onto local roads pass businesses and houses. They stopped at a traffic light and then followed the roadway through a cluster of trees.

Marcia gasped at the transformation in her surroundings. She gazed at the pond filled with geese and ducks that now took the place of the brick buildings she had grown accustomed to seeing along the road. The water reflected the pink, purple and white hues of the trees surrounding it. Lush green grass carpeted the ground on every side. Marcia felt like a character from her childhood reading: Alice who stepped through the looking glass into Wonderland.

"What is this place? Where did it come from?" Marcia marveled.

"I thought you would like it here." Devon grinned, pleased with her reaction. "It takes you by surprise because it's hidden from the street. There is a whole lot more to see," Devon explained as he pulled into a parking spot and shut off the car. He walked around to the passenger side and opened the door for Marcia, bowing deeply. "Mademoiselle."

She giggled. "Monsieur," she replied copying his use of the French language, as she placed her hand in his. Once she was out of the car, she stretched and said, "I'm glad I wore comfortable shoes."

"Good."

"Ready to walk?" they both asked simultaneously.

Laughter.

"Let's go."

They held hands as they strolled along a pathway that encircled the pond. As Marcia looked closer she could see turtles sunbathing on the rocks. She pointed them out to Devon.

"Those are huge. It's been years since I've seen turtles that size."

They got to a fork in the path and decided to follow it away from the pond. Farther along the path, they came upon a circular wall of green hedges. Behind it was a garden where an assortment of colorful tulips was in bloom.

"The arrangement of the flowers reminds me of Hope Gardens in Jamaica," Marcia said.

"Me too. The atmosphere is similar. That's one of the reasons I like it here."

"Do you come here often?" Marcia asked.

"No. I haven't been here in years, actually. But I spent all week thinking of where I would take you, if you agreed to go out with me. I remembered how much you loved being outdoors in lush, green, open spaces, and there is nothing like this in our neighborhood."

Marcia nodded and stooped to inhale the fragrance of a tulip, gently placing her fingers at the top of the stem underneath the yellow flower.

"Dèjá vu," Devon whispered, as an image of Marcia in a similar pose as a teenager flashed across his mind. He remembered being with her at Hope Gardens, a similar place in Jamaica. His parents had taken them there and had walked on ahead of them when Marcia literally stopped to smell the flowers just as she had now. It was around that time that he had begun to think about her as a prospective girlfriend rather than like a sister with whom he had grown up.

"Mm?" Marcia queried, but didn't turn to face him.

"Just remembering, that's all," Devon replied. His fingers closed over a small digital camera as he pulled it from his pocket. "Smile," he said, but he felt a disturbing sense of regret.

Marcia smiled.

They followed the path farther along through acres of green grass observing the sports that people were playing. There were soccer matches underway in one area; in another, teams played softball and baseball. Marcia spotted a group of men on a field up ahead dressed in full white.

"Cricket!" she exclaimed. "Wendy calls it British baseball. Where are we?"

"In a diverse community influenced by immigrants from all over the world. If you listen as people pass by, you'll notice a number of different languages being spoken."

"Come to think of it, I did notice." She counted on her fingers. "I heard Spanish, and French Creole, and Portuguese, so far, besides English of course. Let's go watch the cricket match."

Quick strides carried them over to the field where the players were gathered. They sat down on the grass and watched the match, which had already begun. Like a pitcher in American baseball, the bowler forcefully threw the ball toward the batsman who swung hard. His rectangular bat met the ball with a loud thud before he ran back and forth between two bases marked by sticks standing upright in the ground.

"Now, this is a treat," Marcia said. "I always thought I needed to get on a plane to another country to see a live cricket match."

"No. There are cricket leagues here. In this area, most of the players are from the Caribbean. As a matter of fact, I read somewhere that a professional league is forming to allow players to get paid to play."

"Cool."

"Okay, Wendy," Devon teased Marcia, intentionally calling her by their daughter's name because their daughter often said, 'cool.'

Marcia smiled. "Speaking of our daughter, the baseball game she went to should have started by now. What team are you rooting for?"

"The Mets."

"It takes a true fan to support a losing team."

"And you're on the Yankees bandwagon?"

"Riding it all the way to the World Series," she said with a hoot of excitement.

They laughed.

"Perhaps we could go to a game together," Devon suggested.

"I'd like that," she agreed.

They chatted cheerfully, often teasing each other as they watched the game. When the cricket match was over, Marcia announced that she was hungry.

"The only thing I ate today was tea and toast at six in the morning."

"Me too," Devon said, standing, and reaching out to help her get up.

"Tea and toast? Our mothers would be pleased," Marcia remarked.

They congratulated the players as they left the field.

As they walked back to the car, Marcia commented, "It's so peaceful here. I don't want to leave."

"Okay."

"But, on the other hand, I'm famished. Could we pick up something to eat and come back here?"

"I have a better option."

When they arrived at the car, he opened the trunk and retrieved a picnic basket. "Lunch," he announced.

"Devon! You thought of everything."

He grinned. "I can't take credit for this though. Wendy put this together this morning."

"Is that where she was while I was feeling like no one cared about me?"

"With a family like yours, you should never feel that way."

"I know. I praise God for them."

They chose a spot on the slope overlooking the pond and unpacked turkey sandwiches, fruit, lemonade, and honey bun. Then, they said grace.

"This is delicious," Marcia said, after taking a bite of her sandwich.

Devon chuckled. "You're just very hungry. That's all."

"Probably." She kept eating until she noticed him smiling at her. "What?" she asked.

"Just curious."

"About?"

"You. Are you always so...?" He paused, searching for the right word. "...so holy?"

Marcia giggled. "Why do you ask?"

"I was just wondering. In many ways, you're like the Marcia I used to know, except that now you're so holy." When she didn't respond immediately, he continued. "I mean, years ago, we would not have said grace out loud in a public place. And I was thinking about the play we're going to see tonight. A Bible-story. Don't get offended. I think it's a good thing, but if I had chosen the entertainment for us tonight, I would have taken you to a Luther Vandross concert to set the mood for the evening with love songs."

"First of all, I didn't choose the play for us. I chose it for me and Wendy. Does my being holy…" She made quotation marks in the air with her fingers, "make you uncomfortable?"

"Not at all. In fact, I need to thank you and Wendy and your entire family for my newfound relationship with the Lord."

She beamed. "Hallelujah, Devon! Praise God."

"Weird, huh?" He chuckled. "You see, that brings me back to my question. Are you always so holy? Running around shouting praise the Lord like your mother used to do. I remember that used to embarrass you."

"Yeah. That was before I understood. I don't know if I can explain it to you."

"Okay. Tell me why you chose to celebrate yours and Wendy's birthdays by going to watch a Bible story on stage."

Their eyes locked and held. Marcia searched his, trying to ascertain his motivation.

"The story of Ruth shows how faith helps people survive the unbearable. It's a story I identify with from personal experience. It's about women and loyalty between a mother figure and a daughter figure. I wanted to share its message with our daughter."

"That's why you were so angry with me for changing Wendy's plans. I'm sorry."

"Don't worry about it. I'm glad I'm here with you now."

"Really?" he asked, searching her eyes.

"Yes. Really." Marcia stood up suddenly. "As much as I'd like to just lie down here and relax, I need to walk off the calories from this meal."

Devon began to pack up. "We could follow the trail around the rest of the park, but after that, we need to head south if we plan to get to the theatre on time."

By the time Devon dropped Marcia off at home, he felt confident that they had reached a new phase in their relationship. Over the next few weeks, as they planned for Wendy's graduation, they saw each other often, but there were no more romantic advances, just an easygoing friendship that was reminiscent of their childhood bond.

CHAPTER THIRTEEN

As Wendy got to know her father, she found out that they had a mutual love for amusement parks. Wendy and Paul went at least once each summer. This time, they planned a trip for Devon's birthday and talked Marcia into coming with them.

The parking lot outside the amusement park was crowded. Devon found a spot far from the entrance gate. As the two couples climbed out of his car, he and Wendy argued over which roller coaster ride was the best. Marcia listened thinking about how a trip to the amusement park brought out the child inside of everyone one. Wendy and Devon walked up ahead continuing their disagreement with each other. Marcia and Paul followed close behind.

"What do you think?" Marcia asked Paul.

"Hmm."

"Are you willing to be the tie breaker and settle this argument over the best roller coaster?"

Paul shrugged. He was wrapped up in his own thoughts about Wendy and her father. They reached the entrance and, as they'd planned, Devon paid the fee for everyone to get in. Paul never paid full price to enter an amusement park. He either got in on a group rate, like when he traveled there with the church on a bus, or he used discount coupons. He calculated the cost of tickets for the four of them and realized it was more than he earned working each week at his part-time job.

They had decided in the car that the evening was still warm enough for them to go on the water rides, so they headed to that section of the park. They passed through an arch with letters etched out of iron that announced that they'd arrived in the water park. The lines to get on the rides were long. While they waited, Wendy and Devon did most of the talking.

"Did they have amusement parks back in the olden days when you and Mommy were growing up in Jamaica?" she asked.

Devon was about to answer when Marcia interjected, "Yes, dear-y." She bent her back, slumped her shoulders, and made her voice tremble to imitate a very old lady. "We used to slide down dinosaur backs."

Devon chuckled.

Paul burst out laughing for the first time since they'd picked him up at work.

"Very funny, Mom," Wendy said, pretending to feel hurt. She nudged Paul in the side, "And you, Mister. I see I have to embarrass myself to get you to turn that frown you've been wearing upside down."

"I haven't been frowning."

"Yes, you have. But I'm glad the real Paul is back now."

She wrapped her arm around his waist. Paul draped his arm over her shoulders.

"Rough day at work?" she asked, looking into his eyes.

Devon observed the couple, then, he shifted his gaze to Marcia. "It seems they've forgotten about us."

"Yes. Love will do that to you."

"Yes," he said staring into her eyes.

The people ahead of them moved forward and they followed as another set of passengers boarded the ride. Marcia took a cloth covered elastic clip from around her wrist and used it to secure her hair in ballerina bun.

"Your hair is going to get wet, Mom," Wendy said.

"I'm not getting wet," Marcia replied.

"We're all going to get wet," Paul commented.

"No, no. It's all about where you sit," Marcia explained. "I may get a little sprinkled, nothing more."

"You're going to get soaked," Devon challenged.

They finally got to the platform where they would board the ride. Marcia hurried ahead, so she could be first to choose her seat on the small four-passenger wooden boat. Devon climbed in beside her. Wendy and Paul sat in the other row.

"Here we go!" Wendy shouted.

"Let's do this!" Paul joined her in creating excitement.

Mobile tracks lifted the boat up a steep ramp. It perched at the top of the ramp for a brief moment before sliding rapidly down the other side and creating a huge splash as it landed in the water. Marcia and everyone else on board were soaked. They all laughed at her as they climbed out of the boat. Devon reached out a hand to help her, but she ignored it.

"As if I didn't just take a shower," she said, stepping past him, wearing a broad smile.

"Yeah. As if…" Wendy replied, sputtering.

They moved quickly to join another long line, which led to the area for whitewater rafting. The raft seated eight people, but strangely, there were two groups of eight people who wanted to ride together behind them, so the park worker let them ride by themselves.

The two couples sat on opposite sides facing each other, and tried to control the direction of the raft. They could hear the waterfall rushing and see the water cascading down ahead. Only one side of the raft would get drenched. As they spun the raft, each tried to make sure that the other would get wet.

"Are you ready for another shower, Miss T?" Paul asked.

"I think you and your girlfriend need a bath," Devon replied, defending Marcia.

"As if…" Wendy joked, intending to conjure up memory of how wet Marcia got on the previous ride, after insisting that she would remain dry.

They all laughed.

"Oh, you're laughing at me," Marcia demanded, pretending to be upset with Devon. "I thought you were on my side. Why don't you sit over there with them and get ready to enter the Falls, while I watch you guys from over here on the observation deck?"

"Okay."

Devon surprised her by switching seats, leaving Marcia on the other side of the raft by herself. The combined strength of her three opponents twisted the raft, positioning her to get drenched again.

"You wouldn't dare," she said, staring directly at Devon.

She screamed playfully as the water washed over her. Devon jumped back to sit beside her, so that he could get soaked as well.

Wendy leaned close to Paul's ear and said, "Now, that's an act of love, if I ever saw one."

"What did you say?" Marcia asked, wiping water from her eyes.

"Nothing," Wendy replied, smiling innocently.

"I think I heard that," Devon insisted.

She and her father exchanged looks that Marcia and Paul didn't know how to interpret.

They moved on to the roller coasters, after visiting all the water rides. The lines there were even longer.

Devon checked the time on his watch. "With these lines, there won't be enough time to get on all the rides. We're going to have to choose." He addressed all three of them.

"It doesn't matter," Paul replied for himself and Wendy.

"We're celebrating your birthday. You choose," Marcia suggested.

Devon led the way to a new roller coaster that held the reputation of being the scariest ride in the park. It also had the longest line, but none of them complained. They chatted and joked with each other during the hour it took to get to the platform.

"Get ready for the ride of your life," he advised, as they climbed in.

He and Marcia sat in front of Paul and Wendy. They pulled a thick black harness over their shoulders and chest, which locked and held them in place on their seat. They hooted and waved their hands in the air as the ride moved off. Other passengers called out silly comments as the car began its slow climb. As the car moved higher and higher, people joke and laughed. It seemed like they'd reached the top of a mountain when it came to a sudden halt. For what seemed like a long time, it didn't move. The passengers were silent, waiting expectantly for the drop.

The car plunged. Passengers screamed as they plummeted downward. Just as it seemed like they would crash into the ground, the car leveled off. Before anyone could relax, the car entered a loop. It climbed, turned upside down, and dropped. Then, it did it again. And again. Then, it repeated the entire cycle in reverse. By time the car halted for the passengers to exit, everyone was giddy.

"What a rush!" Paul said, as he climbed out and turned to help Wendy.

"Yes!" Devon agreed.

"Let's do it again," Wendy requested eagerly.

"Won't you look at the time," Marcia pointed out. She felt no desire for a replay. "If we join this line again, we won't be able to do anything else."

Instead, they headed for the arcade, where they could play games.

"Anybody hungry?" Devon asked, as they passed a food stand with funnel cake and cotton candy.

Paul was starving, but he didn't want Devon to spend any more money on him.

"I could share a funnel cake," Marcia said, thinking that if she ate that deep fried pastry covered in powdered sugar she would be consuming much more than her usual calories.

"I'll share it with you," Wendy agreed.

Paul wanted to treat himself and his girlfriend, but as they added drinks and cotton candy to their order, he realized it would be awkward to pay theirs separately. He needed to pay all or nothing, and he would be dipping into his budget for the week. While Paul was thinking it through, Devon paid the bill. Paul found himself wondering what it would be like to have enough money to spend without making choices. He'd never desired to be rich, but at that moment, he longed to be financially stable enough to treat his girlfriend and her family to a snack, without worrying that he was squandering money he needed for something more essential.

They sat at a picnic bench and took turns going to the restroom. Marcia and Wendy went first.

"Look at my hair." Wendy squealed when she saw her reflection in the mirror. She had been enjoying herself so much that she hadn't thought about how she looked.

Marcia stood beside her at the counter washing her hands. Her hair was just as frizzy, but she didn't have a boyfriend outside to impress. She and Wendy were dressed similarly in cut-off denim shorts and spandex tops. Wendy wore a bare swimsuit; Marcia covered hers with a t-shirt and had a bag strapped around her waist. She opened the zipper and retrieved a headband from inside.

"Thanks, mommy. You think of everything."

"Naturally," Marcia replied. She felt relaxed. She'd thoroughly enjoyed every moment of this day.

Once Wendy was satisfied with the way she looked, they returned to join Devon and Paul outside. After they ate, they wandered around deciding which games to play. Devon purchased a roll of tickets, so that they could all play. They positioned themselves in front of a water gun, and when the bell rang, they squirted water at a target that moved objects forward in a race. Devon won and the park worker handed him a tiny stuffed toy.

"Let's play again," he requested.

Other patrons joined them at the counter.

The bell rang. They squirted. Paul won. The park worker allowed them to trade up by returning the smaller toy for a larger one. They played the same game three more times, winning a larger prize each time. Devon won the last round. It was just as well, Paul thought, because it was Devon's money they were spending anyway.

Devon offered the oversized stuffed toy to Marcia. "This one is for you."

She smiled sweetly back at him, but didn't take it. "Wendy loves that character."

At first, Devon felt personally rejected. He'd won it for Marcia, like he would for a girlfriend on a date. He wondered if this was Marcia's way of reminding him that they weren't a couple in the way Paul and Wendy were. With his smile fixed in place, he said, "Oh," and turned to give the stuffed toy to Wendy.

"Thanks, Dad." She hugged him.

Paul watched, wishing he'd won the toy for Wendy. She'd been his girlfriend long before she knew her father. Then, his conscience reminded him that he should just be happy for her. She'd confided in him a long time ago about her desire to meet her father. He wished he didn't always feel like he had to compete.

They moved on to other games. Paul won a prize for Wendy, but as he gave it to her, he felt conscious that Devon's money had paid for him to compete in the game. He prayed that he would shake the feeling.

An announcement aired telling them that the park would be closing soon.

"Are you ready?" Devon asked the group.

"Wait. I almost forgot," Wendy said. She grabbed Paul's hand and pulled him behind her. "Come on, we have to record a song."

They piled into a tiny recording studio near the exit.

"What are we going to sing?" Devon asked.

"Not me," Marcia said, bowing out. "I think the singing voice skipped a generation on my side of the family. I'll wait for you guys outside."

"I'll wait with you," Devon said.

Once they left the room, Paul and Wendy chose the only gospel song for which prerecorded music was provided.

Marcia leaned against a food stand that was closed for the night and yawned. "Where did that come from?" she asked out loud.

"You're tired."

"I don't feel tired. It's been a fun day."

"I'm glad you enjoyed it."

"If anybody should be tired it would be you. Thanks for pitching in and taking care of Uncle Trevor's car today."

"Not a problem. I admire him and Steve. Working on the car gave me a chance to get to know them better. I love spending time with you and your family."

Her eyes ran over the length of his body as he stepped closer to her. He was dressed simply in khaki shorts and a navy blue t-shirt, but she still found him appealing. She always felt attracted to him, no matter what he wore. She hoped he didn't know that.

Devon returned the scrutiny. He hoped she knew that he liked what he saw. "Spending time with you has made this the best birthday ever," he said, reaching for her hand.

How could she not take that personally, she wondered. Sure, the word you could be interpreted in a plural sense to mean her, Wendy, and Paul. Yet, as Devon gazed into her eyes, she could not help but think he meant it to be singular, exclusively for her.

Devon longed to kiss her. The seconds passed as he wished they were dating. He wished they didn't have a past in which her most lasting memory of him was that he had broken her heart.

They heard singing. Melodious voices rang out in harmony causing other people in the area to stop and listen. Devon and Marcia turned their attention to their daughter and her boyfriend.

"Wow! They sound really good," Marcia said.

"Professional. Have they ever talked about dreams of a singing career?"

"No. You know Paul and Wendy. They're conscious that they have a gift and they use it to sing for the Lord."

Marcia held Devon's full attention as he gazed into her eyes. His eyes wandered to her hair, noting how the light danced off its natural highlights. They briefly rested on her nose before focusing on her lips. He knew exactly what she would do if he kissed her. She'd get upset at him, and that would bring an unpleasant ending to their day. Instead, he pulled Marcia to stand in front of him and wrapped his arms around her. She was facing the recording studio with her back to him. She stiffened as their bodies touched.

"Relax," he whispered. "It's okay to lean on me every now and again."

Marcia allowed herself to rest for a moment in Devon's arms. It was a safe indulgence outside in public, where bright lights held back the darkness of the night. The tension eased. She closed her eyes and listened to Paul and Wendy singing. She thought of herself and Devon at their age. She remembered how she had daydreamed back then that she and Devon would be together in New York during the summer after their high school graduation. Perhaps they too could have made music together in an amusement park.

When the door to the recording studio finally opened and Wendy and Paul emerged, everyone applauded, including park workers and other patrons passing by. Devon beat them to the cashier and paid for two CDs.

"I'll have mine autographed and dated now," he said, handing both copies to Paul. "That way I'll have proof that I knew you before you became rich and famous."

"If the Lord leads us to a singing career, our goal would be to win souls for His kingdom, not to make big money," Paul informed him as they walked back to the car.

Devon laughed.

They were all smiling good naturedly, but nobody else got the joke.

"What, Dad?" Wendy asked, suspecting that he was laughing because of Paul.

"Yes, Devon. Tell us what's so funny," Marcia demanded, still smiling as she intentionally bumped into him, setting him off course in his stride.

"Nothing," Devon replied.

"Yeah, right." Paul now looked serious.

Devon didn't want to offend him, so he said, "I just find it interesting the way you and Wendy talk."

Paul mimicked him, repeating exactly what he had said. Everyone laughed, including Devon.

In between giggles, Wendy asked, "What did Paul say that was so interesting, Dad?"

"If the Lord leads us to a singing career..." Devon tried to sound like Paul, triggering more laughter among the group. "I've never met another teenager who talked like that."

"I talk like that," Wendy said. "Would you say that means Paul and I are made for each other?"

Devon chuckled. He'd walked right into that one. "If the Lord leads you to that conclusion, then yes."

They were now in the parking lot, near their car. Many of the spaces that were full when they arrived now sat empty. The area was well lit, and occasionally, other patrons laughed raucously as they returned to their car.

Marcia attempted to give Devon a stern looked, but when he made a silly face at her, she couldn't contain her laughter.

"Okay, seriously," Devon said, putting on a straight face. They had reached his car and he turned to face Paul. "How do you know where the Lord is leading you?"

"I'm glad you asked," Paul replied, genuinely glad for the opportunity to talk about his relationship with the Lord. "I pray all the time and ask God to direct my path. I read my Bible, so I know what God considers to be acceptable behavior, and what is not."

"Like what?" Devon asked.

"Intimacy outside of marriage, adultery, murder… If I feel the desire to do any of those things, I know it's definitely not the Lord leading me."

"Okay, but those are obvious things," Devon countered. "Even people who don't believe in God consider murder to be wrong. Where does God say you can't have a singing career?"

"He doesn't. We just haven't felt called to do that."

"But you feel like you're called to marry my daughter before either one of you turn twenty. I'm not sure I agree with your reasoning."

All traces of humor evaporated. Marcia and Wendy stopped their own whispering and teasing, and they waited expectantly for Paul's response. Wendy moved closer to him.

"I set out to please the Lord in everything I do, Mr. Douglas. That's how I've lived for as long as I can remember. Wendy too. We connect with each other on a level that we don't connect with other people. And when we put our minds and energy together to do something for the Lord, great things happen. When I pray, I feel that peace that comes from Jesus. And when my world is messed up, being with Wendy makes me calm. I could search for another fifty years and I don't expect to meet anyone who is more right for me than Wendy. And I know she feels the same way about me." He turned to face her as she reached for his hand and tiptoed to kiss his cheek.

Devon looked at Marcia.

"You asked," Marcia said, shrugging her shoulders. "Not even breeze can blow between those two."

"I see." Devon unlocked the car doors. He suddenly felt weary. "Do you want to drive?" he asked Paul.

Paul hesitated for a moment because the question took him by surprise. "Sure."

Devon gave Paul the keys. Then, he held the back door open for Marcia and sat beside her in the car.

Wendy went around to the front passenger seat. As soon as Paul started the car, she turned on the radio. Devon had the radio tuned to a jazz station. Wendy digitally scrolled to find something else to listen to.

"Wait. Stop there," Marcia requested, as she heard a song that was playing. "Remember this?" she asked Devon.

He nodded. The song had been a hit when they were in high school. Devon sang along, his mind drifting to old memories of himself and Marcia as teenagers. Almost immediately, he mentally fast-forwarded to the present. He treasured old memories, but today, he was especially grateful for the new.

CHAPTER FOURTEEN

In spite of his renewed friendship with Marcia, Devon still spent far more time with Wendy than with her mother. Marcia spoke to him frequently on the phone and would share a hug or light kiss on the cheek when she saw him, but for the most part, their relationship was still about Wendy. And Devon was the first person Wendy chose to confide in after she heard a rumor that rocked her world.

Like any other rumor, this one started with a morsel of truth that got distorted as it was whispered from one ear to another. By the time Wendy heard it, the story in a nutshell was that Desiree was pregnant and Paul was the baby's father.

"What!" Wendy exclaimed, her facial expression conveying a look of shock, amusement, and disbelief. A girl from their church told her the rumor that was being spread among members of their youth group.

Jasmine pulled her aside while they were on a break at work and spoke to her in confidence. They worked together as cashiers at a supermarket and they also attended the same high school.

"Wendy, I'm sorry to be the one to tell you, but we've grown up together in church and I can't stand to see you get burned like this," Jasmine said.

Wendy sputtered on a laugh, as she thought of how ridiculous such an accusation was against Paul. She didn't believe it for a minute.

"Jasmine. Paul is always with me. Even if he was interested in Desiree, which he isn't, they wouldn't have had a chance to get together."

"Oh, yeah. That's what you think. Have you forgotten about the time when you went away to Jamaica? Girl, if you had seen Paul and Desiree together, like we did, you would believe me when I tell you something was going on. I hear that they always liked each other, even though Paul was in love with you. No doubt, Paul is a nice guy and he probably tried to be loyal to you, but you weren't here and he was mad at you."

Wendy grew serious now. She still didn't believe what she was hearing. She trusted Paul. Yet, she wondered what truth would lie at the root of this rumor.

"How do you know Desiree's pregnant?" she asked, paying as much attention to Jasmine's facial expression as to the words of her reply.

"Oh please, girl. Everybody knows. You're about the only person who hasn't heard. That's why I was getting tired of hearing people talk behind your back." As Jasmine spoke, she did not look Wendy in the eye.

Wendy stared directly at Jasmine, but because the shorter girl gyrated her head and waved her hands as she spoke, it was hard to determine whether she was intentionally not making eye contact. Like Jasmine said, they had grown up together in church. Many of the teens in the youth group had. Paul was the only person Wendy was close to, but she tried to maintain a friendly relationship with everyone else. As peer leaders, it was necessary for her and Paul to interact with everyone.

"Okay," she said coolly. "Thanks for telling me."

"Girl, you know I got your back. What are you going to do?"

Wendy hesitated, unsure of how to answer. She had no intention of telling Jasmine what she planned to do. She suspected that Jasmine was more loyal to the rumor mill than she was to any individual and might even spread the word that they'd had this conversation.

"Let me think about it."

Jasmine pulled her long braids together in a ponytail as she waited for Wendy to say more.

Wendy glanced at her watch. "I need to run to the ladies' room before I get back on the register. Talk to you later."

As she hastily walked away, she heard Jasmine reply, "Okay."

Devon picked Wendy up after work. She got into the car, said, "Hi, Dad," and then sat silently beside him. They were seated in the car for about two minutes when Devon stopped at a traffic light and began questioning her.

"Why are you so quiet this evening? Is everything okay?"

Wendy shook her head.

"Care to talk about it?" The light changed to green and Devon drove off just as Wendy shook her head again.

It was after nightfall, but there were still many motorists driving along the road. A bus pulled over at a stop ahead of them and passengers got on and off. They passed a Laundromat that was open twenty-four hours; inside, several people loaded and unloaded the washers and dryers.

"Dad." Wendy sat up erectly. "Will you do me a big favor?"

"I might. What is it?"

"Do you mind taking me over to Paul's house? I have to talk to him."

Devon glanced at the cell phone Wendy was holding in her hands wondering why she wouldn't use it to call Paul.

"In person, Dad, please."

"Did you two have a fight?"

"No way."

"Don't you have assignments you need to complete for school tomorrow?"

"All done. Please, Dad. Just for a few minutes. Please, please, please."

Devon drove her to Paul's house and they went inside together. Paul met them at the front door, and when his mother saw that Wendy and her father were present, she joined them in the living room.

"Brother Devon," she greeted him, according to their church custom to refer to each other as brother and sister. "This is unexpected. Paul didn't tell me that you and Wendy were coming over. May I get you something to drink?"

"No thanks. We'll only be here for a few minutes. I was driving Wendy home from work when she insisted that she needed to see Paul. I'm giving her exactly fifteen minutes," he stated on a yawn. He looked at Wendy and tapped the face of his watch.

Wendy turned to Paul.

"What's up?" he asked, reaching for her hand.

"Can we be alone for a few minutes?"

She directed her question to Paul, but he checked with both his mother and Devon before he answered. They both shrugged. Paul held Wendy's hands and led her into the kitchen.

"Is Desiree pregnant?" Wendy asked as soon as he turned to face her.

He nodded. "You heard too, huh? Mom was talking about it this evening. She said the ladies in her women's group were arguing over what the church should do about it."

Wendy wrinkled her brow. "So everyone does know. Why didn't you tell me?"

"I just found out this evening. I wanted to talk to you as soon as I heard, but I was waiting until tonight when you got home. We need to talk to Pastor about how to handle it when we meet with the youth group tomorrow night."

Wendy studied Paul's expression. He seemed relaxed and his eyes stayed steadily focused on hers.

"Jasmine said rumor has it that you're the father."

"What!"

"That's what I said."

"That's crazy. Who said that and why me?"

"I was hoping you could tell me. She said you and Desiree got together while I was in Jamaica, that you'd always liked each other and you gave in to your feelings because you were mad at me for going to Jamaica and not spending Easter with you."

"Whoa." Paul brushed his hand across his head.

"Paul, you got some 'splaining to do." Wendy smiled as she spoke to Paul with a Latino accent, mimicking a husband talking to his mischievous wife on an old television comedy called I Love Lucy.

Paul shook his head and smiled back, relieved that Wendy found humor in the situation, which probably meant that she trusted him. "I don't know if I can explain." He paused, but his eyes never left Wendy's. He sighed. "Why me? Trust me, Wendy. I haven't been with anyone. I'm still holding out for our wedding night."

"Why would they name you?"

Again, Paul shook his head. "Desiree and I spent a lot of time together during the week you were gone. That is true. She was taking over for you in the lead role of the Easter presentation. We had a short time to make sure that she was ready."

"Did you rehearse with her alone?"

"Yes. Actually, she did meet me here once, but Mom was here. Nothing happened."

"Why did you need to invite her here?"

"It seemed innocent enough at the time. As I said, Mom was here, and we spent the entire time in the living room. I played the piano and she sang. Maybe we went into the kitchen to get a drink, but that was it."

"Why do you think she would name you?"

Paul shook his head. "I have no clue. I can't believe that she would."

"Did your mother say whether the women's group was aware that she named you as the father?"

"No, but let's go talk to her."

They returned to the living room, but only Devon was seated there.

"Mom. Can you come here for a minute?" Paul called out.

His mother returned from the direction of her bedroom.

"Mom, you won't believe this. Wendy says that Jasmine, from church, told her there is a rumor going around that I got Desiree pregnant."

"What!" Devon's voice boomed, drowning out Paul's mother. "Who is Desiree?"

"The girl who replaced me in the Easter production while you and I were in Jamaica, Dad."

"Did you hear anything about this while you were at church, Mom?" Paul asked.

"No," Madge shook her head incredulously. "The women argued about what they should do about Desiree to avoid sending the message that they condone her behavior. But no one mentioned the guy who was involved. I think they all assumed that whoever got her pregnant was not a member of our church. How did your name get linked to all this?"

"I'm not sure, Mom." Paul wrapped an arm around Wendy's waist and turned to face her father. "Nothing could be farther from the truth."

Devon stared first at Paul, then at Wendy. He couldn't wait to talk to her alone. Perhaps, Paul wasn't as innocent as he presented himself to be. Maybe, Saint Paul wasn't so saintly after all.

"Did Jasmine say that Desiree told her this?" Paul's mother was sitting in an armchair now trying to make sense of what she had heard. Like Wendy, she thought such an accusation against Paul was ridiculous.

"No, she didn't, Mrs. Chambers." Wendy paused for a moment. "I didn't think of asking her that, but I did ask how she knew Desiree was pregnant and she never told me."

"Well, there you have it." Madge was ready to defend her son. "Gossip. That's all it is. We need to put a stop to this before it damages Paul's reputation."

"Has anyone spoken to Desiree?" Wendy asked.

Paul and his mother shook their heads.

"She wasn't at the youth group meeting last week," Paul reminded her.

"We could call her," Wendy suggested, "but I don't have her number."

"We have it. It's on the list with the other members of the youth group." Paul left the room and returned quickly with the list.

Without giving anyone time to hesitate, Wendy dialed Desiree's number. "Voicemail," she said and hung up.

"It's getting late," Devon pointed out. "I think you should discuss this with your mother before you do anything else, Wendy."

Wendy nodded. She started walking toward her father, but Paul reached for her hand. She turned to face him and, for a few seconds, they just stared at each other.

"I love you," Paul said. His words weren't audible, but Wendy could read his lips.

"I love you too." She spoke loudly enough for everyone to hear.

Paul kissed her lightly on the lips.

"We'll talk later," she told Paul. "Good night, Mrs. Chambers."

"Don't worry, dear," she replied. "We'll get to the bottom of this, and we both know Paul had nothing to do with it. Ridiculous!" She hugged Wendy and said goodnight to Devon.

In spite of Devon's eagerness to find out what his daughter was thinking, they drove home together in silence.

"Are you going to call your mother?" he asked, as Wendy unlocked the door and let them into the apartment.

"No. I don't think I'll bother her at work with this. She should be getting ready to leave soon anyway."

Devon watched as Wendy turned on the lights in the apartment and checked the rooms to make sure everything was in place. He felt protective toward her. She was his daughter, and he knew from personal experience that males weren't always as innocent as they seemed. In fact, he felt that men were more likely to cheat than to be loyal to the women they were involved with in a relationship. He expected a teenage boyfriend to be just as likely to stray as some husbands.

"Are you worried that Paul might have cheated on you?" he asked when she returned to sit beside him at the dining table.

"No, Dad. I trust Paul. I don't believe what Jasmine said for one minute."

"Why would someone have started a rumor like that?"

"I don't know, and that's what I plan to find out. In the mean time, I'm not going to worry about it."

Devon was taken aback by his daughter's attitude. The calmness she displayed pleasantly surprised him, although he didn't agree that she should blindly trust Paul.

Wendy was on the computer her father had bought for her, when her mother returned home from work. The computer was an asset, but it also created another area of accountability in their life. Marcia couldn't monitor all the sites Wendy visited during the hours after school when she was in the apartment alone. Before Devon entered their lives, Wendy would use the computer upstairs for school assignments and college applications when her aunt was home. Yet, Marcia trusted her. Wendy had even shown her a MySpace page that she and Paul created, and like everything else Wendy and Paul did, the MySpace page was a platform for talking about Jesus Christ, abstinence, and the other issues they were passionate about.

"You're still up," her mother said, greeting her with a kiss on the cheek.

"Hi, Mommy," Wendy shut down the computer after waiting long enough for her mother to see what she was doing.

"Did you do all your homework?"

"Of course."

"How is your graduation speech going?"

"Good. Daddy's been helping me."

"Okay."

"Mommy, I have something to tell you, but I can wait until you get ready for bed, if you want."

"That's okay," said Marcia, plopping herself down on the sofa. "What's up?"

The computer desk and chair were right beside the sofa, so Wendy turned to face her. "Desiree is pregnant and rumor has it that Paul is the father."

"What!" Marcia exclaimed incredulously. "Okay. What kind of weird joke is that?"

"It's not a joke, Mom. Call anybody from church. It seems like we're among the last people to find out."

"Wait a minute." Marcia paused, still waiting for Wendy to admit that she was kidding. "What? Explain to me what's going on."

Wendy filled her in.

"So I don't have to ask if you believe Paul," her mother commented after listening to her daughter's account of everything she'd heard that day.

"No doubt, Mom. Paul is not like that. I don't care what anybody says. I know my man," Wendy declared, smiling.

"Really now?" Her mother smiled back. Wendy's reaction made the weight of the news seem less burdensome, but Marcia still had some concerns. "Okay, I agree with you that Paul seems to walk around with a halo over his head, but he is human."

"Paul would never do that, Mom."

"Never say never, little missy. When your father and I were your age, just about everyone who knew us would have said we never would have made a baby, but you're here."

Wendy made a grimace. "Mom, we're not like you guys."

"Maybe. You're definitely more saved and sanctified than we were at your age, but you're still human. Paul is a good-looking guy and Desiree is an attractive, bright girl. Who's to say that in a moment of weakness, they couldn't have made love?"

"Mommy, first of all, if Paul accidentally fell into bed with someone else, you couldn't call it making love. He loves me. And I just know it didn't happen."

"Okay. I won't argue with you." Marcia thought for a moment. "I'll give Paul the benefit of the doubt, but I want you to understand that it's naïve to think that this could never happen."

Wendy opened her mouth to respond.

"Wait a minute now. Listen. Your father and I were like brother and sister when we were growing up."

Wendy thought—here we go again—but she tried to focus on listening to what her mother was saying.

"We knew each other all our lives just like you and Paul. Devon used to look out for me. He was my defender and protector. It wasn't until our last year of high school that he became my boyfriend. We made love once in his parents' house and that's when you were conceived. All the while, neither his parents, nor my mother who also lived there—none of them—knew what was going on. And as much as he loved me, we still broke up when I was pregnant."

"You told him it wasn't his baby, Mom."

Marcia eyes filled with tears. She nodded. "Yes. I shouldn't have lied." She blinked back the tears. "My point though is that even when you know someone, and truly love them, life happens. You may still end up hurting them, and you could still end up in relationships with other people."

"Mommy, you said you and Daddy were not walking with the Lord back then. Now that you are, God has restored your friendship. As long as Paul and I keep trying to please God, it's automatic that we will be faithful to each other."

Marcia nodded. She understood Wendy, and she prayed that she was right.

Devon called Marcia the next day.

"How is our daughter this morning?" he asked.

"Calm. She is focused on school, as she should be, but she is determined to figure out what's happening at church. I'm surprised you all didn't call me while I was at work last night."

"I wanted to, but I took Wendy's advice and waited."

"I'm surprised that she could wait. She has total confidence in Paul."

"Yes. Do you?"

"Hmm. Well. Not in the way that Wendy does. He has always been sincere, and I'm going to stand by him until I have a reason not to, but frankly, I'm more worried about Desiree."

"Why?"

"Well, from what Wendy told me, the church is quick to guard their own reputation. God forbid that they should have a pregnant teenager in their midst. Right? And Wendy and Madge are quick to defend Paul. I spoke to Madge briefly this morning and she is outraged that anyone would dare to link her son to such a scandal. I mean, Paul is as close to a saint as any teenage boy could come, but he is human. It is not impossible that he could have made love to a girl and gotten her pregnant. It happens every day to unlikely people." She paused. "It happened to us."

Devon took a deep breath and listened. As obvious as it now seemed, he had not thought of the parallel between Marcia's experience and Desiree's until Marcia mentioned it,.

Marcia continued. "I've known these kids all their lives. If anyone is in trouble, it's Desiree, and no one seems to be worried about her. It must be pretty scary to be in her shoes right now."

Devon felt he should say something, as Marcia paused again, but he wasn't sure what to say. This was a sensitive issue for Marcia, and he knew that anything he said could be taken the wrong way. "Do you think it's possible that Paul and Desiree got together while Wendy and I were in

Jamaica?" he asked.

"Anything is possible, but I doubt it. The bottom line is Desiree's pregnant, and I'm more concerned about what's going to happen to her than I am about whose baby she is carrying. Desiree has nothing but her brains going for her. She is from a poor family. I mean welfare, food stamps, and government housing poor. Her parents aren't even around. Her grandmother is raising her. She is such a bright girl. I can't believe she let this happen."

Marcia laughed as soon as her last words left her mouth, but her laughter carried more remorse than humor. "I can't believe I just said that. Our mothers probably said something like that about me." She changed the tone of her voice to imitate their mothers. "Marcia? Pregnant? Oh, she is such a bright girl. I can't believe she let this happen." There were tears in Marcia's eyes now, but she hoped Devon couldn't tell that she was crying.

"Are you okay?" he asked, knowing he should say more but he felt uncertain of what to say and was afraid to say the wrong thing.

"I'm fine. I'm all grown up now and so is Wendy. But I will not sit by and watch the church ostracize Desiree. It's just not fair. She could have had an abortion and no one would have ever known she was pregnant. It takes a lot of courage for a teenager to keep a baby."

Devon sucked in a deep breath when Marcia mentioned an abortion. Again, he knew that she was seeing herself in Desiree. And again, he wasn't sure what to say. He was the teenage boy who had gotten Marcia pregnant and never had to face any consequences. Somewhere nearby was a boy about to walk away from his pregnant lover and unborn baby, just as he had. Even he had a hard time believing that guy could be Paul.

"I need to see you," he said, hoping he didn't sound as insecure as he felt. He couldn't let this situation involving Desiree come between him and Marcia, and he knew it could. He could hear in Marcia's voice that just discussing it was bringing back a lot of pain, pain that he had caused. They had progressed too much in their relationship for her to slip away from him again. They were friends now, and he prayed that someday soon, they would be much more.

"My schedule is flexible until it's time to go to work," she said. "I was planning to go to the college and use the library first. Do you want to ride the train downtown with me?"

"I can't. I have to teach in a little while. Please let me pick you up after work tonight." He braced himself for her usual excuses.

"Okay."

"Okay?"

"Yes. I feel like I need to see you too."

He wanted to say the words, 'I love you,' but he was saving them for the right time. "I'll see you later then."

"I get off at eleven."

"I'll be in the car outside the building."

"See you later."

"Bye."

CHAPTER FIFTEEN

The idea came as an afterthought, but Marcia acted on it without giving herself time to think it through. She dialed the number she had for Desiree's grandmother. The phone rang three times, and Marcia was thinking of hanging up when someone answered.

"Hello."

"Good morning. This is Sister Marcia. Sister Lorraine?" She addressed her as a sister in the Lord according to their church custom.

"Yes."

"I'm sorry to call at such an unusual time. How are you?"

"I'm fine, Sis. Is there something I can do for you?"

Marcia said a little prayer for God to give her the right words to say. "I was calling because I... I was hoping I could meet with you and Desiree. I was a teenage mother. I mean I got pregnant while I was in my last year of high school too, and I know it's very hard. I was hoping that maybe I could talk to you and Desiree."

"It's too late now. What's done is done. After all the talking and teaching. Everyone has to live their own life. But I tell her, I ain't raising no babies. I'm too old for this. She ain't gonna bring no babies into my house. I done worked too hard to show Desiree a better way. I don't expect her to throw her life away like this. I told her, she and that boy she been running around with better go find a place to live. Laid up in the room like she ain't got no ambition. Desiree!" She shouted her granddaughter's name. "I tell that girl to get up and go to school to get what little education she can get before she has to take care of this baby. No sense lying around feeling shame. She should have thought about that before she put herself in grown folks' business. You can't tell these young people that lovemaking is grown folks' business. They're too fast. Some of them can't even read, but they know how to lay up in their parent's home making babies when they're supposed to be in school trying to get an education. But I tell her, I ain't raising no babies. If she is gonna make a baby, she's gonna have to raise that child."

Marcia listened and was careful not to interrupt. When Lorraine paused, Marcia said, "Sis, do you mind if I come over? I know it's an intrusion, but since you're both home…"

"What you coming over here to do? All the talking in the world can't save her. These young people don't wanna hear nobody. You tell them one thing, they do the exact opposite. And you think growing them up in church would make a difference."

"Please, Sis. I would love to see her and she hasn't been coming to church. I prefer to talk to her privately, anyway. I mean, with you around, not with everyone from church."

"Okay. Even though I don't know what difference it's going to make."

"I'm going to leave my house now and walk over there. It will take me about fifteen minutes."

"We'll be here."

Marcia reflected on what she knew about Desiree and her grandmother as she walked. For as long as Marcia could remember, Lorraine attended church and brought her granddaughter with her. As a child, Desiree became one of the church's youngest soloists, and her grandmother was proud of her. When Desiree did well in school, Lorraine brought in proof of her achievements. There was a tradition in the church of publicly announcing the youngsters' accomplishments, and Desiree was recognized many times.

A cluster of brown brick apartment buildings formed the housing complex where Desiree lived with her grandmother. Since Marcia's arrival in New York, she had heard nothing but bad news about 'the projects.' There was a stigma associated with government housing formed by the public perception that those who relied on government assistance were lazy. The media shaped this perception by broadcasting and printing stories about people who exploited the system. Stories of violence in the projects made the news, especially in the summertime, describing shoot-outs between drug dealers that left innocent children lying dead from the crossfire.

Beyond the media spotlight were people of integrity who needed assistance as a crucial lifeline to alleviate their suffering. Government assistance was a temporary means of survival for them. That type of government assistance painted a different picture of poverty from the one Marcia saw in Jamaica, when she was growing up. It allowed poor people in New York to live in apartment buildings like this one. It provided food to people who might otherwise go hungry. It allowed women with no income or health insurance to receive medical care for themselves and their babies. There was no similar system that Marcia knew of in Jamaica when she lived there.

As Marcia entered the building where Desiree lived, she felt no sense of fear, but she was cautious. She called to confirm that she was in the right place, and for her own safety, she also wanted Lorraine to know that she was there. She boarded the elevator and stood near the front. Liquid pooled to one corner at the back of the elevator. From its stench, Marcia could tell that someone had urinated on the floor.

Lorraine lived in an apartment on the sixth floor. She met Marcia at her front door and invited her inside. The apartment was immaculate. A floral sofa, armchair, and loveseat were neatly arranged around a glass-top center table. In front of that was a wall unit containing a television. The adjoining dining room held a table for six that was covered with a white lace tablecloth and a bouquet of flowers sat in the center.

Marcia examined the pictures that covered one wall. She focused on a woman who resembled Desiree.

"My daughter," Lorraine said.

"Desiree looks a lot like her mother," Marcia observed. She faced Lorraine. "And they both look like you. Beautiful women."

Lorraine smiled and accepted the compliment, but she was still trying to assess Marcia's intentions. She knew that people at church were gossiping about Desiree. She expected them to express their disapproval and dreaded their complete condemnation. Marcia's call had taken her by surprise. She had not expected a call of support.

"Desiree!" she shouted.

Dressed in sweatpants and an oversized t-shirt, Desiree entered the living room. "Yes, Grandma."

"Sister Marcia is here to see you."

Marcia could tell by Desiree's expression that the girl was surprised by her presence. "Hi, Desiree."

Desiree glanced back and forth from her grandmother to Marcia, wondering what they were up to. "Hello, Sister Marcia," she replied softly.

Marcia prayed for wisdom again. Perhaps being forthright was the best way for her to win Desiree's confidence. "How are you feeling?"

"Fine."

"Really? Then you're doing better than I was when I was pregnant with Wendy."

Desiree wrinkled her brows, but gave Marcia her full attention.

"I was around your age when I got pregnant," Marcia continued, "and I was terrified. I hadn't planned on having a baby. I had planned to finish high school and go to college. I was going to be an advertising executive and eventually own my own business. I was bright enough to do it too."

Marcia paused. She was standing in the living room. Desiree stood a few feet away from her in the short passageway that Marcia assumed led to the bedrooms. Lorraine had walked into the kitchen. They could hear water running from a tap.

"I looked a lot like you do. For many months, I could hide my pregnancy with baggy clothes. I got sick a few times, but thank God, I didn't have morning sickness every day. Are you having morning sickness?"

"Sometimes," Desiree responded in a mere whisper.

"Can I ask you something?"

Desiree nodded.

"How does everybody know? You're not even showing."

Instead of answering, Desiree started crying. Marcia wrapped her arms around her and held her. As Desiree sobbed, Marcia stroked her hair. Marcia closed her eyes as she pictured her own mother trying to console her when she was younger.

"Everything is going to be alright, Desiree. Believe me. I doubt that pregnancy is what you wanted for yourself at this time, but it's not the end of the world."

Desiree looked up at her with tears streaming down her face. "Sometimes, I feel like I could kill myself for being so stupid," she said softly. "I let everybody down. There I was acting like the Virgin Mary when I was already two months pregnant. It was like I was trying to fool myself. As if acting like I wasn't pregnant would make it go away." She sobbed again.

"I understand," Marcia said. "I did the same thing. I mean I also pretended I wasn't pregnant, until my mother found out and that forced me to face the truth. Is that what happened to you? Did your grandma find out?"

"No. I mean yes. She wasn't the first to find out. I told my best friend. Well, she used to be my best friend, but we're not friends anymore—not after she told everyone my business."

"Did your baby's father already know?"

Desiree nodded but offered no further information.

"When I was pregnant with Wendy, I didn't tell anyone who the father was. I even lied to Wendy's father and told him that he was not the baby's father."

Desiree stared at Marcia with wide eyes.

"I did. I'm not proud of my actions, but at that time, it seemed like the right thing to do. It was such a confusing time. Do you feel confused?"

Desiree nodded.

"Do you want to talk about it?"

Desiree stared at Marcia, unsure that she could trust her. She felt comfortable talking to her right now, but she'd also felt comfortable confiding in her best friend who'd let her down. Wendy's mother had always been friendly to all the children in the youth group, and they thought she was cool. She looked young and dressed nicely. Desiree wanted to trust her, but wasn't sure she could trust anyone ever again.

Marcia smiled at her. "You don't have to tell me anything, if you don't want to. Just remember this. I have been in the position you're in right now, and I survived; praise the Lord. It wasn't easy, and I didn't do it alone. In fact, there were times when I felt like I could have killed myself. Every time I read about a desperate teenager who hurts herself or her child, my heart goes out to her because that could have been me. Thank God, I didn't do anything to hurt myself, or Wendy. Hold on to your faith, Desiree. Don't stop going to church because you feel like you've sinned, and definitely don't stop going just because people are talking about you."

Desiree sobbed. "It's so hard. I can never go back there."

"Yes, you can. Jesus isn't in the business of condemning sinners. He wants to save us. If ever you needed the Lord before, you need him now. Believe me when I tell you, Jesus saved me."

"I can't face them again."

"Okay. Fine. Let's talk about school. Today is a school day. You should be in school."

Desiree shook her head.

"You can't just hide yourself away from the world because you feel ashamed. I did that and it was a mistake. I had already finished high school, though. If you stop now, you won't graduate."

"I'll get my GED."

"Easier said than done, Desiree. You're so close to graduating. Just finish the school year. You're going to make life much harder on yourself if you don't get your high school diploma."

Desiree stared back at Marcia. She knew what Marcia was saying about finishing high school was true. But she would rather take the examination to get a General Equivalency Diploma than face her peers in order to earn her diploma the traditional way.

"Please go back to school, Desiree. I promise you that, one day, you'll be glad you did. You may feel embarrassed now, and you may feel like you don't have a friend in the world. But this is where everything your grandma has tried to teach you can help. Think of the words of those hymns we sing in church on Sundays like 'What a friend we have in Jesus,' and 'Closer than a brother my Jesus is to me.' Jesus knows all about what you're going through and He will give you the strength and peace of mind to bear the unbearable. I'm telling you that from experience. And you know the best part? He knows the future. He knows how much better life is going to get for you, if you just hold on and trust in Him."

Desiree continued to stare at Marcia with tears streaming down her face. She wondered where this woman had come from on this morning when she was locked up in her room feeling so depressed. Had God heard the prayers that she couldn't bring herself to say? She noticed that her grandmother had walked back into the room and was watching them.

Marcia turned to Lorraine, but she held one of Desiree's hands. "Can we pray?"

"Oh yes!" Lorraine replied.

They joined hands. Marcia asked God to let each of them feel His presence. She prayed that God would touch Desiree and carry her through this experience the way He had carried her. She apologized for their disobedience, and praised God for forgiveness and mercy.

When they were finished, she asked Desiree if she had a favorite scripture.

Desiree shrugged.

"She has always loved the twenty-third Psalm," Lorraine said. "Ever since she was a child, she liked to picture people as little sheep and the Lord as their shepherd."

Desiree sobbed.

Marcia placed an arm around her shoulders and started reciting the Psalm. Lorraine joined her. Desiree stood in between them with tears streaming down her face.

The Lord is my shepherd, I shall not want.
He maketh me to lie down in green pastures.
He leadeth me beside the still waters.
He restoreth my soul.
He leadeth me in the paths of righteousness for His name sake.
Yeah though I walk through the valley of the shadow of death,
I will fear no evil for thou art with me
Thy rod and thy staff, they comfort me.
Thou preparest a table before me in the presence of mine enemies.
Thou anointest my head with oil, my cup runneth over.
Surely goodness and mercy shall follow me all the days of my life,
And I will dwell in the house of the Lord forever.

When they were finished, Marcia hugged Desiree. "I'm going to write my cell and house phone numbers down for you," Marcia told her. "Call me please. If you need anything, or you just want to say hello, call me. I'm praying for you. I love you."

Desiree didn't say anything else, but waved slightly as Marcia retrieved her bag and got ready to leave.

Lorraine walked Marcia to the door and thanked her profusely.

Later that night, Devon met Marcia outside of the building where she worked. He was leaning against his car, and as she approached, he straightened up and took a step toward her. She ran into his arms. He laughed and wrapped his arms around her.

"Wow! If I knew I'd get a greeting like this, I'd wait here every night."

She looked up at him and he saw that tears were seeping into the corners of her eyes. He brushed a hand across her cheek and kissed her lightly on the lips. Minutes ticked by, as they stood there holding on to each other.

Finally, she said, "I'm okay now."

He stepped back so he could see her face properly under the streetlight, but he kept his hands on her waist. Again, he felt the overwhelming urge to tell her he loved her. Instead, he leaned forward and kissed her gently. Deeply. Then, he opened the car door and waited until she was seated inside. They held hands for most of the drive back to her house.

Wendy was waiting up for them when they arrived. Devon and Marcia listened attentively as she gave them a detailed description of what happened at the youth meeting at church that evening.

Desiree hadn't shown up, but her absence was no surprise to the other teens. Every other member of the youth group was present and most thought Desiree would not have the nerve to face everyone ever again. Some of the other girls would have loved the chance to play the role of Virgin Mary and resented that she'd had the nerve to accept the part while knowing that she was pregnant.

Reverend Walker brought the group to order. Normally, he would let the youth minister lead the meeting, but this was a special circumstance. They opened with prayer before he focused their attention on one verse of scripture.

"Does everyone have a Bible?" Reverend Walker asked. He looked around at the group and noticed that a few people were sharing. "I need each one of you to open your own Bible to Romans, chapter twelve, the first verse. If you didn't bring a Bible with you, there are extra copies on the shelf." He waited for everyone to find the verse, then he read, "I beseech you therefore, brethren, by the mercies of God, that you present your bodies a living sacrifice, holy, acceptable to God, which is your reasonable service."

He stopped reading and looked up at their expectant faces. The chairs were arranged in a circle so that each person could see the faces of all the others. Many had listened to the gossip, and now they couldn't wait to hear directly from the reverend his verdict on the situation.

"If you're using your personal Bible," Reverend Walker continued, "highlight this verse." He watched them and waited as some underlined the verse or shaded it with a highlighter. "Now, I want you all to read it out loud with me. All together."

They read the verse.

"What do you think that this means, Dennis?" The reverend addressed his teenage son who was also a member of the youth group.

"It means we shouldn't abuse our bodies," Dennis replied.

"Anyone else? Stacy, what do you think it means?"

"The speaker is begging the people to live pure with their bodies," Stacy explained.

"Okay. Good. There has been a lot of talk about lovemaking around here lately. Most of the time we talk about why you shouldn't be making love. Right?"

A few people nodded.

"Remember, God is love, and God's love never fails. When we rush to make love without the commitment of a loving marriage that is centered on God's love, we end up alone and broken hearted. Yet, we now have evidence among us that some of you have chosen not to wait." He paused as he surveyed the faces of each of the teens. Some looked down at their Bibles. Few met his gaze head on. "Each of you sitting here is between the age of thirteen and eighteen. To your parents or guardians, you're children. You live in their homes and depend on them to support you. Yet, many of you get upset when your parents try to tell you what to do. Am I right?"

Some shrugged. Others nodded. "It depends," someone replied.

"During your life in this church, you've been told that fornication, which I'll remind you means lovemaking outside of marriage, is wrong. In other words, unmarried people should not be making love, and if they are, God will punish them for it. Isn't that what you've been taught?"

They nodded.

"That's what the Bible says," Paul offered.

"Yet, rumor has it, Paul, that you and Desiree have been intimately involved with each other, and that you're the father of her unborn baby."

Some of the teens squirmed in their seats. Some smiled awkwardly and glanced at Paul and then at their peers to view their reaction. No one had expected Reverend Walker to be so candid as to come out and just say everything in front of everyone.

"I've heard, Pastor," Paul responded. He appeared cool and collected. "I don't know who started the rumor, and why, but I can tell you that I am still a virgin."

Some of his peers guffawed.

"I have not betrayed the trust you put in me and Wendy when you appointed us to lead our peers and encourage them to wait until after they get married to make love. I take the responsibility you gave me seriously. I believe the Bible and I fear God. According to first Corinthians six, verses nine and ten, fornicators aren't getting into heaven, and that is where I'm trying to go."

Reverend Walker tried not to smile, but Paul's response pleased him. Paul had always held strong convictions about living according to the word of God, convictions that made him weird to many of his peers.

"I believe you, Paul," Reverend Walker said. "Yet, we all have moments of weakness. We adults can attest to that. We may not set out to sin, but sometimes it happens in spite of our best intentions. Grown men cheat on their wives, and guys cheat on their girlfriends."

Reverend Walker's attention remained fully focused on Paul even as he could hear the other teens become restless. Paul looked directly back at him, maintaining eye contact except when he glanced over at Wendy. From her seat beside Paul, Wendy shifted her attention back and forth between Paul and the reverend.

"So much of our wrongdoing is done in secrecy," Reverend Walker continued. "My son tells me that at age thirteen, many of the boys he knows already claim to be making love."

Many of the other teens nodded and wore expressions that said, "No surprise there."

"So, they're man enough to be making love at thirteen, as long as their parents don't know about it. Right? Especially if they're in the church, they're under pressure to hide their sexual activity. And many succeed. Until something like this happens and a woman, or girl, cannot hide her pregnancy."

There were murmurs among the group.

"So Desiree is pregnant." Reverend Walker slowly scrutinized the faces of each teen. "This isn't news to any of you. Neither is the allegation that Paul got her pregnant. Paul says he didn't, and Desiree isn't here to speak for herself."

After a moment of silence, the reverend continued. "Parenting is a tough job. I was twenty-five years old and married to First Lady Valerie when we had our first child. Now, thirty years and three children later, I'll tell you it has not been easy raising children. It's been a blessing, but it's still a tough job. Finances alone make it difficult. And it's even harder when you have no education, no money, no job, and no place of your own to raise a child in. For these reasons—in addition to the fact that God commands it—we urge each and every one of you to wait until you're older and married to make love. Do you understand why?"

They nodded.

"Commit your lovemaking unto God because He is love. If you're sexually active now, stop. Don't wait until you get pregnant, or get a girl pregnant. Don't wait until you start feeling symptoms and you're too scared to go to the doctor to find out what sexually transmitted disease you picked up."

Reverend Walker paused again, giving the teens time to reflect on what he was saying. He had no doubt that he had their attention. Many of them sat erect, and each one looked directly at his face. Some looked shocked at his boldness in addressing them so candidly. He prayed that he had the support of the parents on this. If their children thought they were old enough to do it, then they certainly were old enough to talk about it.

"Lovemaking is a beautiful thing when shared with the right person at the right time. And making a baby is a miracle. Children are indeed a gift from God. Each of you sitting here is a blessing to the grown-ups whose lives you've touched. I'm personally glad that you are who you are and not an abortion statistic. You're a blessing to me. I've watched you growing and felt the same pride I feel in my own son and daughters." Reverend Walker sighed and rested his head in his hands.

"Do you understand that we love you and we want what's best for you?" When no one answered, he repeated, "Do you?"

Many of the teens nodded; a few said yes.

"Now I am asking you—we can't control what you do—but I'm asking you to stop. Stop the lovemaking, if you're doing it, but also stop the gossiping. Desiree, Paul, and Wendy are sons and daughters of this church. You all are. We don't want to lose any of you. We want Desiree to come back to church, and the more you talk about her behind her back, the less likely she is to return. God is a forgiving God. The thing to do when we disobey Him isn't to run away from Him. You can't hide from God even if you try. When we have sinned, we need to seek Jesus more than ever. His grace and mercy can make a bad situation better, but without Him, things will only get worse."

Again, Reverend Walker paused and looked around the room. Most of the guys wore jeans and t-shirts. The girls also wore jeans, with a fashionable blouse. Reverend Walker usually wore a suit when he had official business at the church, but today he donned jeans, t-shirt, and sneakers. He hoped his casual attire made him seem more approachable to the youth. "I've been doing a lot of talking. Do any of you want to respond? Feel free even if you think I won't agree with what you have to say."

Jasmine timidly raised her hand.

Reverend Walker smiled at her and said, "Go ahead, Jasmine."

"So, you're telling us not to make love, but it's okay for a pregnant girl to be all up in the church."

The reverend took a deep breath before he answered. "Jesus welcomes sinners. He tells them to go and sin no more. Stop what you're doing that you know is wrong, but don't stop trying to get close to Jesus. Do you understand?"

"I think so," Jasmine replied.

"I'm meeting with the grown-ups too, this week. They have also been gossiping. Some have already condemned Desiree and Paul. That's not what the Bible teaches. Jesus said, 'Let he who is without sin cast the first stone.' We all sin, and that's why we need a Savior to help us in our weakness. We don't want another teenage girl to get pregnant, but we also don't want to lose the one who is already pregnant to the streets. Do you understand me?"

Nods.

"If you're a friend of Desiree's, or if you used to be her friend—and it's okay with your parents—call her and tell her what happened here this evening. Tell her we want her to come back to church. I also hear she has stopped attending school. Encourage her not to drop out. If your parents instruct you to do otherwise, then listen to your parents. I don't want you to disobey them, but do not go out of your way to make Desiree feel unwelcome in this church."

Reverend Walker stood up and invited everyone to stand and join hands. "I love each of you. My door is open. Feel free to talk to me, or to my wife if you're more comfortable talking to a female. If you have more to say on this matter but don't want to speak in front of everyone, you can always call me or catch me when you see me." He paused again and waited in case anyone else wanted to speak.

"Grab hold of your neighbor's hand, if you haven't already done so," he suggested. "Let's bow our heads in a word of prayer."

The group dispersed quickly after the prayer.

Marcia was first to speak after Wendy finished retelling what happened at church. "Praise God for Reverend Walker," she said. "I wish I'd had a pastor like that when I got pregnant with Wendy."

They were all seated at the dining table and Devon placed one hand over Marcia's.

"Mommy, I know you feel sorry for Desiree, but don't you think that if Pastor is too soft that it will send the message that what she did is okay?"

Marcia shook her head. "Desiree will have to face many consequences for her actions, regardless of what Pastor says and does. But I think loving her back into the church will help prevent her from making more bad choices."

Devon squeezed her hand. "Your mother is right," he said. "Any word on how Paul's name got linked to Desiree's?"

Wendy shook her head. "Mom, did she tell you?"

Marcia shook her head.

"I'm standing by Paul," Wendy affirmed.

Devon smiled, impressed by the conviction with which his daughter stood by her man. He prayed that Paul deserved his daughter's vote of confidence.

Marcia stood up. "Well, this isn't going to be resolved overnight, so I suggest that we all get some sleep." She faced Devon as he stood up. "I'll sleep a lot better once I know that you're home safely."

Devon kissed her lightly on the lips. Then, reaching for Wendy's hand, he said, "A family that prays together stays together." They prayed.

CHAPTER SIXTEEN

Marcia visited Desiree again on Saturday. This time when she arrived at their apartment, Desiree's grandmother informed her that Desiree had just left.

"Come on in, Sister Marcia," Lorraine invited her. "I have to apologize for Desiree. These young people are going to do what they do, no matter what we try to say and do about it."

"Did she know I was coming?"

"Yes, of course. But just a few minutes ago the phone rang, and the next thing I knew Desiree was fully dressed and headed out the door. I believe it was her baby-father who called."

Marcia sat down on the sofa. She was disappointed that Desiree had not wanted to see her, but she also realized that this might be her chance to learn the baby's paternity. "Sister Lorraine," Marcia entreated in a soft voice, "Do you mind saying who the baby's father is?"

Lorraine removed her glasses and peered at Marcia, examining her from head to toe. "I don't know why, but I trust you. I have prayed and I believe that you're not here just to pry. I think you really know what Desiree is going through, so I'll tell you."

Lorraine sat beside Marcia and lowered her voice, although there was no one else in the apartment to hear them speaking. Tears filled her eyes. "I pray that together we can turn Desiree back from this path that she is on before," Lorraine's voice cracked, "before she ends up like her mother."

Marcia reached out and held her hands. She looked at Lorraine with compassion in her eyes as she waited silently for her to continue speaking.

"I won't know for sure until Desiree comes back, but chances are she went to the beauty salon to get her hair and nails done. She goes every weekend, and that boy Keith that she's been running around with pays for it."

"Is Keith one of her school mates?"

"Keith is a twenty-five-year old high school dropout who is making big money on the streets. I don't know exactly when Desiree started hooking up with him, but a few months ago was the first time one of the neighbors told me she saw Desiree in his car. Desiree won't talk to me, and I cannot be everywhere that she is. All I can do is pray."

"Did you ask her about him?"

"Yes, of course. I asked her, I warned her, I begged her not to get involved with this man. At first, she said okay. Then she started showing up every weekend with her hair and nails done, and she couldn't tell me where she was getting the money to pay for it. Then, she would go out, supposedly with her girlfriends, and a few times she didn't come back until the next morning."

"Oh dear. What did you do?"

"Cry and pray. What else can an old lady like me do? The moment I try to talk to her, she rolls her eyes and bops her head, and walks out of the room and slams the door. What can I do? She is too big now for me to spank her. And I'm too old to get in a fight with my granddaughter."

"Is there anyone that you could call? Perhaps another family member could influence her. It also sounds like a change of environment might do her good."

"Hmm. Let me tell you something. You come in here sounding like a social worker. You think you've got all the answers." Her words scolded Marcia, but her voice sounded more weary than angry. Lorraine paused and sniffled. "Let's see. I could call Desiree's father, but, the last I heard he was in prison serving time. Again... Hmm. I could call my daughter, Desiree's mother, but she is a crack-head and a prostitute... a mere shadow of what she used to be... a walking skeleton. She has about six kids now, scattered throughout the foster care system, growing like weeds, raising themselves. Desiree was her first and the only one my health would allow me to take."

"I'm sorry," Marcia said. Her words were inadequate, she knew, but she couldn't think of anything else to say.

"Desiree's mother was just a kid when she got pregnant the first time. I thought I was going to save her. I took full charge of Desiree so that her mother could go back to school. But she wouldn't give up the streets and the man she was running around with. Once he got her hooked on some stuff, she was lost to the world." Lorraine sobbed. "I'm afraid that the same thing is going to happen to Desiree."

"We won't let it," Marcia insisted.

"Oh yeah. How are you going to stop it?" Lorraine tilted her head and impatiently brushed the tears from her face.

"Spiritual warfare. Prayer, faith, and aggressive intervention."

"Child, I done been on my knees so much I wore a hole in the carpet."

"Yes, but you've been praying alone. From now on, we're going to pray with you, and fast too, and God will bring about a change. I know He will, whether or not, we live to see it."

The next morning, Devon waited in his car in front of the building while Marcia went upstairs to get Desiree. It was half an hour before the service and Lorraine met her at the door dressed and ready to leave. She motioned toward Desiree's room where she said Marcia would find the teenage girl fast asleep.

Marcia requested that Lorraine wait. She knocked loudly on the girl's door. There was no answer. Marcia asked Lorraine for a credit card which she used to pick the lock.

As she opened the door, Desiree jumped out of bed. "Rise and shine and give God the glory," Marcia announced cheerfully, switching on the light. Desiree had opaque curtains drawn casting darkness throughout her room.

Was it the shock of Marcia breaking in, or had Desiree been awake all along? Both, Marcia surmised, as they confronted each other.

"Good morning, Desiree." Marcia smiled cheerfully. "What are you going to wear to church this morning?"

Desiree folded her arms and faced Marcia, silently challenging her.

Inwardly, Marcia prayed. She refused to back down. Lorraine, Devon, Aunt Pat, Uncle Trevor, Wendy, Paul and his mother had joined her in fasting and praying that Desiree would go to church with them this morning. Marcia didn't plan to leave the apartment without her.

"This is nice." Marcia pulled out a skirt and blouse. The skirt was long and beige with an elasticized waist. The oversized blouse and accompanying jacket would not draw attention to her belly. Marcia placed the outfit on Wendy's bed. "Get dressed," she said firmly.

She turned her back to leave the room when she heard Desiree softly say, "I can't."

"Why not?"

"I... I haven't taken a shower yet," responded Desiree, still shocked that Marcia had the nerve to break into her room.

"I won't tell anyone, if you won't."

Desiree's face contorted into a look of shock and amazement. How dare this woman?

"I'm going to church this morning, Desiree, and I'm not going without you," Marcia stated. "Now, please get dressed so we won't be late."

Desiree just looked at her.

"Please. I'll be standing in the hallway. I'm giving you ten minutes."

From where she stood in the corridor, Marcia could see Lorraine standing in the living room. Marcia placed her index finger against her lips urging Lorraine not to say anything. Then, she clasped her hands and bowed her head in a posture of prayer. Lorraine did the same.

Whether it was their prayers, fasting, or the phone calls from her peers earlier in the week that moved her, ten minutes later Desiree emerged from her room fully dressed.

"You look great," Marcia complemented her. Then she added, "I brought you a muffin."

"I'm not hungry," Desiree said.

"You should eat something… for the baby."

Again, Desiree just stared at her. Marcia met her gaze with a look of compassion. On the surface, Desiree's body language was resistant and rebellious, but as Marcia gazed into her eyes, she felt she also saw a silent appeal for help.

They arrived at the church a few minutes late and had to wait in the foyer while the choir marched down the aisle and the singers took their position in the choir stand.

"Keep your head up," Marcia whispered to Desiree as they entered the sanctuary. Devon escorted Lorraine while Marcia and Desiree walked side by side. They found seats in the same pew as Marcia's family. Each time Marcia looked at Desiree, her attention was either focused on the altar, or on the Bible or hymnal in her hand. She didn't look around to notice the curious glances from other members of the congregation.

Reverend Walker preached about forgiveness, and when he did the altar call, Marcia was certain some members would have liked to see Desiree publicly throw herself on the mercy of the church. She didn't.

After the service, Marcia stood with Desiree as she returned the smiles and greetings from her church family. Reverend Walker himself came over.

"It's good to see you, daughter," he said.

Desiree gasped.

"Don't stay away." Reverend Walker turned his attention to someone else and moved on.

Marcia invited Desiree and her grandmother to dinner at Aunt Pat's house, but they declined.

After Devon dropped them off, he and Marcia were seated in the car together, when he said, "You did good today, Sister Marcia."

"Praise God. We have to continue to pray and fast for Desiree."

Devon nodded. "Don't take on her burden though, Marcia," he cautioned. "Desiree is going to have to live her own life."

Marcia was tempted to retort, "What's that supposed to mean?" but she didn't. She believed that God would turn Desiree's life around the same way He had saved hers. The circumstances were different, but God was the same.

Marcia soon discovered that although she and Desiree shared the common experience of being pregnant at age seventeen, Desiree was determined to deal with her situation differently. She refused to return to high school. Instead, she took the test for the General Equivalency Diploma. She also continued to attend church on Sundays, but no longer attended the meetings of the youth group. She seemed to have cut all ties with her peers in the church.

Wendy and Paul ran into her outside of a shopping center one evening, and were surprised when she beckoned them over to meet her boyfriend.

"Hi, Wendy. Hi, Paul. Come meet my Boo."

Desiree was standing with an unfamiliar man in front of a dark tinted sports utility vehicle when they saw her. He was leaning against the SUV; she was leaning against him, and they were facing the store as though they were waiting for someone to exit when Wendy and Paul walked out.

"Hey, Desiree." Wendy and Paul held hands as they walked over to her.

"I'd like you to meet Keith, my boyfriend and soon to be baby-father." She stepped aside as she made the introduction. Keith was a little taller than Desiree with a thick, muscular body and light brown skin. They both wore sweats and sneakers accentuated with gold necklaces and earrings.

"What's up, man?"

"What's up?"

Paul and Keith acknowledged each other with a nod.

"Finally, the mystery man has a face," Wendy said looking at Desiree, then Keith, then back at Desiree again.

"Mystery man?" Keith questioned Desiree.

"Yeah. Remember, I told you. Paul is the guy from church who Miss Busy Body Ex-Best Friend of Mine told everyone was my baby-daddy. She was running her mouth like she was all up in the cool-aid and didn't even know the flavor." Desiree shifted her weight from one hip to the next, and made a circle with the index finger of her right hand as she spoke.

Keith eyed Paul suspiciously.

"Don't worry about him," Desiree continued. "You might as well call him Saint Paul. Wendy, I know you didn't believe the hype, but I still wanted you to meet my man. I don't want your man, never have. This is my Boo." She linked her arm with Keith's. "The only thing Paul and I ever did together was to rehearse for the play."

Wendy nodded. "I thought so," she replied.

"So, we're cool?" Desiree asked.

"Always," Wendy replied.

"Look, man," Paul said to Keith. "The young adults are having a special service this Sunday at four. Why don't you come on out, you and your

Boo?"

Keith smiled but declined. "I don't do the church thing."

"It won't be a typical church thing," Paul countered. "The choir will rock the house with uplifting music you can dance to. It's going to be tight. Think about it. You got a ride. If you decide to come, Desiree knows where the church is."

A quiet moment followed in which no one said anything.

Then, Wendy said, "Take care of yourself," as she and Desiree shared a quick embrace. "Nice meeting you," she told Keith who smiled and nodded in return.

They said goodbye.

CHAPTER SEVENTEEN

When Wendy announced her decision to attend a state college instead of the Ivy League university her father had attended, she and her father had their first argument.

"Dad, I don't need an Ivy League degree to work as a missionary in Africa," she told him.

"No, you don't, but what if you wake up one morning and decide that's not what you want to do with your life? I changed my mind about my career path while I was in college."

"That supports my point, Dad. You invested so much into getting a Columbia degree and you're not even using it."

Wendy's comment struck deeper than Devon would ever tell her. In fact, she echoed his father's words.

"God called Paul and me to be missionaries long before you came into my life, Dad. I know this is God's plan for me. I am not going to change my mind."

"So you're saying that the fact that Paul did not get accepted into Columbia has nothing to do with your decision."

"It was a factor, but not a primary one. This college is offering us free tuition. We're not pursuing lucrative professions, so it doesn't make sense to acquire student loans."

"I've told you a thousand times, I'll pay for your education."

"Thanks, Dad, but no. Please understand. I've always expected that when I finished high school, I'd go to college, but I knew that Mommy didn't have the money to pay for my education. I thank God that you're here now." She hugged him. "But I also take pride in knowing that I don't need your money to do this. By God's grace, I am making you and Mommy proud by finishing high school without getting pregnant, and I'm a straight A student. I don't have to rely on my parents or student loans to pay for my college education. Do you know how good that makes me feel? This is a major hallelujah moment in my life."

Devon sighed. "You're right, Wendy. I am sorry I wasn't always there for you. I'm here now and trying to help you in any way I can. I'm proud of you, and I'm here if you need me. As you said, this is indeed a hallelujah moment. Praise God, but I'm sure…"

"No buts, Dad. Please," she pleaded. "This college has a top notch Africana studies program and study abroad arrangements with colleges in Africa. I've gone over their program carefully, and Paul and I think it will give us the background we need."

Devon let the conversation rest, remembering Marcia's advice that trying to dictate what Wendy should do with her life would only alienate her. Later, he mentioned the conversation to Marcia.

"It bothers me that she doesn't want my help. I'm her father. It's my responsibility to pay for her education, especially because I can afford it."

"You have to understand that Wendy fashioned these goals long before she knew what it meant to have a father."

Devon dropped his head into his hands. He could never regain the time he had missed with Wendy, her childhood, most of her adolescence. And like her mother, she was a woman who didn't want his money. He wondered how much Wendy's attitude was influenced by Marcia's comments declining "Douglas charity." He hadn't realized he had spoken his thoughts out loud until Marcia walked over to the sofa where he was seated and knelt down in front of him. Their eyes met.

"I would never put you down in front of our daughter, Devon. I've never spoken badly to her about you or your family. And regardless of how well we're getting along with each other, I promise not to interfere with your relationship with Wendy. I think you want what's best for her as much as I do."

He looked at her for a moment wishing that he could rewrite the script on this aspect of their lives, wondering if he would ever have the opportunity to raise a child—but when he spoke, he simply said, "Thank you."

"I'm glad you're here now," Marcia added.

"Me too."

As Devon was leaving home to pick up Uncle Trevor for Bible study one Wednesday evening, the phone rang. The domestic helper who worked in his parent's home called from Jamaica to tell him that his father had been rushed to the hospital after suffering a heart attack. Devon got the name of the hospital from her and called his friend Troy, asking him to go there. Then, Devon left for Bible study with the volume high on his cell phone because he expected Troy to call back. He planned to ask the study group to pray with him, but before he reached the house to pick up Uncle Trevor, his cell phone rang. He pulled over to the side of the road before answering.

"Hello."

"Devon."

"Yes, Troy. Did you find them? What's happening?"

"I'm at the hospital with your mother, and my parents are on their way here."

"Good. Thanks for calling them. Mommy will appreciate their support. How is she holding up and how is my father doing?"

Troy hesitated.

"Troy?"

"Where are you now, Devon? You're going to need to come home on the earliest flight you can get."

"I figured that much. Is my father in intensive care?"

Troy evaded the question. "Is there any other family nearby who I can call to come be with your mother until you get here?"

"No. No one close anyway. In spite of all the children my grandfather had, my father grew up as an only child and has always kept to himself. He and my mother tend to live like all they have is each other. You know their love."

"Yes, but your dad's siblings…"

"They might as well be strangers. Ah. If you and your parents could rally around Mommy until I come, I'd appreciate it. I'll go to the airport on standby and should be able to get a flight there in the morning. Of course, I'll stay until my father gets out of the hospital. Actually, they'll need me around after that too."

Devon rambled on, voicing his thoughts until Troy interrupted him. "Devon."

"Yes. What?"

Troy cleared his throat and when he spoke, his voice sounded hoarse. "Devon, your father won't be coming out of the hospital. I'm sorry. He passed away before I got here."

Devon dropped the phone. His head fell forward hitting the steering wheel and blasting the horn. He had expected a miracle tonight. He had not expected this. Ever so awkwardly, he picked back up the phone again as he heard Troy repeatedly calling his name.

"I'm here." Devon took a deep breath and sighed his answer.

"Why didn't you tell me you were on the road? Pull over if you're still driving, please. The last thing we need now is for you to have an accident."

Devon shook his head as though Troy could see him.

"Devon. Are you alright?"

"Yes."

"Are you still driving?"

"No."

"Good. Listen, man, I'm so sorry. I'll do everything I can on this end. Just take care of yourself until you get here tomorrow. Okay?"

Devon assured him that he would be fine and promised to call back later that night. He had barely hung up when the phone rang again.

"Yes," he answered abruptly.

"Dad, it's me, Wendy. We're at the hospital. Aunty Blossom is in labor. She is having the babies. Can you and Uncle Trev come to the hospital please? Everyone else in the family is here. Uncle Steve is with Aunty of course. And Mom and Aunt Pat are in the waiting room. The only ones missing from our family are you and Uncle Trev." Wendy spoke rapidly in a high-pitched voice.

"Whoa. Slow down," Devon replied, amazed that he was smiling, in spite of the grim news he had received moments before. Hearing how much Wendy accepted him as a part of her family lifted his spirit. A rush of joy filled him at the sound of her voice, and her excitement began to take the place of his grief. He knew that tomorrow would probably be the most difficult day of his life, but today, he wanted to share in Marcia and Wendy's joy.

"Oh my goodness, Dad. The twins are on their way. I can't wait to see them. Uncle Trev is with you, right? Let me talk to him, please."

"I'm on my way to pick him up."

Wendy glanced at her watch. "You're late, Daddy. You're never late. Hurry up! Uncle Trev knows how to get here."

"Okay, boss lady," Devon agreed, smiling. "We're on our way."

"See you soon. I love you."

"I love you too."

Devon could not explain the turnaround. The news of his father's death had hit him like a blow to the gut, causing a rush of pain and fear that felt like it would cripple him. But before he could submerge himself in sorrow, Wendy's call pulled him up from the abyss. The pain his father's death caused was still there, somewhere deep inside him, but for the next few hours he mentioned it to no one as he shared in the joy and anticipation of new life.

Hours later, they stood in front of the nursery ogling the twins. As Wendy tried to convince Aunt Pat and Uncle Trevor that the babies resembled her, Devon moved closer to Marcia and wrapped one arm around her waist.

"What are you thinking about?" he asked, his voice low enough that only she would hear.

She looked up at him, her eyes wide as they met his. "The miracle of life," she said.

"Does this bring back memories of having Wendy?"

She nodded. "Sad ones, in a sense, but I realize now how blessed I am. When I look at Wendy standing over there and remember what my life was like in the days before and after she was born, I just feel so grateful." Tears seeped into the corners of her eyes.

"You made it through those difficult days," Devon said with a smile.

"God has been so good to me. I was alone when I had her, Devon. I mean the hospital workers who had a job to do were there, but no family. No one who loved me was there."

Devon glimpsed downward instinctively; he felt ashamed. He wanted to say he should have been there, but saying so wouldn't make up for his absence.

Marcia continued. "I remember feeling afraid and lonely like I've never felt again in life. And just when I thought I couldn't bear it anymore, something strange happened. I felt peace. I know now that it was God's presence."

Devon reached for both her hands and faced her.

"I remember the last time I saw my mother before she died. She came to visit me shortly before I had Wendy, and when she left I cried hysterically. I thought I was going to die just from heartache alone."

Devon embraced her, but she gently pushed him back and looked up at him.

"I'm okay, but that night I got on my knees feeling desperate. Mommy had left the Bible open to a page where she had underlined these words: Be anxious for nothing, but for everything by prayer and supplication with thanksgiving let your request be made known to God and the peace of God which surpasses all understanding will guard your heart and mind through Christ Jesus. That peace is what rescued me that night. Those words, taken from Philippians four, verses six and seven, have become a memory verse for my life."

She paused briefly, and continued when Devon said nothing. "It was that inexplicable peace that came over me when Wendy was born. That's when I knew Jesus was real."

As Devon listened, he thought of how Wendy's phone call had rescued him. He understood. He drew Marcia close to his side and rested his head on hers, but still he said nothing.

It was after midnight when they said goodnight to Uncle Trevor and Aunt Pat outside the hospital, and Devon insisted that Marcia and Wendy ride home with him. Back at his house, he told them about his father's passing and that he would be leaving for Jamaica that morning.

"I want to go with you, Dad," Wendy said.

"School is almost over. It doesn't make sense for you to miss out on the days leading up to graduation," Devon replied, firmly.

Wendy gasped and quickly paced the length of the living room with one hand on her head. "Graduation. You're going to miss my graduation."

Devon grabbed her hands and pulled her to stand still in front of him. "I promise you this. I wouldn't miss your graduation for the world. I want nothing more than to see you graduate, and get married when the time is right, and to share in every other milestone in your life. Trust me, I've missed enough already."

Wendy started sobbing and her father hugged her.

Marcia rose from her seat on the sofa where she sat watching them. She had opened her mouth more than once to respond, but decided not to interfere. The interchange was the result of months of bonding between Wendy and her father, and despite the sadness of the moment, Marcia's heart sang at their display of love for each other.

She walked over and touched Wendy on the shoulder. Facing Devon, she spoke, "I have a suggestion."

Wendy turned to face her and Devon reached for her hand.

"The funeral is likely to be next weekend, right?" she asked Devon.

He nodded.

"And Wendy's graduation is on the following Wednesday. Wendy could fly down for the weekend to be with you and your mother, Devon, and if you cannot return with her, you could probably get a flight back during the week, before her graduation."

Wendy nodded and seemed satisfied. She asked to be excused so that she could call Paul.

"It's two o' clock in the morning, young lady. You need to get some sleep," Devon said.

"Paul is probably sound asleep," Marcia added.

"I promised I would call him, no matter what time I got back," Wendy replied. She was already walking down the passageway toward her bedroom, her cell phone in hand.

"He is still the number one man in her life," Devon said, smiling at Marcia for the first time since they had returned to his apartment.

"I don't know about that. You're in pretty close competition. I would say she loves you, very, very much." Marcia smiled back at him.

He took her hand and pulled her in the direction of his bedroom. "Help me pack," he stated.

For the next two hours, they talked, as he threw some of his belongings into a suitcase, took a quick shower and made a list of favors for her to complete. Stop delivery on his mail and daily newspaper, and mail out payment on a few bills. It felt good to count on her as his friend again. After she showered and returned from checking to find that Wendy was sound asleep, he told her so.

"Thanks for being here. I'm just sorry I wasn't there for you when you needed me most."

"Devon Douglas. If you apologize to me one more time, I'm going to scream," she declared, with a pretense of anger, and flopped backwards on the bed. "Seriously though, I praise God that you're here now and already, you've been such a positive influence on our daughter."

"And you?"

"Me?"

"Yes." He finished setting the alarm clock and came and sat next to her. "What effect has my presence had on you?"

Her eyes met and held his. "At first, seeing you brought back a lot of painful memories. But then you gave me a chance to mend my broken heart. Instead of dwelling on the distant past each time I think of you, I have new happier memories now, of you being a good father to our daughter."

"Thank you," he said, as he trailed his index finger along her cheek. "It's like you gave my life new purpose when you forgave me. I promise that I will never do anything to hurt you." He trailed his finger across her lips. Kissing her right now would be the most natural thing in the world, but could he resist going further as he stretched out beside her on the bed?

He changed the subject completely, forcing his thoughts away from the two of them to the bleak reality facing him later that day. "When your mother died, it was pretty sudden, right? Like what's happened to my father."

She nodded as the grim reality of losing a loved one sank in, replacing the momentary disappointment she felt that he hadn't tried to kiss her.

"How did you cope?" he asked.

"Badly. I blamed myself. In my weakest moments, I wanted to kill myself for causing her so much grief."

Devon's eyes searched hers for the details she didn't explain in words. "Was this before or after Wendy was born?"

"Wendy was born in December. I didn't find out immediately, but Mommy died the same day."

"I'm sorry." Devon sighed heavily, and then continued. "There's one thing I don't understand. You said at the hospital that when Wendy was born, you felt God's peace, but you're now saying that shortly after that you felt suicidal. You mean that your mother's death caused you to feel that you couldn't go on, even for the baby, in spite of your faith?"

Marcia thought for a moment before she answered. "Back then, I didn't have much faith. It's only now when I look back that I realize that God sustained me during a time when I had no hope for a better day. You know, like in the poem on Aunt Pat's dining room wall; it was His footprints in the sand—not mine. Sometimes you might feel God's presence when you're alone, but sometimes God has to send someone to rescue you. What I felt at the hospital helped me through the desperation of that moment, but when things got worse, I needed something more. I needed a shoulder to cry on. Someone had to literally pick me up. That's when God sent Aunt Pat and Blossom."

"Do you think that's why He's brought us together right now?"

"Perhaps."

He sighed. "I feel like I let my father down, Marcia."

Marcia propped herself up on one elbow and looked down at him, and for the first time since they were teenagers, she saw Devon crying. Tears streamed from the corners of his eyes and ran along his face, back into his hair.

"He and my mother gave up so much to allow me to follow my dreams, dreams that took me farther and farther away from them, when all my father really wanted was for me to look up to him and follow in his footsteps."

Marcia touched his cheek and angled his face toward hers. "Your father was always proud of you when we were growing up. I'm sure he was no less proud of the man you have become."

"I let him down. He wanted nothing more than for me to work with him. That was the plan when I went off to college, you know. All the marketing, economics, and accounting courses I took were geared toward expanding our hotel. But by the time I earned my degree, I was no longer interested in doing that. Even though I went home each summer to work with him, I did so grudgingly, and he knew it. We argued often last summer when I was there. It was like his last big attempt to get me to see things his way. When I went home with Wendy for Easter, he said nothing about it. Now, I can't believe he's gone. I don't know how I'm going to face Mommy later today." He was surprised at himself for crying, but he felt strangely comforted that it was Marcia alone who was seeing him like this. He wouldn't expose his deepest feelings to anyone else.

"Promise me something," she said.

Again, his eyes met and held hers. He felt comforted by her friendship.

"Promise me you'll have faith, no matter how guilty or sad you feel."

He nodded, but wasn't sure he knew what she meant. When she spoke again, it seemed as if she'd read his mind.

"I didn't think I could survive after losing my mother. But, I'm glad I kept going, even when I thought only more pain lay ahead. As Wendy grew, she brought so much laughter and joy into my life. And the most amazing gift was her blind faith. She trusted in God from day one, and as I watched her grow and listened to her, I learned to do the same."

"I love you so much," Devon whispered.

Marcia closed her eyes as she leaned forward and kissed him. Then without making eye contact, she rested her head on his shoulder and snuggled close. The alarm would go off soon, signaling the start of another phase in their lives.

But Marcia didn't fool herself. Tonight, Devon needed her because he was vulnerable. When he said he loved her, she remembered how he'd told her so before in a private, passionate moment as they made love. This wasn't the first time he had confided in her either, exposing his insecurities. He had done that often when they were teenagers, causing her to feel in those moments like the most important person in his life. But once he was back with his friends who talked down their noses at Marcia because she had no father and her mother was a domestic helper, he became distant. So, unless Devon had truly changed, she had no doubt their love would remain secret.

CHAPTER EIGHTEEN

Wendy's graduation day arrived sunny and hot. The possibility of a thunderstorm threatened to dampen the late afternoon. For now, however, Wendy and her family left for the graduation ceremony under brilliant blue skies. Marcia drove Devon's car, with Wendy seated beside her in the front passenger seat. Uncle Trevor and Aunt Pat sat behind them. Blossom and Steve stayed home with their babies.

"What time is your father coming, Wendy?" Aunt Pat asked.

"I'm not sure, Aunty. Dad called last night after his flight got held over, but I didn't speak to him today."

"His flight was rescheduled for this morning," Marcia added. "He is going to take a cab from the airport and meet us at the theater. I will keep my cell phone on vibrate, so he can call me to bring his invitation out to him once he gets there."

"I wish he would answer his phone though," said Wendy. "Say a quick prayer with me that he is okay please."

They prayed.

"Don't worry, honey," Marcia assured her, placing one hand on her daughter's arm. "He'll be here. Your father would not miss your graduation for the world."

Later, as the graduates filed into the theater, Marcia took a quick look at the screen of her cell phone to make sure she hadn't missed Devon's call. Where was he? She said another prayer for his safety.

She was seated near the aisle, with Aunt Pat and Uncle Trevor on one side, and an empty seat reserved for Devon on the other. She moved into Devon's seat and positioned herself to take a picture of Wendy as she approached.

Wendy wore a white robe over her summer dress now, and a graduation cap covered her hair. She smiled and waved at her relatives, but as her eyes rested on the empty seat, her smile faded.

"Where is Daddy?" she asked, as she got closer to where they were seated.

Marcia shrugged, but tried to reassure her as she passed by. "He is probably on his way."

Wendy and her classmates sat down and the ceremony began. There were introductory speeches. Administrators lauded each other and the student body for their performance throughout the year and acknowledged alumni contributions to the high school.

Marcia checked the time. She prayed that Devon would arrive before Wendy made her speech. He had pledged to be there recording the event, so they would be able to watch it again in the future. Now, Marcia's concern grew that he would miss the ceremony altogether.

"Something must have happened to him," whispered Uncle Trevor.

Minutes passed.

The principal introduced Wendy, congratulating her on her near-perfect grade point average. He informed the audience that Wendy had been accepted into five of the top universities in the country. The crowd applauded as Wendy approached the podium. Paul stood and whistled loudly to show his support. The stage lights shining on Wendy prevented her from seeing the audience fully, but she stood confidently with faith that the people she loved most were there.

Wendy opened her speech, bucking societal convention, by praising God for her success and thanking Jesus for her loving family and Paul Chambers, her best friend. She mentioned highlights of common events she and her classmates had shared over the past four years. She thanked the teachers for their dedication and challenged the entire graduating class to use their education to benefit their community.

"This high school will always hold a special place in my heart for many reasons," she concluded, "especially because it was a the place where I first met my father."

After the ceremony, Wendy and Paul stopped to pose for pictures with friends as they worked their way outside to meet their family. The guests of the graduates stood in groups outside the theater. As Marcia waited for Wendy, a fleeting thought of Desiree crossed her mind. Desiree had not returned to school to graduate with her peers, but she had earned a General Equivalency Diploma when she passed the alternative exam.

Paul was first to find his mother in the crowd and he left Wendy's side to meet her. Wendy's eyes rested briefly on Paul as he embraced his mother. Sounds of laughter and squeals of excitement filled the air as the scene was repeated over and over again by other graduates. As Wendy completed her survey, her eyes met her mother's, and she noticed that only

Aunt Pat and Uncle Trevor stood by her side.

"He's not here," she whispered as her eyes welled up with tears. "I was so sure he would be here. I prayed and I knew God would answer, that Daddy was there beside you, Mom, listening to my speech." She sobbed.

Marcia hugged her, looking over her shoulder at her aunt and uncle, tears forming in her own eyes. Until this moment, she hadn't realized how much Devon meant to them. If he had been there, she would have felt redeemed, like her mother Ruth was smiling down on them pleased that both of Wendy's parents were together supporting their child. But in Devon's absence, Marcia ached for herself and her daughter.

Wendy should have been elated at this moment. It broke their hearts to see her crestfallen.

"Lord, have mercy," muttered Aunt Pat.

"Never mind, baby girl. We're here," Uncle Trevor assured Wendy. "And I'm sure there is a good explanation for your father's absence."

What excuse could be good enough? Marcia wondered, as she tried over and over again to reach Devon. Only death could cause her to miss her daughter's graduation. She would sooner arrive in a wheelchair, or on a stretcher, than to not get here at all. She hoped Devon was well because, as she tried to comfort Wendy, anger welled up inside her, and she wanted to kill him.

Paul noticed Wendy crying and abruptly walked away from someone who was in mid-conversation with him. A few steps brought him to her side and he embraced her. Wendy cried even more now as she rested her head against his shoulder. Neither one of them said a word to the other. He understood more than anyone else that this was a matter of faith for her. She had believed God for this. She had faith that her father would be there because she believed it was in God's will for her. In the upcoming days, her disappointment over her father's absence would cause her to question how much she really knew about God's plan for her life.

They heard from Devon late that evening after all the festivities were over, after Marcia, using a gift from her aunt and uncle, had treated the family to dinner at a restaurant near their home. Paul and his family dined with them. His antics brought laughter to everyone's lips. He even cheered up Wendy, who eventually joined him in telling jokes. Marcia and Wendy were at home getting ready for bed when Devon finally called.

"Dad!" Wendy exclaimed, when she heard his voice. "Praise God! Are you okay? We've been so worried about you."

Devon sighed. They couldn't see the tears that filled his eyes. His head was pounding, but he wouldn't burden Wendy with his problems, especially not after the way he had let her and her mother down. "Honey, I'm so sorry I wasn't there." He paused and took a deep breath. He needed to sound apologetic, but calm. Devon Douglas was always composed. Devon Douglas believed that big men don't cry. Devon Douglas always retained control of a situation, until now. Never before had he felt more aware of his own weakness.

"What happened, Daddy?" asked Wendy. "Where are you?"

Marcia had been putting clothes away in the closet, but when she heard Wendy talking to her father, she came and sat beside her on the bed and held her hand.

Devon cleared his throat. "I'm still in Jamaica," Devon said. His voice sounded husky and he felt a lump rise up in his throat. "Mommy, I mean your grandmother is not doing so well. We had an emergency situation this morning just as I was leaving for the airport and I had to see that she got proper medical care. I've been with her all day."

Wendy's emotions hung on every word. Her heart went out to her father, who was still adjusting to the loss of his father, and now faced another health crisis involving his mother. Since returning from dinner, she had spent some time alone reading her Bible and talking to God, and it had prepared her to put aside her own disappointment and comfort him. "I'm sorry, Dad. I know this must be hard for you. Is Grandma going to be alright?"

"I hope so, Wendy. I want you to know how proud I am of you. I don't have to ask how well you delivered your speech; I know you were exemplary. It hurt me to miss it. I love you very much and I hope you'll find it in your heart to forgive me."

Tears streamed down Wendy's face and a sob escaped her lips as she answered him. "It's okay, Daddy. I understand. I love you too, and I wish you had been there, but I'll get over it. Take care of Grandma, okay."

"Okay." Devon hoped his daughter wouldn't realize that he was crying too. He was exhausted and emotionally drained. Again, he inhaled deeply. "Is your mother there?"

"Yes. Hold on." Wendy removed the receiver from her ear to hand it over to her mother when she noticed her shaking her head vigorously and mouthing the word, "No."

"Dad, Mom can't talk on the phone right now."

"Alright. Give her my love. I'll call again in the morning, okay?"

"Okay. Dad, I love you."

"I love you, too, Wendy."

Marcia had not taken the phone from Wendy because she had not trusted herself to speak. She marveled at her daughter's compassion and forgiveness, but Wendy's display of true love only made Marcia angrier at Devon for hurting their daughter. Marcia knew she was wrong to feel that he did not deserve their forgiveness, but for now, that's how she felt. After all the heartache Devon had caused her, he now compounded it by breaking their daughter's heart. And she didn't agree that being with his mother should have taken priority over being at their daughter's graduation ceremony.

Devon kept calling until he caught her off guard later the next day. Wendy had gone to work and Marcia answered the phone, just in case Wendy was the one calling.

"Marcia, it's me Devon. Please don't hang up."

"Wendy isn't here right now. I'll tell her that you called."

"Wait. I wanted to talk to you."

"Save your breath, Devon. There is nothing that you could say to me to make up for your absence yesterday. You should have been here. End of story."

"Listen, please. This isn't easy for me, you know. What would you have done in my situation?" he asked. "An only child whose father died and his mother has a nervous breakdown on the day of his daughter's graduation."

"I would not have hesitated to be there for my child. Children are dependent. They need their parents. Adults can find their way."

"So, you're telling me that if, God forbid, you lost your Uncle Trevor, and Aunt Pat needed you the way my mother needs me right now, that you would have no problem leaving her?"

His example struck a chord with Marcia. Now, the choice didn't seem so easy. The decision no longer seemed clear cut.

She didn't answer, but he could hear her breathing. "Marcia, my mother is an emotional basket case right now. She drove her car off the road two nights ago. By some miracle of God, she didn't get hurt. Then, she was prescribed medication and overdosed yesterday morning making her violently ill. I don't know what would have happened to her if I hadn't been at the house. I don't want Wendy to know all these details because I think it will only hurt her more, but I couldn't leave Mommy without fearing that I would have another parent to bury when I got back."

"How is she now?" Marcia asked, shaken by the details Devon just shared.

"Still depressed."

"Why didn't you call sooner? We were expecting you all day, believing that sooner or later, you'd get here."

"I'm sorry. I should have called earlier. I spent the morning reacting to what was happening here. But I'm guilty of waiting longer than I needed to call because I was afraid to hear how much I had hurt Wendy. And I knew you would be mad at me, but I'm asking you to try to understand. I really need your forgiveness."

"And Wendy really needed her father at her graduation. Actually, no she didn't," Marcia lashed out at him. She felt unable to control her desire to hurt him for the way that he had hurt them. "You have never been there for her and she has done well this far in life, so I don't know why we brainwashed ourselves into thinking she needs you now."

Devon gasped, but he didn't try to defend himself. He was defenseless against the truth. "You're right," he said. "I'll talk to you later."

Tears stung his eyes as he hung up the phone. He didn't have time for this. He had a hotel to run, his father's affairs to attend to, and a mother to keep on a discreet suicide watch. He said a simple, silent prayer, "Lord, help me," and threw himself into his work.

Wendy spoke to her father every day, but instead of joining him in Jamaica for the summer as they had initially discussed, she used the credit card he had given her to buy a round trip ticket to Africa. She found information on a web site on the Internet and made arrangements to spend time with a host family while doing volunteer work in a community there. The next day, she broke the news to Paul while he was walking her home from work.

"You're joking, right?" Paul asked, as he stopped in his tracks and turned to face her.

"No. I'm serious. I was thinking about this for a few days, and last night I was up late surfing the Internet when I decided to use my credit card to charge the ticket."

"You can't go to Africa without me."

"What do you mean? This does not interfere with our plans. At least I'll be able to bring you feedback. This can help us prepare for our life together there."

"Why didn't you tell me this before, Wendy? Why didn't you tell me you were thinking of doing this?"

"I don't know. I have been doing a lot of soul searching lately. I haven't talked to anyone about it. It's hard to explain what I'm feeling. I just need to do this. I need this time alone."

"We are supposed to get married this summer."

"Pastor won't marry us yet. He has told us that much."

"There is always City Hall."

"Paul, that is not what we planned."

"No. Life is not happening according to our plan, or what we thought was God's plan for us. I know that's why you're upset. Ever since your father missed graduation, you've been so withdrawn."

Tears filled Wendy's eyes. "I thought he would be there. I was sure that he would be there. That's the reason God brought Daddy into our lives at this time, wasn't it? He should have been at my graduation and he should have given me to you in marriage this summer." Tears streamed down her face.

Paul swallowed hard and wetness seeped at the corners of his eyes. "It's like he came along and spoiled everything."

Wendy shook her head. "Don't blame Daddy. I think we were a little hasty, that's all."

"What are you saying? That you don't want to marry me anymore."

"I do, but we have to wait. We can't get married without the blessings of our parents and Pastor. I don't think God wants us to do that."

Paul sighed. "I love you so much. I want to marry you. I don't need to wait another ten months or ten years to figure that out. I have never been interested in any other girl. I don't even want to spend the next few weeks without you. Please don't go to Africa without me."

"I paid two thousand dollars for the ticket. It's non-refundable."

"Two thousand dollars! Where did you get that kind of money? Oh, I know, Daddy, of course." Paul shook his head and started to walk away. He couldn't compete, and he was tired of trying to measure up to Devon.

"Paul, please understand why I need to do this."

He turned to face her again. "I don't understand you anymore," he said softly. "The Wendy I know and love wouldn't impulsively spend two thousand dollars like that, but then again, my Wendy didn't have that kind of money. The Wendy I know would have asked me what I thought before she made a decision like that. My Wendy cares about me." Paul swallowed hard, but met her gaze.

Wendy stepped forward and reached out to touch his cheek. "I do care about you. I love you." She sniffled.

"We are supposed to go to Africa together, as husband and wife. That's our dream, God's plan for our life together." Tears seeped from his eyes.

"Is it?" Wendy cried harder now.

Paul felt powerless to convince her. He had no money. All the money he was earning from his summer job would go toward his college expenses. He was hoping to scrape together an extra five hundred dollars to join her while she was in Jamaica visiting her father. He had learned about an organization there where he could stay and volunteer his services feeding and caring for the poor. He had not told her of his plans yet because he wasn't sure he would have enough money, and he didn't want her to be disappointed if he couldn't go. Now, it no longer mattered. He had been worried about her, when she hadn't given his feelings any thought. Was it Wendy, or the situation, that was undermining his manhood?

When he spoke, he tried to exercise control over the one thing that remained in his grasp. "I love you, Wendy, but if you can't wait for me, I can't promise that I'll be here waiting for you when you get back."

Wendy gasped. They were standing on one corner of the intersection at the end of the block where she lived. Tears were streaming down her face, as she extended her hands toward him and then withdrew it. "That's not fair."

He said nothing, but continued to look at her.

"You understand me better than anyone else, Paul. I need you… I need you to support me on this."

He shook his head. His voice was hoarse when he spoke. "You know me well enough to know why I can't. It's like you're breaking us apart. We are supposed to do this together."

She was weeping now and he hugged her. Standing on the street corner with cars passing by them, he held her. Neither of them noticed whether there were any pedestrians around. After a while, she pulled away.

"I am going to Africa," she whispered.

He nodded and wore a serious look on his face. "Okay." A pause and then, "I'll wait here until you get inside your house."

"I love you, Paul."

"I love you too, Wendy."

"Call me when you get home please."

He nodded. Standing on the street corner on one side of the intersection, he watched her until she entered her front door. She paused to wave to him before she went inside. Then, he crossed the street and walked in the opposite direction. Each step brought him farther away from her, into a new phase in their lives.

Wendy left for Africa in the beginning of July. This time, Marcia drove to the airport with Uncle Trevor, after Paul politely declined to go with them. Aunt Pat lectured them before they left, calling Wendy's decision to travel alone to an unfamiliar place "sheer madness" and saying that her mother was equally crazy to allow her to go. Aunt Pat finally acquiesced after Uncle Trevor insisted that they needed to let the youth find their own way. Devon also opposed the trip, but he was powerless to influence his daughter from Jamaica, and her mother was still not responding to his phone calls.

CHAPTER NINETEEN

He couldn't believe that she was gone. Paul banged the keys of the piano sounding out his loneliness and frustration to an empty apartment. For the first time in his life, Wendy wasn't just a phone call away. He'd had a feeling that ever since Wendy found her father things had changed between them, but he hadn't expected this. Africa was their dream, God's plan for their lives, something they were to experience together. He felt both hurt and angry that Wendy had gone ahead of him.

He spent the first couple weeks after graduation working, but the job wasn't giving him enough hours. He needed to get away from everything that reminded him of Wendy. He got up from the piano and stared out the front window trying to imagine where she was at that moment, and wondered whether she missed him as much as he missed her. Had he left Wendy like this, he knew she would be crying, but instead she'd left him, and he wouldn't cry—not anymore anyway. He prayed for her, and about his own bitter feelings because he knew that he had no choice but to forgive her. He was about to give in to the urge to just run away when the phone rang.

"Paul, this is Reverend Walker."

"Hello, Reverend Walker. What's up?"

"I just got a call from Michael Morrison, the young man we were trying to put you and Wendy in touch with, who goes to the college you'll be attending."

"Yes, Pastor."

"Well, he is in his senior year now. He lives in an apartment near the college campus, and he plays in a band. One of their band members had a motorcycle accident and is in the hospital. They're not sure when he'll be on his feet again, but Michael wants to know if you can fill in for him."

"Yes!" Paul said emphatically without taking time to think about his answer.

Reverend Walker chuckled. He knew Paul had been pining over Wendy like a lovesick puppy, so when Michael proposed the idea, he expected that Paul would accept. "You can live with him until school opens and you move into the dorms. The gigs pay, but not much, but all the retail stores there are hiring, so you shouldn't have a hard time getting a summer job."

"Yes!"

"He's expecting you to call him." Reverend Walker gave Paul the number.

"Thank you, God!" Paul shouted when he hung up with Reverend Walker. "Thank you! Thank you!"

A week later Madge Chambers struggled to hold back the tears as she said goodbye to her only child. Paul's decision to move away now cut short the time she'd have preferred having to prepare herself to let him go.

"If Wendy were here, I don't think you'd be leaving." Madge noticed that Paul was wearing the navy blue and white Yankees baseball cap that Wendy had bought him along with an accompanying jersey.

"But she isn't, is she, Mom?"

"No, but I hope you're not doing this just to get back at her."

"Mom, this is a great opportunity."

"Did you tell Wendy?"

"I haven't spoken to her."

"There was another message from her on the machine."

"I heard it. It's not my fault I keep missing her phone calls. And she's never left a number where I can reach her."

"The message said there is no phone where she's staying."

"I know. I know."

"You two children love each other so much. Does this mean that you're breaking up?"

"We already broke up, Ma. Our relationship was over when she boarded that plane to Africa."

"I don't believe that." Madge stared directly into her son's eyes, and she could see the pain there, behind his tough façade. "I'm going to miss having you around."

"I know." He hugged her.

Madge squeezed him tightly. "Is there anything you don't know, young man?"

"Lots. That's why I'm going to try to get me a college education." Paul grinned at her.

She smiled and tried again to hold back the tears.

Paul picked up his backpack and oversize duffel bag. He planned to ride the subway into the city and catch another train out to the college-town where Michael would pick him up.

The moment he left, Madge dialed Marcia's number. She needed a shoulder to cry on and she knew Marcia would relate to what she was feeling right now.

Paul wasn't at the airport when Wendy arrived from Africa. Wendy was disappointed but not shocked that Paul wasn't standing with their mothers as she approached them after she disembarked the plane. She hadn't spoken to him in four weeks, and she guessed that he would be upset, but she prayed that he'd understand. She'd tried to reach him many times, calling both his cell and house phone numbers, but he was never available.

"Praise God you're home safely," her mother said, locking Wendy in a tight embrace.

"Welcome home," Madge greeted Wendy as she turned to hug her too.

"I'm happy to be home. Praise the Lord. Where's Paul?"

Both mothers exchanged glances. Neither one had wanted to break the news about Paul moving away to Wendy over the phone.

Wendy didn't miss the look they shared. "Is Paul okay?"

"Yes. Paul is fine," Madge reassured her. "And you know he loves you very much."

"But?" Wendy asked, waiting to hear the reason for his absence. "Is he at work?"

"Yes," both mothers answered, seeming almost relieved to have Wendy provide the explanation.

Wendy shrugged, puzzled by their behavior. Then, she started walking with them to the area of the airport where she would retrieve her luggage.

"You lost weight," Marcia commented.

"You look good though, but slim. How was the food over there?" Madge asked.

Wendy smiled. She followed along with their line of questioning as they picked up her bags and made their way to the car. The moment they were all seated in the car together, she switched the subject back to Paul.

"Paul is still mad at me, right? That's why he didn't come to the airport and didn't answer my phone calls." She longed to see him and felt certain that once he saw her again, he would let go off any negative feelings he had about her trip. Plus, there was so much she wanted to tell him about the places she'd been, the people she'd met, and the things she'd seen that would help them plan more realistically for their future together. "Let's drive by his job so I can surprise him."

"Paul changed jobs, honey," Madge said, meeting Wendy's eyes in the rearview mirror of the car. "He got an offer to play in a band with Michael Morrison, so he moved out to Michael's apartment and got a job in retail nearby."

Wendy's mouth hung open. Then she demanded to know, "When did this happen?"

"About two weeks ago."

"Mommy, you couldn't tell me?"

Wendy's mother turned to face her from the front passenger seat. "We knew you'd be upset, so we tried not to worry you while you were so far away."

Wendy pulled out her cell phone and dialed Paul's number. His voicemail picked up. "Hey, Paul. It's Wendy. I'm back. I miss you. Call me back, okay?" She tried to sound upbeat, but as she hung up the phone and stared out the window, tears threatened to fill her eyes.

Paul didn't return Wendy's call. His mother fussed at him because she didn't agree with his behavior. She reminded him of how he was always striving to live righteously and told him that Jesus wouldn't agree with his behavior. Still Paul refused to call Wendy or to answer her incoming calls.

After trying to reach him for a few days, Wendy hung up the phone one evening and started to cry. When her mother walked into the bedroom and saw her, the look on her face just made Wendy cry harder.

Marcia held Wendy as she sobbed brokenheartedly, and as Marcia tried to console her, an image of Marcia's own mother came to mind.

Marcia pulled back and looked at the tears streaming down Wendy's face. Wendy's shoulders shook as she sobbed. Marcia said out loud the Bible verses about the peace of God that her own mother had shared with her. Those words were one of her dearest memories of her mother.

In many ways, Ruth lived on in Wendy. Wendy's passion for Jesus Christ was just one trait she shared with her maternal grandmother.

Gradually, Wendy's sobs lessened and she calmed down.

"I know how you feel," Marcia told her.

Wendy looked back at her thinking her mother had no clue.

"Believe it or not, I was once your age too, and sadly enough, I was just as brokenhearted."

"Because of daddy?"

Marcia nodded, but she didn't want to sully Wendy's thoughts of her father. "Yes, but look how things turned out. God brought Devon back into my life, and look how much he has done to show us how much he loves us."

Wendy nodded. "Do you still love him?"

Marcia nodded. She didn't need to hear Wendy ask her why she hadn't answered or returned Devon's phone calls. Marcia had been treating Devon exactly the way that Paul was treating Wendy. "I'll call him tonight," Marcia said. "Sometimes, we have to go backward in order to move forward."

Later that night, when Wendy was asleep, Marcia picked up the phone to dial Devon's number. "Let love be without hypocrisy," was the piece of Scripture that spoke to her at that moment. The last thing she wanted to do was admit that she was a hypocrite. A Bible toting, scripture quoting Christian who had not acted Christ-like toward the man she loved. She credited her own survival to the fact that God had forgiven her, and shown her grace and mercy. She also considered herself righteous enough to lead others to the Lord, yet when it came time for her to display the Holy Spirit working within her, she failed to react with faithfulness, gentleness, and self control.

In her heart, she said a silent prayer, but she knew that repenting before God was not enough. She dialed Devon's number.

Devon answered the phone on the second ring.

"Hello." He sounded sleepy.

Marcia's eyes widened as she noted the time displayed on her digital alarm clock in her room. "I'm sorry. I didn't realize it was two o' clock in the morning."

"Marcia?" Devon sounded fully awake now.

"Yes, it's me," she whispered.

"Is everything okay?" Devon sat up in his bed.

"Yes. I... I wanted to know how you are doing?"

He exhaled. "I'm fine." Silence and then, "Say something, please, so I know I'm not dreaming."

"You're not dreaming. Ah... Did you talk to Wendy recently?"

"Yes, she told me about what's happening with her and Paul."

"Will you be here to help us move her belongings over to the college?"

Devon's heart raced. Up until that moment, he had not known Marcia would welcome him. "I want to be there."

She knew the cause of his hesitation. "How is your mother?"

"Marcia, she is wasting away. Is that what it means to truly love someone? It's like she gave up on living when my father died. I just see this void when I look into her eyes. She hasn't done anything else to harm herself, but she isn't healing either. Her grief is as raw as it was on the day she lost her husband."

Marcia gasped. "Jesus!"

"Yeah. If only she had Jesus. I know she'd be better off. I'm experiencing His strength for myself right now."

"Wow!"

"I'm so glad you called. There is so much that I want to tell you that I can't tell anyone else."

"Wait, Devon." She paused. "I love you so much. You're not even waiting for me to apologize. I'm talking to you now for the first time in weeks, and here you are acting like I never hurt you, like I am your best friend."

She could picture him smiling as she heard his breath escape his lips.

"You are my best friend. You understand me like no one else I've ever met," he said.

"But I still owe you an apology. I'm sorry for being so insensitive. It was hard enough to lose your father, without me getting on your case."

"I deserved it."

"No, you didn't. Don't ever say that. There is no doubt in my mind that you love Wendy and wanted nothing more than to be at her graduation. It's unfortunate that things didn't work out that way, but I'm proud of you for standing by your mother when she needed you so desperately. You probably saved her life."

"Praise God."

"There is more. I didn't stand by you. Let's say I could learn a lot about forgiveness from our daughter."

"She is special."

"And so are you, Devon. I'm sorry I hurt you."

A pause and then he said, "I wish you were here. I need to take you in my arms right now. To look into your eyes and tell you how much I love you, how empty my life feels without you. I need you, Marcia. I can live without you because God is carrying me, but I don't want to."

Tears streamed down Marcia's face. "What do you want me to do?"

"Come see me."

"What do you mean?"

"Come to Jamaica. I don't care if you stay for a day, a week, or for an hour. I just need to see you and I can't come to you right now. Please say you'll come."

"Okay."

"Yes!" Devon jumped out of bed. "I could get you on a flight later."

Marcia giggled. "I can't come immediately. Wendy is back, remember?"

"Bring her with you."

"She needs to tie up loose ends here and get ready to move. Give me a few days to spend with her and then I'll come spend a week with you there."

"Yes! Hallelujah! Marcia, you don't know how much this means to me."

"I do."

On the night before Marcia left for Jamaica, Wendy offered her some tips. "Mommy, if you do nothing else while you're in Jamaica, make sure you visit Dunn's River Falls, go sailing on a glass bottom boat, and go white water rafting."

"Yes, Ma'am." Marcia smiled at her daughter who was lying on the bed. She'd slept little during the days leading up to her trip to Jamaica.

She tried to spend as much time as she could with Wendy, realizing that these were days of letting go. Her job as Wendy's primary caregiver was over. Although she would never stop being a parent, she no longer had a youngster to worry about. Wendy was now a young adult who was making decisions independently. The trip to Africa was Wendy's most radical decision yet, creating the longest separation she had ever had from her family and her boyfriend.

"I know you know all about Jamaica because you grew up there, but it has been almost two decades since you left," Wendy reminded her mother.

"You're right. I'm sure a lot has changed since then. Now, are you sure you don't want to come with me? If the flight isn't full, we could still get you on."

"I'm sure. You and daddy need this time together. I hope you'll decide to make us a complete family." She also hoped that a happy ending for her parents would have a spillover effect and would bring about a happy ending in her and Paul's relationship.

"Honey, for now, we're just friends. Okay?"

"Good friends, I hope. You'll need someone to take care of you when I'm gone to college."

"I can take care of myself, young lady."

"Yes, I know. But it's nice to be loved."

"It sure is."

CHAPTER TWENTY

A wave of heat engulfed Marcia as she stepped off the plane at Sangster International Airport in Montego Bay. She entered the terminal, retrieved her luggage, and queued up with the visitors to pass through customs. The customs officer took her American passport, glanced at her picture, then back at her and stamped it.

"Welcome to Jamaica," he said.

"Thanks," she replied. Without further comment, she picked up her suitcase and travel documents and followed the crowd heading outside. She politely refused to have any of the porters carry her luggage.

As she exited through sliding doors, pulling her luggage onto the pavement, assertive men swarmed around her offering, "Taxi, nice lady?"

A bronze arm reached forward grabbing her suitcase, and she gasped as she felt someone's palm against her lower back.

"I'm here, babe." It was Devon.

She smiled up at him and he kissed her lightly on the lips, before steering her toward where he was parked.

"Welcome home," he said, as he placed her suitcase inside the trunk of his car, closed it and turned to face her.

"I can't believe I'm actually here."

"Believe it," he said, pulling her into his arms.

Hot air fanned their faces as they held each other. Moments later, Marcia pulled back to look around her, surveying the tropical landscape adorned with palm trees and colorful flowers. Lavender morning glory bowed its head beneath the afternoon sun, which mirrored the brilliant yellow of the marigold, and beamed down on the radiant red of the hibiscus. Hardly a cloud dotted the clear blue sky as another plane came in for landing over crystal clear waters. The mountains covered with thick green foliage interrupted by a few buildings formed a backdrop to one side.

"It's even more beautiful here than I remembered."

Devon held the passenger door open for her and said colloquially, "Ah nuh nutten."

"Devon Douglas, since when do you speak patois?" Marcia asked, knitting her brows at him.

"This is nothing. You have not yet begun to explore our beautiful island."

He switched on the ignition and turned down the radio, but left it playing loudly enough so that in between their conversation, Marcia could listen to a local talk program. He was grinning from ear to ear.

Marcia laughed. "So this is what it means when Mommy used to say, 'Your glad bag burst.'"

Devon chuckled. "No, actually. She didn't sound so refined. She used to say, 'You glad bag bus'.' A wha' do you? You nuh 'member how fi chat patios? A twang you deh twang? A must foreign you just come from."

Laughing out loud, Marcia corrected him. "My mother may not have been an educated woman, but she did not sound like that."

Devon sobered a little, but still smiled as he said, "Seriously though, if you don't want to pay inflated tourist prices for everything while you're here, you better find your Jamaican accent. Just because you're a naturalized American citizen doesn't mean you can't sound like a born and bred Jamaican."

They reminisced about their Jamaican childhood as images they passed brought memories to life.

Devon pointed to the vendors selling fruits on the side of the road. "The mango sweet eh man," Devon commented colloquially. "Watch him." A satisfied customer peeled a mango with his teeth and sucked all the orange-colored fruit from the inside until the mango seed was bare.

Devon pulled over in another area and purchased pepper-shrimp.

"You remembered," Marcia stated as she took a small bag of the spicy seafood from him, appreciating that he had not forgotten how much she loved them.

"As if I could forget anything about you," Devon replied smugly.

"Then you know that I'm not going to even taste this until I get some coconut water."

"Of course." Devon stopped the car again, this time to purchase two coconuts. The vendor chopped off the top of each coconut with his machete revealing holes from which they gulped down a cool drink of coconut water.

"Let's just eat the shrimps here," Marcia suggested.

"Like old times," Devon remembered.

Marcia nodded, biting a chunk of pepper-shrimp and pealing off the remainder of the shell.

"Hot and spicy?" Devon asked.

"Just right," Marcia replied. "Eat some."

Once they'd drained the last of coconut water from each coconut, they handed them back to the vendor who chopped each one in half. He handed their coconuts back to them with a piece of the husk to use to spoon out the jelly.

"Delicious," Marcia observed as she savored the first mouthful.

"When was the last time you had a snack like this?" Devon asked.

"Right before we graduated from high school," Marcia replied, but she smiled realizing that the memories no longer hurt.

Devon pulled up in front of his family's hotel and gave his car keys to a valet. Built above cream-colored sand, there was only a single, broad, six-story building on the two hundred acre property now, but Devon planned to fulfill his father's dream of developing a massive resort. Much of the property remained undeveloped and guests enjoyed tours through its natural tropical foliage on horseback, but construction was scheduled to begin soon on two dozen three-bedroom to seven-bedroom villas. There was just one large swimming pool now, but the more upscale villas would have their own pool, each with private access. Tennis and golf were among the sports offered, but many guests preferred water sports or simply relaxing on the beach.

Devon introduced her to the workers as he showed her around. "Did you decide yet if you're going to stay here or at the house with Mommy and me?"

"I'd like to stay here if you don't mind. During the time I lived in Jamaica, I never had the chance to stay in a hotel."

Devon checked her in and asked one of the workers to take her luggage to her room. Then, he got called away for a quick meeting.

Marcia took her tote bag to a restroom and changed into a swimsuit. She walked onto the beach, rested her bag on a lounge chair, and ran into the sparkling waters of the Caribbean Sea. She splashed and played and swam with the carefree joy of a child.

Unsure of how much time had passed, she finally noticed Devon watching her from the shore.

She beckoned for him to join her.

He smoothed his hands over his white shirt and khaki shorts. Then he tipped his straw hat and bowed slightly and extended a towel toward her.

Marcia laughed and slowly walked toward him.

"I don't need that," she said and hung the towel around his neck. She preferred to let her body air dry in the heat of the sun.

Devon chuckled.

Hand in hand, they walked along the shore, each one silently saying a prayer of thanksgiving. Neither of them had imagined that a day like this would come. Both of them felt like there was no place else they'd rather be.

Marcia marveled at their footprints in the sand and thought of the famous poem that spoke of the Lord's footprints being the only one there because He carried her when she couldn't carry herself.

"As my mommy would say: Praise the Lord! Hallelujah! Thank you, Jesus!"

Devon looked at her and smiled. "Amen."

As they strolled along, Marcia said, "Wendy made me promise to take a ride on one of those glass-bottom boats."

"Oh yeah. We did that with my parents when Wendy was here. Do you want to go now?" Devon asked.

Marcia shook her head. "Later," Marcia replied, feeling content to walk hand in hand with him on the beach. The ebb and flow of the sea caressed their feet.

"I'll take you to that church over there on Sunday," Devon said.

Marcia noticed the building across the water with the cross of Jesus in front. "I can't wait. Is that where you worship?"

"Sometimes. Mommy is a member of another church up in the hills, so I go with her there when she goes, but she hasn't gone for a while. We should encourage her to come with us when we have dinner with her tonight."

Marcia nodded, and then exclaimed as she saw someone on horseback riding toward them.

After talking to the rider who was a worker from the hotel, Devon told her that he needed to head back. "You could stay longer if you'd like."

"No thanks. It's about time for me to see my hotel room."

Marcia's mouth fell open as she entered her hotel room. Positioned against one wall was a canopied four-poster king size bed. The room was spacious, painted peach with a plush sofa and television in a seating area against another wall. But it was the vista that caught her attention. She opened twin glass doors onto the balcony and gasped as she looked down at the beach. Her view of the sea extended for miles. She said a prayer of thanksgiving and stood there mesmerized watching guests enjoy windsurfing, parasailing, swimming, and sunbathing. Eventually, she went inside, showered and stretched out on the bed, where she drifted off to sleep.

Devon lived on a hillside, away from the commercial hustle and bustle of the tourist district. There were few houses in the area, each tucked away amid acres of fertile land. He drove up to a large iron gate and stopped to talk with the guard who opened it for him.

As they entered the driveway, Marcia commented, "Twenty-four hour security."

"Overnight. Mommy feels safer having him out here since my father died."

"I see," Marcia nodded.

Devon drove his BMW up the driveway pass a cluster of trees, which formed a green background on their left. To their right, Marcia looked downhill at the ocean and skyline, which radiated brilliant blue through the trees. The Douglas family's sprawling two-story concrete and steel house loomed up ahead. The bay windows at the front of the house provided a panoramic snapshot of the horizon.

Marcia climbed out of the car, overcome by a wave of nostalgia. She remembered what the house looked like on the inside. Paintings of outdoor Jamaican marketplaces, rural wood houses, and farm life hung on the walls throughout the foyer. During the daytime, sunlight beamed directly into the room through the convex glass ceiling covering the second floor. An open staircase led up to that level which housed five bedrooms and three bathrooms. One room was Devon's, the room where Wendy was conceived.

Marcia approached the house slowly, hesitant at first. The emotional conflict she had struggled with as a teenager resurfaced. She should have been able to call this place home because she had grown up there, but she only enjoyed that privilege because it was her mother's workplace, and her employer was kind enough to let Marcia live there too. Such an arrangement for a domestic helper's child was rare, if not unique. The bedroom she and her mother slept in was not on the second floor with the others; it was on the first floor behind the kitchen and laundry rooms. As Marcia entered the house, she almost expected to find her mother there, dusting the Douglas family's fine mahogany furniture or sweeping the floor.

Devon reached for her hand.

"Relax," he said. "I'm so happy you're here."

Her tension eased at his touch. Confidence and peace replaced her feelings of sadness, nervousness, and uncertainty about meeting Mrs. Douglas.

"Mommy, we're here," Devon called out, raising his voice.

They heard the click of heels against the ceramic tile floor and a petite lady appeared. Mrs. Douglas had been a dancer when Devon's father first met her in New York, and she still stood tall, her posture ramrod straight. Silver hair shone where it had once been jet black. She wore her hair pulled back to reveal high cheekbones and slim features. Her poise and vigor belied her sixty-five years.

"Good evening, Mrs. Douglas," Marcia said softly.

"Marcia Tapper. As I live and breathe." Mrs. Douglas opened her arms wide and wrapped Marcia in a tight embrace, kissing her hard on the cheek. "I didn't know I'd live to ever see you again. Let me look at you." She gestured toward Marcia with one hand and Marcia twirled in front of her. "Lovely. If your mother could see you now…" Her words brought tears to their eyes. "It is so good to see you. Welcome home."

"Thank you. It is good to see you too, Mrs. Douglas. Thank you for having me." The affectionate greeting moved Marcia. She had remembered Devon's mother as being too sophisticated for such a demonstrative display.

Marcia's only regret at that moment was that she couldn't also hug her mother. Ruth had been like a fixture in that house and Marcia kept expecting her to appear.

Devon placed one arm around his mother and the other around Marcia and guided them toward the dining room. "Ladies, this way please." He appeared unaffected by the poignant moment, but it affirmed that he needed to have Marcia as his wife. She belonged here with him, and he took the fact that his mother had welcomed her so warmly to mean that she would agree.

Marcia looked for her mother's face as the housekeeper turned to face them, but a stranger's eyes briefly met hers.

"This is Dottie," Devon said. "She replaced your mother."

Marcia blinked back tears.

Dottie led them into the dining room where the walls stood two stories high, with glass windows covering all of one side. In the center sat a cherry wood table with twelve chairs above an area rug. Suspended from the ceiling above the table hung a crystal chandelier.

Devon said grace before they sat down to dinner and talked about old times. As they shared fond memories, talk of Wendy brought laughter to his mother's lips. Devon felt certain he saw a glimmer of hope in his mother's eyes.

"Marcia, your daughter is truly delightful. I wish you'd convinced her to come with you."

"I tried, but you know she just returned from Africa, and she's leaving for college soon."

"Yes, yes. She filled me in on the phone. I must tell you in person that I'm proud of you for raising her as you have."

"Praise the Lord." Marcia humbly accepted the compliment.

After dinner, they moved into the family room where Marcia was first to start perusing old photo albums looking for pictures of her mother. Mr. and Mrs. Douglas' wedding album was among the stack. Marcia glanced from Devon to his mother before she opened that one.

"Bring it here," Mrs. Douglas said. "I've been afraid to look at it since

I lost my husband." She patted the space beside her on the settee for Marcia to sit down. "Have you ever looked at these, D?" she asked her son.

"Not recently, Mommy."

She waved him over to sit next to her on the other side. As they looked at the pictures, Mrs. Douglas talked about how she and her husband met and fell in love. In less than six months after she had met Devon's father, she went from being her daddy's girl to being Mrs. Donovan Douglas. She defied her father by marrying so soon after she had met Devon's father, but she never regretted it.

Devon's father turned out to be a one-man woman. He had grown up witnessing the heartache his own father, Mass Dev, inflicted on his mother with his repeated extramarital affairs. He made up his mind that he would protect his wife and children from that kind of distress. Devon's parents were best friends, loyal lovers, and confidential companions until they were parted by his father's death.

"I don't think I can go on without him," Mrs. Douglas said, sobbing, as tears streamed down her cheeks.

Devon wrapped an arm around her and Marcia handed her a tissue from a box on the coffee table.

"I know it hurts, Mrs. Douglas. I can only imagine what a blessing it was to have a husband who loved you so much. I'm sure he wouldn't want you to stop living because he passed on first."

"We were one, Marcia." She sobbed. "Do you know what it is to find the one person in this world who completes you?"

Marcia glanced over at Devon, who was looking directly at her.

"I think she does," he said.

"I'm alone in this world without my husband. He was my strength, my inspiration, my reason for living. There is nothing here for me now."

"You have your son," Marcia said.

"Of course. Thank God for him." She clasped Devon's hand in hers. "And his love alone has sustained me since his father died."

Marcia knelt down before them. "Mrs. Douglas, if I may."

The older woman looked at her son, then back at Marcia. She nodded but a puzzled look wrinkled her face.

"You said thank God, just now, Mrs. Douglas. Do you believe in God?" asked Marcia.

"Of course."

"Do you believe that Jesus is Lord and Savior?"

"I understand why some people feel they need a Savior."

"Sometimes, it takes losing everything you thought was important to realize that Jesus loves you and He's always there. His love alone can sustain you. Mrs. Douglas, your husband loved you very much, but he was not your Savior. Your life can go on without him."

Mrs. Douglas shook her head. "You don't know what you're saying."

"Mommy," Devon interjected and held her hand.

"Your son loves you dearly too, but he is not your Savior." Marcia paused to choose her words carefully. "Mrs. Douglas, if your parents had expected you to sustain them, if they had relied as heavily on you, like they couldn't live without your constant presence, they would have prevented you from fulfilling your role as wife and mother. Devon is here for you, but you have to also stand on your own."

"I can't." Mrs. Douglas inhaled shakily and her voice was feeble.

"With Jesus Christ you can. I know you don't understand yet, but all I can tell you is that without Jesus as the source of my strength, I would have died a long time ago."

Mrs. Douglas gasped. "Don't say that."

"It's true. When I found out I was pregnant with Wendy, I couldn't face my mother. I couldn't face you, after the way I let you down. I had nowhere else to go and I had no money. Then, when Mommy died, I felt like it was my fault. I thought I didn't deserve to live. I was that weak, that unsure and pessimistic about the future." She paused. This was the first time she had discussed that period of her life without crying. "In the absence of faith, there is suicide, and a whole lot of other ways of giving up, but a little bit of faith gave me hope that as I lived each day, things would get better. By some strange miracle, I cried and I prayed and trusted in God and He brought me through to this day when here I am in front of you."

Mrs. Douglas leaned forward to touch Marcia's cheek. "You've been through a lot, dear. You've grown up to be a strong woman."

Marcia shook her head. "No, not at all. Devon can tell you, I'm a big crybaby. Jesus. He is the source of my strength."

"Pray for me, please," whispered Mrs. Douglas.

The three of them joined hands. Marcia prayed asking God to help them feel His presence and to help them know Him like they have never known Him before. She quoted Philippians, chapter four, verse thirteen, "I can do all things through Christ who strengthens me."

At the end of the prayer, she stood up and hugged Mrs. Douglas. "There was a song that kept me going after Mommy died. It's based on that scripture. The chorus says, 'His strength is perfect when our strength is gone. He carries us when we can't carry on. Raised in His power the weak become strong. His strength is perfect. His strength is perfect.' I'll have to get you a copy of the CeCe Winans' CD that it's on."

Mrs. Douglas wiped a tear and smiled at Marcia. "Thank you, my daughter. Thank you."

Devon escorted his mother up to her room, leaving Marcia to wander around the house.

"God works in mysterious ways, son. Marcia is everything I would have wanted her to be, and much more, even though she didn't do things my way."

"Why did you care so much, Mommy? You're the only person I've ever met who has done so much for your domestic helper's child."

Mrs. Douglas thought quietly for a moment. "Someone saw talent in me and paid for my education when I was young. His only request was that if I ever had the opportunity to help someone else, I should do it."

"What if, Mommy? What if you had known then that I was the father of Marcia's baby?"

"I don't know, Dev. I would have been disappointed at first. I love you both so much, I would think you were throwing your lives away by not waiting to become so intimately involved. Some things are worth waiting for, and I wish you and Marcia had waited."

"Would you have been opposed to us having a relationship?"

"Hmm. You always considered her as your sister, so knowing that you had a romantic interest in her would have taken some getting used to. But I think your father and I would have accepted it. She was as cultured and intelligent as any of the girls you brought home, and far more kindhearted. Once she completed her education, I think even your father would have approved. Come to think of it, your father and I tried so hard to have more children. Perhaps, we might even have considered adopting Wendy and raising her as our own."

Her words stimulated feelings of remorse as Devon realized that back then, he would have pressured Marcia not to have his baby, without even thinking of how many failed attempts his parents had made to provide him with siblings. He praised God that things turned out the way they did. Praise God for Marcia and Wendy.

He cleared his throat and spoke in a hushed voice. "And now, Mommy?"

"That's up to you. Not many people remain as devoted to each other as your father and I were. I would love for you and Marcia to experience that. If my parents had leaned on me the way I've been leaning on you, it would have put a great strain on my marriage." She sighed. "Thanks for all you've done, son. Marcia's words were not lost on me tonight. It's not going to be easy, but I know that, somehow, I'm going to be okay. There is a mother and daughter out there who need you more than I do."

Her son towered over her as she held him.

"Go now," she said, giving him a gentle shove.

"Thanks, Mommy."

Devon found Marcia standing on the back porch overlooking the swimming pool.

"I see you've made some changes," she said, turning to face him, as she heard his footsteps approaching. She waved her hand toward the deck that was lit up with fluorescent lights.

"Yes. I like to swim at night, so I had the pool enclosed." He slid one arm around her waist. Their bodies were close, sides touching. As he stared into her eyes, he felt overcome by emotion.

"Marry me, Marcia." His proposal took both of them by surprise. Then, Devon got down on one knee, determined to do this right. "Marcia Angelique Tapper, will you marry me?"

Marcia closed her eyes tightly. Devon's proposal was her teenage fantasy fulfilled. She should be ecstatic, but she was not. She believed that Devon really loved her, but the timing wasn't right. Too much had happened too fast. There were too many changes happening in their lives. Marriage was a lifelong commitment and she was afraid that a year from now, when the novelty of their relationship wore off and they settled into the drudgery of daily living, he would revert to his old ways.

Devon's eyes met hers as she opened them. "You're going to turn me down," he said. Devon dropped his head, looking down at the floor. He spoke softly and slowly. "I wouldn't want to marry me either, if I were you, not after all the heartache I caused you."

She placed both her hands on either side of his face, as she sat down. "That's not what I mean."

"Let me guess. You're going to say our relationship is about Wendy. But it's not about Wendy. It's about us: you and me. Long before Wendy was born, you loved me. And, if I'd had any sense back then, I would have realized it and returned your love. I'm not that foolish boy anymore. I love you. All I'm asking is that you give me a chance."

"I do want to marry you," Marcia said, smiling, "just not yet. Not until I finish college. It matters to me that I come to you as an equal."

Devon glanced heavenward and back at her.

She tried to explain further. "It matters to me. I need to complete my education on my own before I marry you. Ask me again in three years, if you still want to marry me."

"Three years!"

"That's when I'll be graduating. It will also give us time to get to know each other again and decide if we are really in this for keeps."

Devon sighed. "Why does what you're saying sound so familiar?"

"It's the same sober advice we gave to our daughter and her boyfriend. Are you ready to practice what you've been preaching?"

"Wendy and Paul are teenagers. We've known each other for a lifetime. We'll be almost forty if we wait as long as you want to get married."

Marcia shrugged.

Devon sighed. "Do you really love me?" he asked.

"You know I always have."

He smiled, more sure of himself, now. He kissed her and then said, "Let me pay for you to go to college full-time. You'll finish in a year or two and we can get married sooner."

"No. I have to do this on my own."

"No more charity," he said with a smirk.

"No more charity," she affirmed.

"You can work at the hotel without pay to pay me back, after we get married," he suggested with a grin. "Deal?"

Marcia looked serious. "Deal."

"Two years is still a long time," he said, returning to his seat beside her. Words his mother uttered earlier echoed in his mind: "Some things are worth waiting for," she had said. "You're worth the wait," Devon told Marcia and kissed her.

On Marcia's last evening on the island, Devon's mother gave her a package to take back to New York for Wendy.

"Thank you," Marcia said, embracing her. "Are you sure you don't want to come with us? Wendy was so excited when we told her that you might be coming."

Mrs. Douglas smiled. "I know. I talked to her earlier today and she was still trying to convince me. But I'll visit her some other time, once she has settled in at the university." She held on to Marcia with one hand and reached for Devon with the other hand. "You and Wendy—the three of you—need this time together as a family."

CHAPTER TWENTY-ONE

Wendy watched for the limousine from the living room window of Blossom's apartment. Finally, there was going to be a wedding in her family, and the bride would travel to the church in grand style. When she and Paul had talked about getting married, they hadn't planned to hire a limousine. They'd wanted a simple ceremony at the church they'd grown up in, surrounded by their relatives and church-family.

From the window, she focused on the corner where she and Paul had stood, a couple years before, when she told him she was planning to travel to Africa. That moment changed everything between them, she remembered. Even though she saw him almost every day during their first two years of college, after her trip to Africa, he treated her like a casual acquaintance instead of his closest friend. Nowadays, he was always with another girl.

The back of her eyes burned, but Wendy refused to cry. It was her parent's wedding day, and she was happy that they were getting married.

"The limousine is here," she announced, as the car she was watching for came into sight. She took one last look at herself in the mirror surveying her straight, ankle-length pink dress with lightweight transparent sleeves shaped like butterfly wings. "Let's go," she added cheerfully, reaching for her matching purse.

Blossom emerged from the bedroom dressed in a violent gown, holding hands with her twin daughters, one on each side. "We're ready! Your father must be anxious by now, given the fact that we're over an hour behind. Come on, Marcia."

Alone in the bedroom, Marcia stared at her reflection. She inhaled deeply, placing a hand on her stomach. Her white silk dress felt soft against her fingers. She closed her eyes. In a few minutes, she would live out her teenage fantasy of marrying Devon Douglas. Again, without realizing it, she'd called the shots. Devon had waited patiently until she was ready to get married. She set the terms and fulfilled them by earning a Bachelor's degree before becoming his wife. She was also the one who insisted that they get married in New York.

Yet, there was one issue over which she was finally ready to surrender control. She looked down at her body, past the sweetheart neckline of her wedding gown. She turned sideways, pressed her hands against her belly and looked in the mirror. She remembered clearly how her belly bulged when she'd been pregnant with Wendy. How alone she'd felt, ashamed and afraid.

Teenage pregnancy was no longer a source of great shame, but she still viewed it as a hindrance that delayed dreams and caused lost opportunities making life more difficult for the young girls who experienced it. Wendy and Desiree were the same age, yet Desiree's pregnancy had set them on divergent paths. Wendy was halfway along the journey to earning a Bachelor's degree. Desiree was taking classes when she could, but she'd had another baby and her baby-daddy Keith had also gotten someone else pregnant.

Marcia thought of herself and Devon and felt thankful that God had brought them to a place of total reconciliation. More than trusting Devon, the decision for her to marry him and possibly have another child meant completely trusting God.

She heard a soft tap at the door.

"Ready, Mommy?"

"Yes, Wendy. Let's go."

Sunshine brightened that clear, cool afternoon. Wendy stood in the doorway of the white church where she and Paul had grown up together, certain that holy matrimony was in God's plans for their lives. She smiled at the usher, but as he took her hand and escorted her down the aisle, her eyes filled with tears. She was ecstatic for her parents but sad for herself. Paul should have been by her side. Even though they hadn't married each other as quickly as they'd planned, he should still have been her date for her parents' wedding. But she could only guess as to his whereabouts at that very moment. She got to the pew where Paul's mother stood taking pictures.

"You're so pretty," Madge Chambers told her and blew her a kiss. Madge regretted that Paul wasn't the young man escorting Wendy down the aisle. She'd called him while she was waiting for the ceremony to begin, and she scolded him again for not accepting the invitation he had received from Wendy's parents.

Wendy smiled back at her and wished the sight of Paul's mother didn't make her want to cry even more. Mrs. Chambers loved her and she knew it. The older woman had told her that she was praying that they would work out their differences, and that Wendy and Paul would still marry each other and give her some grandchildren one day.

Wendy took her place on one side of the altar, while the usher took his place on the other side. Wendy smiled at her grandmother who was seated near the front. She had flown in from Jamaica for the wedding. Devon's mother held a wallet-sized picture of her husband as she watched the proceedings. It was her way of including Devon's father in the ceremony. She still missed him terribly, but she was stronger and felt that he would have been as proud of their son as she was at that moment.

Blossom entered the sanctuary, a striking maid of honor wearing violet. She ran her manicured fingers through her hair and placed her hand in her husband's. Wearing a black tuxedo, Steve escorted his wife down the aisle. As they reached the front of the sanctuary, they turned to face the doorway.

The doors opened revealing their two-year-old daughters dressed in lacy white dresses.

"It's Mommy," shouted one of the twins.

"I see Daddy," the other pointed and waved.

The congregation roared with laughter as the girls raced down the aisle, tossing flower petals from their basket. They met their parents with a high-five, and Blossom and Steve escorted them away from the pulpit.

As the organist began to strum the notes of the traditional wedding march, Marcia positioned herself just outside the doorway of the sanctuary. She smiled at Uncle Trevor and resolved that she would ride each wave of emotion today without shedding any tears. She held a bouquet of lilies in one hand and smoothed the front of her straight silk gown with the other before looping her arm with Uncle Trevor's. He was her give-away father, and although she had been almost an adult when she met him, he had truly treated her like a daughter since then.

Only two other men had played a paternal role in her life. Devon's father had been a constant male presence when she was growing up, but he hadn't interacted with her much. His grandfather Mass Dev had been much more talkative and loved to tell them stories when they visited him. She hadn't given much thought to the identity of her biological father. Had he been half the man Devon was, he would have found her in the same way that Devon had found Wendy.

A ray of sunlight beamed through a glass window and glistened on the faux diamonds that lined the heart-shaped neckline of her dress. Matching diamonds lined the tiara that crowned her upswept hair. She exhaled, and the air from her lips lifted the long, spiral curl from her hair that dropped down on one side near her chin.

"Relax," Uncle Trevor whispered, patting her hand. "You're gorgeous."

"You don't look too bad yourself," she joked, as they began their journey down the aisle.

As she got closer to the altar, her eyes met Devon's and filled up with tears. She closed them briefly hardly believing that this day had finally come.

Devon grinned at her, tearful himself, and proud that she was the woman he would marry.

Uncle Trevor took Marcia's hand and placed it in Devon's. He gave Devon a nod. They'd talked, and he felt assured that Devon would take good care of Marcia and Wendy. He took a seat beside his wife who held on to his hand and said, "Praise the Lord."

Devon squeezed Marcia's hands as they faced each other. "You look stunning!" he whispered, and they turned to face Reverend Walker.

Wendy and Blossom adjusted the train of Marcia's gown, and laughter erupted among the audience again as the twins ran forward to throw flowers on the train.

During the ceremony, Uncle Trevor and Aunt Pat, who were celebrating their fiftieth wedding anniversary, read from Ephesians five.

"Wives, submit to your own husbands, as to the Lord," Aunt Pat read, "for the husband is the head of the wife, as also Christ is head of the church, and He is the Savior of the body." Her eyes met Marcia's, and Marcia looked at her first, then at Devon.

Uncle Trevor read, "Husbands, love your wives, just as Christ also loved the church and gave Himself for her... So husbands ought to love their own wives as their own bodies; he who loves his wife loves himself." He spoke directly to Devon, who accepted the challenge and smiled reassuringly at Marcia.

Steve stepped forward with the wedding ring.

Devon's eyes remained fixed on his bride as he reached for the ring. As he slid the ring onto her finger, he was acutely aware of God's grace in his life.

"With this ring, I thee wed."

Their vows were traditional and heartfelt.

Wendy watched closely as her parents placed rings on each other's fingers. She uttered a prayer of thanksgiving to God, whose plans were so much better than hers. Her mother and father had made it to the altar, and Wendy was still hopeful for herself and Paul. She prayed and had faith. She didn't know what God had in store for their future, but as her parents leaned forward to share a kiss, Wendy felt satisfied that her Savior had her life in His hands.

*****THE END*****

THE HEART TO LOVE

ABOUT THE AUTHOR

Shauna Jamieson Carty is a born-again Christian who writes fiction and non-fiction to show how people are strengthened to endure life's toughest situations when they trust in God who loves us so much that He gave us JESUS. Born and raised on the island of Jamaica, she began her career as a writer while living in the United States, where she earned a Master's degree in journalism from Columbia University and a Bachelor's degree in political science from Lehman College. She has edited her mother's books, co-authored a book with her husband, and encourages their children to also write and publish their work.

NON-FICTION BOOKS

Praying in the Moment: Reflections on the Election of President Barack Obama, by Shauna Jamieson Carty, spans the generations. Eight of the reflections are told through the eyes of Americans who have experienced race relations at its worst, but have now lived to witness progress beyond many of their expectations. The ninth reflection documents the experience of a young adult who attended the inauguration. The tenth gives voice to three children under age ten who express how they feel about the election of America's first black president.

By Faith: A Marriage Building Devotional with prayers, activities, and discussion topics, by Ricky and Shauna Carty, conveys the perspective that a lasting, happy and faithful marriage is a gift from God for which we should glorify Him, and not a direct construction of man for which we should credit ourselves. It can be used as an individual or couples' devotional, or it can be a workbook for married couples whereby they can record their own stories and store keepsakes as a legacy of the Christian marriage for younger generations.

www.ingramcontent.com/pod-product-compliance
Lightning Source LLC
Chambersburg PA
CBHW071246130626
46556CB00003B/1185